Escaping Reality

By LUCY WADE

ISBN: 978-1-9993751-0-2

First published 2019

Escaping Reality is a work of fiction. Although the events described loosely follow real-life scenarios, the characters within this book are not representative of any person, alive or dead, and are purely fictional constructs.

CONTENTS

PREFACE

Ever since I was a little girl, I have loved reading and writing. As a child, I would imagine being someone else, re-enacting certain characters. As I grew older I really enjoyed art and would tell everyone that I wanted to be a record cover designer. Instead, I entered into the normal 9-5 job brigade. Looking back, I wonder whether I could have carved out a better career in a more creative role, maybe something like fashion design, portraits or interior design, all of which I love.

In 2017, I was fortunate to be able to work part-time in the care industry and decided to take the opportunity to attend a writing course in London. I was so inspired by what was presented to me that I enrolled in the mentoring programme straight away. It's been an experience I've really enjoyed. It hasn't been easy, and the actual writing was much harder than I could ever have imagined. Yet, sixteen months later, here it is. My book is complete. It feels surreal and hugely rewarding.

People have asked me, why write a fiction novel? And why this subject? Well some of the novel is based on similar experiences to my own, so why not base my first book on something I already know about?

If I had to choose two things in my life that I am most proud of, the first would be my son. He's an incredible individual, and has overcome so many obstacles in his young life.

The second, would be my sobriety. It's been nearly five years since I stopped drinking. There were dark times, some of which I cannot fully remember, due to blackout periods. Ultimately, I had to make a choice – carry on and lose everything, or seek help. Thankfully, I chose the latter.

If you are suffering from a mental health problem, whether it's anxiety, depression, domestic violence, insecurity, self-loathing, an eating disorder, or anything else, please know that there is always support available, and that you can find strength, hope, and faith in acknowledging and learning how to deal with these problems.

I would like to thank all my family for their support in helping me reach my goal. Thank you to my husband for the hours and hours of silence, for ensuring evening meals were made, and for walking the dogs when I didn't have time. Thank you to my friends, who will support me by reading my book, and by always being there for me.

I would also like to thank Richard Mcmunn and Jordan Cooke from The Book Publishing Academy, I couldn't have done this without you.

And last but not least, I want to thank Alcoholics Anonymous and all my friends I have made along the way. Without this programme my life would have been very different.

If anyone who reads this is struggling, always remember, if something is important enough to you, I guarantee you will overcome the hardships in life to achieve what you need to.

I hope you enjoy the book. It's not about the money or the recognition, to me it's about the accomplishment and helping others.

Sincerely,

Lucy Wade

CHAPTER 1
The Early Years

Alma looked around the room. It was small and dark. In the corner of the room a stool was tucked beneath a table, and on top of the table was a sewing machine. It looked old and worn. A line of cotton thread hung through the eye of the machine needle. On many occasions, Alma had watched her mother sitting at the machine, sewing for what seemed like hours on end. She imagined the needle swinging back and forth, the precise movements of her mother's hands over the fragile cotton...

There was a photograph on the table. A man and woman smiled and held hands, against the backdrop of an old house. Mami had her hair set perfectly. She wore a turquoise dress, low cut, showing her ample cleavage. Alma's father was a handsome man. He wore a military uniform, with a row of medals above his left breast pocket. His eyes shone through the glass of the photo frame, and his chin was slightly tilted, as if to show the pride he was feeling at that particular moment.

'Almita!'

Alma whirled around, startled. Voices were coming up the dirt track.

'Almita!'

'Yes, Mami, I'm here!'

Alma swung her legs off the armchair and threw open the door, running down the track to meet Mami and Aunty Maria. They were swinging a hamper, between them, that carried all of the food for that night's meal. It was Uncle Oscar and Aunty Maria's anniversary, and there was a feeling of excitement in the air.

Mami brought the hamper up onto the kitchen counter and opened the lid. On her tiptoes, Alma stretched out, trying to reach the top units.

Aunty Maria laughed, 'Almita, you are only four years old. Soon, you will be big enough to reach all the way up there.'

'I'm nearly five!' Alma said sulkily.

During the celebrations later that evening, Alma could not help venturing outside the house, gazing out down the dirt track, listening for the tell-tale sounds of a car engine. She hadn't seen her father for days now. Every time she thought she heard his voice, her stomach would turn, riddled with butterflies. He didn't show. That night, she laid in bed next to Mami, and for the first time she heard Mami cry. It was a quiet cry at first, but when Mami could not hold in the tears any longer, her sobs became wild and uncontrollable. Alma never stirred. She held her yellow dolly tightly in her fist, and stared into the darkness.

Days passed. Mami had been sewing furiously. Every afternoon, strangers would come by, and purchase the finished garments from Mami. On occasion, Alma heard Aunty Maria express her dismay at how little people were paying for the clothes.

'We could go to Belize?' Aunty Maria said.

Mami shook her head, 'No. Things will be okay here.'

One evening, when Mami stood up, Alma noticed that her chair had blood on it. The next day, Alma woke up to find an empty space beside her in the bed. She rolled off the mattress and walked tentatively out into the hall. Mami was on the floor, with her hands on her tummy and her knees up against her chest. The carpet had spots of blood on it, just like the chair. Mami was groaning in pain.

Alma ran. She ran as fast as she could, until she reached Aunty Maria's house.

'Aunty Maria, please come quick! Please, something's wrong with Mami!'

After that, Mami spent a lot of time in bed. Aunty Maria and Uncle Oscar spent more time than ever with them, cooking and cleaning and looking after the house.

A few weeks later, Alma heard a familiar sound outside the door. She ran down the track and saw a gleaming black truck. A man got out. He beamed, and stretched out his arms. Alma was dizzy with happiness. She threw herself into his chest.

'Papi, Papi. Where have you been?'

Papi kissed her on the head. He smiled at her, and his eyes twinkled. Then, all of a sudden, he was lifting her up and putting her down.

'Wait here, Alma. I need to speak to Mami.'

Alma watched as he turned to go inside the house. He walked confidently up the dirt track, and opened the kitchen door. Moments later, there were raised voices. The voices got louder. Mami was shouting something. Alma leaned against the truck, clutching both hands together and scuffing her right foot against the tyre. It wasn't long before Papi came back out. He was holding a black bag. He put the bag on the back seat, turned towards Alma, and put her in the passenger side of the vehicle. He closed the door.

Suddenly, Mami's face was at the window. Her cheeks were streaked with tears. She leaned in and took Alma by the hand, kissing her on the forehead.

'I will see you soon, Almita. I promise.' She then looked at Papi and said, 'Por favor Carlos, regrese mi hija temprano oye.' Alma understood perfectly, *Return my daughter early, please.* Papi nodded, and got into the truck. Alma watched as her mother became a small figure in the distance. She did up her seatbelt, and looked at Papi.

'So, Papi, where are we going?'

...

The next few days were a blur of excitement. Alma loved spending time with her father. He would take her to his place of work, a shabby porta cabin, with lots of books. In the cabin, other soldiers were smoking and talking in loud Spanish. Papi would fetch Alma a burrito and a bottle of Coke, and then sit her on his knee, while he talked about the other soldiers and the war in El Salvador. He would pick Alma up and swing her round and call her 'daddy's princess', and say that he loved her very much. He would tickle her toes and make her laugh out loud. And then, all of a sudden, it was time to go back home. Alma said goodbye to each of the soldiers individually, as she had learnt their names by heart, and promised that she would see them again. She left the cabin and got into Papi's truck. He climbed silently into the seat beside her, and put his big hand on the top of her head.

'Let's go home, Almita.'

Not long after that, Mami left to go to work in Belize. Alma stayed with other relatives, but she missed her mother terribly. Every night she would wake up drenched in sweat, after nightmares of both Mami and Papi being killed. When Alma saw her father again, she told him about the dreams. In response, he crushed her towards his chest.

'My Almita, they are just silly dreams. Nothing will ever happen to me or Mami. I wouldn't let it.'

Almita looked up at him and smiled, glowing with reassurance.

'Can you stay this evening, Papi?'

Papi looked over at Aunty Maria and Uncle Oscar. Uncle Oscar muttered something disapprovingly.

'Papi has somewhere else that he needs to be,' said Aunty Maria.

Alma understood. She hugged Papi as tightly as she possibly could, and watched him walking down the track.

Shortly afterwards, Mami returned. To Alma's delight, she seemed much happier. She told Alma that she was waitressing at a dance club, owned by her friend Tia. Mami gave Aunty Maria a purse full of money, and Alma heard them talk about buying food and clothes. And then, as quickly as Mami had arrived, she was gone again. Aunty Maria took Alma up to bed, promising her that she'd see Mami again soon.

A few weeks later, Alma started attending school. She would attend in the mornings, but to her horror the teachers said that her dolly could not come with her. Every afternoon, Alma would rush home in anticipation, pick up Dolly and spin her around the room. It wasn't right, leaving her. They went everywhere together.

It seemed like months before Mami returned. When she did, she was very excited, and Alma heard her talking to Aunty Maria about someone she had met.

'Oh, Maria, I hope you will like him. He's so funny and seems to really want to get to know everyone. He's always asking about Almita and the rest of the family.'

'Does he make you happy?'

'Oh yes, yes he does.'

They giggled, then would suddenly go quiet and burst out laughing. Alma came into the room several times, only to be told to go to bed, as it was late. She noticed a marked difference in her mother. Mami looked pleased with herself. When she dressed and did her hair in the mornings she would slip on her high heels and look at herself in the mirror with a nod of approval. Alma, in the meantime, was still not happy about having to leave Dolly behind, and spent several mornings telling Mami about this.

One Saturday, Alma woke up late. She picked up Dolly and ran to find Mami, but she wasn't in the house. Aunty Maria was downstairs.

'Mami has gone out to get her hair done,' she said. 'It's going to be a special day!'

'Why, Aunty Maria?'

'Mami is meeting someone today, and you will be too, so you must behave courteously. Do you understand that?'

Alma nodded, but she thought nothing more about it. Instead she carried on with her usual routine, playing with the chickens, dressing up in silly outfits and making sure Dolly enjoyed herself too. Later that day, Aunty Maria helped Alma to bathe, and then put her in a pretty dress. Mami helped too, and she braided Alma's hair into two French plaits. Alma was delighted with this. She put her feet into her black, shiny shoes and clicked them together. She held Dolly up in the air and swung her around, pretending to dance. Then, all of a sudden, there was a knock at the door. Mami rushed to open it.

When the door opened, Alma could see a tall man, holding a book in his hand. Mami squealed with delight, and ushered him into the house. Aunty Maria and various other relatives jumped to their feet, rushing to shake the man's hand.

Mami brought the man over to Alma. 'Alma, this is David. He is from Inglaterra – England.'

David smiled down at Alma. He put out his hand.

Alma stared at him. She quickly ran behind Mami, hiding behind her skirt. Mami laughed, and escorted David over to the dinner table. Alma followed. She couldn't help staring at David. He was quite slim, with dark hair and dark eyes. He was wearing a red t-shirt, and Alma could see that the book in his hand had big, white writing on the front cover.

David sat down opposite Alma. He turned and looked her in the eyes, and said, 'Hola, Almita.'

Almita smiled. 'Hola, David.'

By that point, everyone else had taken their seats at the table. Alma and David continued talking in broken Spanish. Every time David pronounced something incorrectly, Alma found herself warming to him. Even at that age, she could appreciate that he was trying.

Later that night, when David had left, Mami sat down with Alma.

'David will come back tomorrow, and we're all going out for something to eat and drink.'

Alma nodded. She played with Dolly's hair.

'Almita, what do you think of David?'

Alma thought for a moment. Then, she ran straight into Mami's arms. She pushed her head against Mami's chest. Mami laughed and cuddled her.

'Do you think he is nice?' she asked.

Alma nodded her head. 'Very!'

Mami smiled. She picked Alma up with both arms and carried her to the bedroom. She laid Alma down on the bed and kissed her on the forehead.

'Buenas noches, princesa.'

As she turned to sleep, Alma noticed that the photograph on the table had gone. She resolved to ask where it had gone, the following day.

Following that, David and Alma spent lots more time together. David told Alma that he was learning to speak better Spanish, and that when he returned to England he was going to try even harder, so that she could understand everything he said. He even seemed to like Dolly too, which Alma was very happy about.

When David left to return to England, Mami cried. She cried like Alma had never seen her cry before, and then eventually she had to return to Belize. On the day she left, Alma cried too. Alone in her room with Dolly, she wiped the tears on the mattress, and started looking again for the photograph. It wasn't there, or in any of the drawers. The next time she saw Aunty Maria, Alma asked:

'When will I see Papi again, Aunty Maria?'

Aunty Maria put her hands on Alma's shoulders and looked deep into her eyes. 'Almita, your father has gone away with his job. He probably won't be around for a while.'

Alma stared back at her. 'Where is the photograph of Mami and Papi?'

Aunty Maria turned her head and looked at the empty space, where the photograph had been displayed. When she turned back, there was a curious look on her face, but Alma didn't know what it meant.

'The glass encasing broke, little Almita. They just had to get it mended, that's all. Now, get ready for bed.'

A few weeks later, when Alma was out playing with her cousins, she saw a bright yellow bus pull up outside their neighbour's house. Mami got off the bus. She was pulling her case behind her, and carrying several bags. She looked tired, but as soon as she saw Alma her face brightened. Alma ran towards her. She fell into Mami's arms and inhaled the scent of her perfume. Mami's cheek was wet with tears.

'I am home now, Almita. Everything will be alright. But later tonight we need to have a proper chat, okay?'

Later that evening, as Mami got Alma ready for bed, she said, 'Almita, I have something I want to discuss with you. Do you remember where David is from?

Alma nodded. 'Inglattera...England.'

'Yes, that's right. Alma, we'll be going there soon, with David.'

'Why, Mami?'

'Well, because that's where David lives, and he wants to show it to us. Just like Papi, David is a soldier, so we'll be living with all of the other soldiers too, in a special area.'

Alma held Dolly against her chest.

'What about you though, Mami?'

'I'll be there too, Almita, of course.'

'Okay, and Dolly can come too?'

'Yes, Dolly can come too.'

Alma smiled. She pressed her face against Mami's chest. She knew she would sleep well that night – just her, Mami, and Dolly.

The next day, Alma was eating breakfast. Dolly was sat at the table next to her. Mami came into the room. She sat down opposite Alma and gave her a serious look.

'Alma, we need to talk.'

Alma picked up Dolly and pressed the doll against her chest. She ran her hands through Dolly's hair.

'Now, Alma. Did you think about what I said yesterday?'

Alma nodded, slowly.

'So you know, if we all go to England – me, you and David… it's a long way away. Are you ready for that?'

Alma nodded, again. Mami smiled.

'David is going to show us where he comes from. Won't that be lovely? And you'll meet lots of other children too, who can teach you how to speak English.'

'I can teach them Spanish too.'

'Yes! That's a good girl. Now, I've spoken to Papi, and he wants to see you this evening, before we go away. Go up and get some of your things ready, Almita.'

That afternoon, sitting in the truck, Papi seemed very quiet. When they eventually stopped, it was outside a house that Alma had never seen before. Papi helped her out of the car and guided her to the front door.

Inside the house, Alma took off her shoes. Papi showed her into a lounge, with three chairs and a TV. There was a parrot perched on one arm of a chair, and it was chattering noisily. It stopped abruptly when they came into the room. A woman was sitting in one of the chairs.

'Alma, this is Consuela, a good friend of mine.'

The woman smiled at Alma. She got to her feet and tried to hug her. Alma froze. She clung to Dolly. Papi sat her down in one of the chairs. He stood next to Alma, squeezing her hand gently.

'Almita, I hear you are going away with your mother for a while.'

Alma nodded. 'We are going to England, Papi.'

'Do you want to go?' Papi asked. He looked at Consuela as he said it. She smiled, got up, and walked into the kitchen.

Alma thought for a moment. 'Why can't you come with us?'

Papi smiled, 'My work is here, Alma. And besides, Mami will bring you back soon.' Alma stared into his eyes. For a moment, she thought that they seemed very sad.

Papi took her hand again. He brought it to his mouth and gently kissed her knuckles, 'Promise me, Almita. Promise me that you will always do what your mother asks.'

Alma nodded. Consuela came back into the room, with a tray of tortillas, cheese and ham.

'Alma, would it be okay for me to hold Dolly?' Consuela asked.

Alma stared at Consuela. She hugged Dolly close to her chest.

'Almita,' Papi said, stroking Alma's hair, 'it's okay.'

Consuela smiled, 'I promise I won't hurt her.'

Alma handed Dolly over, somewhat reluctantly. 'Dolly is very excited about going to England,' she said, watching Consuela carefully.

The drive back home seemed to take hours, and again most of the journey was in silence. Outside the window, everything seemed dusty. The wind was picking up, and litter was flying along the dirt road as if by magic. Alma thought about England. She imagined what it would be like to play with other children, and not understand a word that they said. Papi's hands were gripping the wheel tightly. Alma could see the gun in his holster, next to his pocket.

Her mind went back to Consuela, and the house they had just been to. Did Papi live there now? Why didn't he come and stay with her and Mami anymore? She opened her mouth to ask, but then thought better of it, and went back to staring out of the window.

When they arrived back home, Alma ran straight indoors. From outside, she heard angry voices. It was Mami and Papi, they were arguing, and soon Aunty Maria and Uncle Oscar were joining in. Alma peered through the curtain.

The front door was slightly open, and she could see her father's face. He was in some sort of pain or distress and seemed to be pleading with Mami. Eventually, he got very angry. He started shouting, louder than Alma had ever heard before, and then he turned around and got into his truck. He sped off, with the tyres screeching, leaving Mami crying and Aunty Maria trying to comfort her.

Alma let the curtain fall back into place. She sat on the bed with Dolly, stroking her hair and wondering why there had been so much shouting. After a while, Mami popped her head around the door.

'Almita, are you not changed yet?'

Alma quickly got off the bed and changed into her pyjamas, not taking her eyes off Dolly, who was laid out across the mattress. Dolly's hair was a mess, and both her eyes were closed. Mami walked over to Alma, took out her plaits and started to brush her hair.

'Mami…' Almita said quietly.

Mami continued brushing Alma's hair.

'…why were you and Papi shouting? Is Papi okay?'

Mami stopped brushing for a moment. 'Yes, Almita, he is fine. We just have some things to sort out before leaving for England, that's all.'

'How long are we going for?' Alma asked.

'Not long, just a few months, that's all. We'll meet some of David's friends and then we'll be back before you know it.'

Mami started brushing again. She hummed a bedtime tune, and Alma started to feel her eyes getting heavy. Smiling, Mami bent down and hugged Alma tightly, before lifting her onto the mattress.

The following day was very hectic. Mami was pacing a lot, biting her fingernails, and looking at the clock. Alma spent her time outside. It was hot, and she played with a bucket of water, giving Dolly a bath and changing her clothes. Then, suddenly, she heard a shout from Aunty Maria: 'He's coming, he's coming!'

Alma looked up the road, and saw David. He was getting out of a taxi, waving and smiling, and carrying a case. Mami rushed out of the house and ran towards him. They hugged and then Alma saw them kiss. On the way back to the house, Mami and David held hands. Alma ran up behind them. She took David's hand away from Mami and wedged herself in the middle of them, grabbing Mami's hand herself. Then, she realised that Dolly was still in the bucket of water. With a terrible shout, she ran back to rescue her, and then sprinted back into the house. Everyone was extremely excited, and there was lots of talk about the next day. Alma heard Aunty Maria say, 'You'll need to be there at two o 'clock,' but she didn't know what that meant, and when she asked Mami, Mami just smiled and said that it wasn't important.

When Alma woke up the next day, Mami had gone, but she returned later that afternoon. She was with David. David had a little flower on his jacket pocket and Mami looked very pretty in a blue skirt and silky blouse. They both hugged and kissed Alma. Other people started arriving at the house with bottles of drink and food and saying congratulations.

That night seemed to last forever. Alma enjoyed showing everyone her dolly, and telling them about their trip to England. Then, one relative said, 'Almita, are you all packed?'

Confused, Alma said, 'Not yet.'

'Well you better hurry up,' he said, 'as you are going tomorrow!'

Alma looked around to see if she could find Mami, but she wasn't in the room. She wasn't in the bedroom either. She ran outside, and saw Mami and David talking.

'Mami! Mami! Are we leaving tomorrow?'

Mami bent down and kissed Alma on the cheek, 'Yes, Almita, we are. Tomorrow evening we will be leaving to travel to England, so we will pack in the morning. Go inside now and get dressed for bed, we have a very long journey. I will be in to say goodnight shortly.'

Alma looked at her mother and then at David. They were both beaming. Alma turned and walked back into the house, saying goodnight to everyone. She picked up Dolly and got ready for bed. She laid in bed for ages, staring at the dark ceiling, thinking about England. She wondered whether Dolly would like England. What would happen if she didn't?

Later that night, when Alma woke, she reached out. Her mother was there beside her. Alma brushed the soft skin of Mami's back. She pushed Dolly out between them, letting her share the pillow, before closing her eyes once more.

CHAPTER 2
Inglaterra

It was really cold. Alma tried to wrap herself up in her long cardigan, but it wasn't making any difference. She was tired too. This journey seemed so long. Where was this place that David lived? Mami had been crying for a long time now, and the goodbyes had lasted all morning. Alma stared out the window of the monstrous machine. She had never seen anything like it. It had a funny shape, and big, wing-like arms. She couldn't believe it when David told her that they were flying through the clouds. Her ears had started to make funny noises, and at one stage she couldn't hear anything at all. Then they became painful, and she had to fight back tears. Mami still looked really sad. Her eyes were red and she was sipping from her hot drink. Dolly was sad too. She told Alma that she was scared, and wanted to go home.

The big machine came to a halt. Everyone got up and started walking down the aisle. Soon, they were queuing, coming down the steps and out into the dark night. There were lots of people and a few children too, chattering in Spanish and English. One girl also had a dolly. Alma stared at her, then at her dolly. The girl stared back, then looked away. Alma held onto Mami's hand tightly, as everyone started moving. When they reached the bottom they were ushered into a line and started walking towards a big building.

They walked and walked, and Alma felt her legs wobble underneath her. She needed to sit down, and tried tugging at Mami, but all Mami kept saying was that they had to keep going. Alma couldn't take another step, and she stopped in her tracks. Dolly fell before Alma did – she lay in a crumpled heap, crying. David looked around and ran back to pick Alma and Dolly up. He lifted her into the air, and they carried on walking. Dolly clung tightly to Alma's chest.

The next thing Alma knew they were on some moving steps that carried them upwards. David put Alma down, and she cried out loudly as she nearly lost her balance. He put his hand out to the side, so that she could steady herself. Mami had a worried look on her face. At the top of the steps, Alma saw a sea of people waiting.

'What is everyone waiting for?' Alma asked.

'Passport control,' David smiled down at Alma.

Alma looked at Mami, 'What's that?'

'We have to show those men some papers, Alma. It's very important, otherwise they won't let us go to England.'

They arrived at the front of the line. David walked up to the glass window and spoke to the man behind it. The man looked at the papers, then shook his head. He came out around the side of the booth and gestured for them to follow him. Alma, Mami, and David followed the man through and into a room, where they sat and waited. Eventually a man with dark glasses came in, and spoke to Mami and David. The man was looking at Mami's paperwork, and David was trying to explain something, but Alma didn't really understand. She knew that she needed to go to the toilet, but as she stood up to ask, the man looked at her in an angry way, so she sat back down again.

Eventually they were allowed to leave. Alma just made it to the toilet, but when she got into the cubicle she didn't understand what to do. Mami showed her where the flush was. Alma jumped back in surprise. It made such a big noise, and there was so much water!

The next stop was picking up their bags and cases. They had so many, Alma looked around at everyone else and they only seemed to have one or two. She counted seven cases in total, and David and Mami struggled to get them onto a trolley. After some more paperwork checking, they found themselves outside in the dark, looking for a big car to take them wherever they were going.

When a car finally did arrive, David put out his hand, but a man and a lady stepped out in front of David, trying to get into the car. David said something in English. He sounded cross. The man started shouting at David, and then suddenly David was shouting back. Alma burst into tears. Mami was pulling David away, and the other lady was trying to get in between both of them. Alma could see David, he was pushing his face into the other man's face. The man from the big black car ran around to their side and calmed everyone down. Alma, Mami and David got into the car, and all the bags and cases were put in the back. Alma's heart was pounding so hard, she scrunched Dolly towards her chest, and huddled up to Mami in the back. David sat in the front with the man. They were both shaking their heads and muttering something. Alma looked at Mami, but she did not look at Alma – she was shivering and rubbing her hands together.

Alma looked out of the window, there were so many people around, most of them were wearing coats and hats. As she looked out, she pulled up the hood of her coat and sunk back in the seat. It wasn't long before she fell into a deep sleep.

Alma awoke in a strange bed in a strange room. She still had her coat and her shoes on. Dolly was lying next to her. Alma picked up Dolly and got out of bed. She could hear voices coming from downstairs. Outside, there was a long hallway and then stairs leading downstairs. Alma held onto the rope coming down the stairs. There were lots of them, and she felt tired by the time she reached the bottom. A short corridor led to another room, and in the room stood Mami, David, another lady and another man.

'Almita,' Mami called out. 'Come here and meet David's mum and dad.'

Alma walked towards Mami, still half asleep. She smiled up at the strange new people.

'Hello Alma,' said the lady. She had white hair and wore a pink dress, tied tightly at the waist, making her look very slim.

'Hello,' Alma replied.

David came over to her and held out his hand. 'Alma, look what Nanna and Clive have got for you.' He pointed to a small pram in the corner of the room, 'It's for Dolly.' He pulled Alma over towards the pram, and opened up the blankets inside. Alma tucked Dolly into the sheets, cautiously. David showed her how to push the pram, and then she followed them all outside into the garden. Alma looked around in bewilderment. It was a long garden, with lots of different flowers and potted plants. Mami smiled at Alma and ruffled her hair. David, Nanna and Clive all spoke in English, and Alma and Mami stood there looking at each other, not really knowing what was going on.

They spent a few weeks with Nanna and Clive. Alma felt very comfortable in her new surroundings, but it wasn't long before she started wondering when they were going to return home. She asked Mami on several occasions, only to be told that it would be soon, and to just enjoy herself, as they were on holiday. Alma decided to make the most of it, and even met another girl from the house next door, although she didn't have a clue what the girl was saying. Her name was Sarah. They played by pointing and laughing at things, and Sarah's mum would often make them both little sandwiches. Alma decided that she liked the food in England, but Mami seemed to be finding it a bit more difficult. On top of that, it was so cold! Alma found that she was always wearing a coat, tights and shoes, and sometimes even a woolly hat. When they weren't out, Alma wore a big house coat that Nanna had bought for her. She loved this, as Dolly fitted perfectly in the pocket.

Soon, it was time to move on. They were going to a place called Telford.

Alma dressed Dolly up for their trip, using the new clothes that Nanna had bought her. She brushed Dolly's hair and washed her face. Dolly was super excited for the journey. David had a new car, and Alma watched from the bedroom window as David and Clive put their cases and bags into the back.

It was a long journey to Telford, and when they did get there it was almost dark. As she stepped into the house, Alma gasped. It was really big! She ran around with Dolly, going from room to room and then upstairs. The floors had funny material on them, just like Nanna's house. It felt really cold inside, and David and Mami quickly brought in the cases and numerous bags.

Alma took her small bags and put them in one of the rooms. Each room already had furniture inside, and upstairs there were lots of beds. The bathroom was so big that Alma just stayed there for ages, taking it all in, and wondering whether anyone else was going to be living there with them.

Finally, Mami told Alma that it was bedtime. Alma ran upstairs again and chose a room with two beds. All her bags had been put on one bed, and the next day Mami said they would sort everything out. She also said that the following week Alma would be starting English school.

'Why do I have to go to school?' Alma asked.

'Well, because you have to go…it's just like in Honduras. You went to school there too, remember? All children have to attend school from a certain age, Almita,' Mami said, as she tucked Alma into bed.

'I won't know anyone, and I won't understand what they are saying.'

'Don't worry, Almita. There will be someone there who will be helping you,' smiled Mami.

'When are we going home?'

'Soon,' Mami said. Alma grumbled under her breath. *Mami always says that,* she thought.

Alma lay in bed in the dark, listening to Mami and David speaking downstairs. She tried hard to make out what they were saying, but their voices were muffled. She could not fall asleep, and kept tossing and turning, trying to close her eyes and drift off. Her mind drifted back to Papi, in Honduras. When would she see him again? She imagined being back home, and cuddling him, telling him about her adventure in England. Alma smiled to herself. She would tell him all about her new toys and this big house, and of course school when she started. The thought of school wiped the smile off her face. She was scared. Her heart started racing, and soon she started to feel panicky. Clutching Dolly, she imagined how she would try and communicate with the other children. Would they like her? Would she like them? Would she be able to take Dolly? What if she couldn't take Dolly? Alma squeezed her eyes shut and pressed Dolly tightly against her breast, pulling the covers over both of them. It won't be for long, she told herself. They would be going home soon.

That night she had a terrible dream. She was in a Coca-Cola factory, holding onto Dolly tightly. Tears were streaming down her cheeks. She sobbed and shouted, 'No, no, no!!!' The soldiers were tying Papi up, and slapping his face. David was there, so was Mami, and she was crying too. One soldier stormed over to Alma, grabbing her arm and making Dolly drop to the ground.

'You must choose, which one are you going with?' the soldier shouted. 'Do you want this one…?' he pointed at Papi, 'or this one?' he pointed at David. Mami started crying out. The soldiers moved over and dragged her out of the factory, screaming. Alma felt her throat tighten. She couldn't get the words out. She felt dizzy, Papi was disappearing into the darkness.

'Please, Papi, please don't go,' Alma whispered.

She woke with an awful ache in her chest. She was very hot, and her clothes were wet with sweat. It took a while before her heart slowed to a normal pace.

The rest of that week was spent sorting the house out and unpacking. They went out food shopping and then clothes shopping, to buy Alma and Mami some warm jumpers, and of course Alma's school uniform.

A week later, Alma started school. The first day was awful. Alma cried several times, and had to be taken from the classroom more than once. There was no communication between her or any of the children, but she stayed behind after school with a nice lady who was helping her with her English. It wasn't easy, she would practice at school and then when she came home David and Alma would sit at the dining table and he would teach her his way. He would sometimes get angry and shouted at Alma if she didn't understand things quickly enough. Alma would cry and run to her bedroom and then she would hear Mami and David argue and shout.

One morning, when Mami was walking Alma to school, Alma asked her again when they were going home. Mami stopped and bent down next to her.

'Almita, we are not going home. We have decided that we are going to make a new life here in England. You will have a better future here.'

Alma stared back at her mother. She could not believe what she was hearing.

'I hate it here,' Alma shouted. 'I want to go home, I want to see Papi, I don't want to live here in England. Please Mami, please can we go home?' Alma started crying.

'We have to stay here and make things work. We have better prospects here. You will do well at school, and later on get a good job. You may decide when you are older that you want to go back and visit the family, but for now it's my decision and I will do what's best for you. Now, come on, otherwise you'll be late for school.'

Mami held her hand, and they walked along in silence. Alma stared in front of her. She felt an overwhelming ache inside her tummy. She wished she had Dolly with her, but the school had confirmed that no toys were allowed.

As they approached the school gates, Alma could see all the children playing. Mami let go of her hand and bent down to kiss her.

'Alma, be strong and try to enjoy school, okay? Make friends and take part when your teacher asks you to.' Mami smiled at Alma and ushered her into school.

Alma turned and walked through the gates, keeping her head down. She knew what was about to happen. She looked up and saw the same children that would always greet her. They all held hands and made a circle around her, and started singing a song. Then they all laughed. Alma didn't know what they were saying, but she didn't like it. She waited for the bell to ring, so they would go away.

Alma did not really want to do much for the rest of the day. She sat in the classroom listening to the teacher, trying to make out what she was saying. During their art lesson, she drew Dolly wearing a pretty dress, and one of the other girls came over and expressed their delight – pointing at Dolly's long hair. Alma smiled, and looked at the girl's picture. She'd drawn two figures, a small dog and a big sun in the corner.

At the end of the day, Mami was waiting at the school gates. Alma noticed how pretty she looked. Mami's face was rosy; she wore a dark coat, and at least two jumpers underneath. She wore jeans and boots and looked small compared to the other mums. She was holding Dolly, and waved her at Alma. Alma ran quickly towards the gates and reached out to grab Dolly. She could smell Mami's perfume on Dolly's hair, and she felt so happy to have Dolly back in her arms. Alma span around, waving Dolly around. Nothing else mattered at that moment. It was just her and Dolly, reunited.

CHAPTER 3
Eleven

'Alma, where is your lunchbox?!!'

In her bedroom, Alma froze. What was she going to say? She would just have to lie and say that she'd left it at school.

'Almita,' Mami shouted again, 'where is your lunch box? It's not in your school bag.'

Alma made her way downstairs. 'I must have left it at school,' she said, looking down.

'Why didn't you show us these letters? I found them in your bag.' Mami held up three envelopes. Alma winced. She had forgotten all about them. Two of them were fine, but the third one Mami would definitely have something to say about. Luckily, Mami would have to wait until David got home to read them, as she was still not confident in understanding written English. Mami and David always spoke Spanish, and Mami would always speak to Alma in Spanish too, with a few English words thrown in. Alma called it 'Spanglish'. Here in Ireland, it was even harder to understand people, but Alma had gotten used to the accent.

'Well?' Mami was waiting for Alma's response.

'Sorry, I must have forgotten about them,' Alma replied, taking the letters from her mother's grasp. 'I will put them by the clock, so David can read them.' She walked away sheepishly.

'You will have to take your lunch in a bag, make sure you bring your lunch box home today.'

Alma nodded, 'What time is my party tomorrow?'

Mami looked up from washing the dishes.

'We thought about one o'clock to four o'clock, that's what it says on the invitation…you did give them out, didn't you?'

'Yes, I know Trudy, Katherine and Mandy are coming,' Alma smiled. She knew that because they had been teasing her about her presents.

'Ammmmaaaar,' she heard her sister shouting from her high chair.

Alma looked over at her and laughed, 'Hey, Yoli, why have you got so much food on your face?'

Mami held out a small flannel. Alma wiped Yoli's face and then removed her bib. Yoli began to cry. 'Come on Yoli, you need to be clean!' Alma exclaimed. Yoli looked up at her with big brown watery eyes, and then started to rub her face, whimpering. Alma lifted her out of her high chair and they walked over to Mami in the kitchen. Mami rolled her eyes and smiled.

'Come on, Almita, we have to go, otherwise we will be late,' Mami picked up Yoli and put her in the push chair. She held Alma's coat out.

'Ammmmaaaar,' Yoli wanted Alma to push her. Alma obliged and they all made their way to school. Alma recalled how her little sister could be so naughty and clumsy, she would always be running into things, hurting herself, crying and then doing the whole thing again. Alma peered over the push chair. Yoli's face was flushed, she looked around at everyone and everything, mesmerised.

As they walked to school, they were joined by Daniel and his mum, Elvera, who spoke Spanish too. Daniel was younger than Alma, so she didn't see him around school too much. Elvera was one of Mami's Spanish friends, they lived just around the corner.

Approaching the school gates, Alma was overwhelmed. She felt anxious. Her tummy was knotted together, and started to ache. She thought about how to tell Mami that Tamsin and her friends had taken her lunch box. Tamsin was taller than most girls at school, she had ginger hair and freckles. Alma felt nauseous every time she saw her. Sometimes she would hide or turn around, so she wouldn't have to face meeting her. Tamsin and her friends would steal lunch boxes, money and other personal things from other kids at school. Alma knew she wasn't the only one it was happening to. She thought back to when it first happened, a few weeks ago. She'd been walking through the playground, with Trudy, when suddenly they'd heard voices behind them…

'Hey, you! Oi, we are talking to you…hey Indian girl, wait up!'

Alma and Trudy were ushered to a quiet part of the playground. The ginger haired girl whispered to Trudy to get lost. At first Trudy looked at Alma, hesitating, but Alma nodded for her to go.

'What's this then?' Tamsin grabbed Alma's school bag and took out her pencil case. She emptied all the other contents on the ground, looking through just in case there was anything that took her fancy. She pinned Alma back, hard against the wall and started rifling through her pockets, discarding tissues and holding onto some coins which didn't really amount to much.

'Tomorrow you are gonna bring me more of these, Indy,' Tamsin held up the coin to Alma's face. Her friends started laughing. Alma could smell Tamsin's breath on her face. She slowly nodded in agreement.

'Oh and make sure you don't sit near any of us during classes, we don't like smelly Indians anywhere near us, okay?!' Tamsin shoved Alma away from her. The girls laughed as they kicked the contents laying on the ground. Tamsin walked away, stuffing the pencil case under her coat. She looked back at Alma with a smirk and a nod, as if to warn Alma not to forget the money she had demanded.

Alma knew Tamsin and gang would not forget about the money, and when Alma came into school the following day without it she was terrified of the consequences. The girls cornered Alma in the toilets. When they realised Alma didn't have the money, Tamsin squeezed Alma's wrist so hard that she left fingernail marks on the skin. Fortunately for Alma a teacher was approaching the toilets, and told the girls to get a move on, as classes had started.

The stealing had escalated in the past two weeks. Recently it had been her lunch box – Scooby Doo, bright yellow, red, and orange. No-one else in school had that one, not in those colours. Alma knew Mami would be very cross about it going missing. There had been pens taken, even Alma's PE kit had gone missing. It was getting more and more difficult for Alma to keep making excuses at home. One evening, Alma had frantically emptied David's ashtray of change, hoping that no-one would notice, just as long as she left a couple of coins.

'Don't forget your lunch box,' Mami said as Alma passed through the gates. Mami turned the pushchair around and started heading back home.

Alma saw Trudy and Katherine in the playground, and they were shortly joined by Mandy.

'You okay, Alma?' Mandy asked

'No, Mami found the letter in my bag…the one about me not going to PE because I didn't have my kit,' Alma looked down at the ground.'

'Why don't you just tell Mrs Peel the truth?' said Trudy. 'Just tell her that Tamsin took it.'

'I can't, I'm too scared.' Alma put her hand in her pocket and took out some change. She showed her friends, they looked worried.

'Here,' said Mandy, handing Alma three coins, 'that's all I could get.' Alma smiled appreciatively. Then, the bell sounded.

Alma found it hard to concentrate that day. She just sat there, looking into space. Mrs Little was talking to the class, but Alma was not listening. She was imagining running through cornfields, with Dolly tight in her grasp. She felt the wind through her hair, fresh on her face. The sun beat down on the top of her head as she ran faster, dainty stems of corn tickling her legs. Alma looked ahead, a tractor in the distance seemed so small. Her feet were beginning to feel tired, and the tractor seemed to be moving further and further away, instead of getting bigger. Alma felt herself gasping for air. Dolly was urging her to keep going, but her legs felt weak.

'Alma, please can you read the next paragraph?'

Alma looked around. The whole class was looking straight at her. She had no idea where the last pupil had left off. 'Err sorry, Miss, can you tell me where we've got to?'

The class erupted in laughter. Mrs Little walked over to Alma and pointed at the third paragraph in the book. 'Alma, please pay attention.'

'Sorry, Miss.' Alma began to read. She pretended to be in character, as if she was reading to Yoli. Her book collection at home was vast. Nanna and Clive would always bring a couple more books when they visited, and would often buy them for birthdays and Christmas too. Her favourite was a big book with all different stories by Hans Christian Anderson, *the Ugly Duckling*, *the Princess and the Pea*, and *the Little Mermaid*, all favourites for Yoli too.

At the end of the day, Alma slowly put her books away in her bag. As she did so, she noticed a piece of folded paper inside one of the pages. She slid this out and opened it up. It showed a drawing of an Indian girl, with a feather in her hair. Next to her were the letters *STINKS*. Alma looked around to see if anyone had noticed, but the classroom was almost empty. Alma once again looked at the piece of paper, folded it up, and put it in her coat pocket.

She walked out of the classroom towards the toilets. She entered one of the cubicles and sat down on the seat for a moment. Her heart ached. She couldn't see for a few seconds, and stifled a sob, frantically searching for a tissue in her pockets. Mami always stuffed Alma's pockets with plenty of tissues, and she was grateful this time round. Blowing her nose and wiping away the tears, she washed her hands and looked into the mirror. She had to find a way to stop this. Alma knew she was different. She wasn't like the other children, but she didn't dress like an Indian girl. Yes, her skin was darker, but Mami said they were olive skinned, not dark. She looked like someone from Honduras, not an Indian. Maybe she did smell? She put her arm up to her nose just in case she hadn't noticed, but all she could smell was a faint waft of baby powder which Nanna would always buy her. It reminded her of Yoli.

Alma looked at her hair. She hated it. Cut too short by Mami, she looked like a boy. Her eyes were big and she had stubby lashes. Her nose was too wide, her teeth were wonky, and her lips were enormous. Looking at her reflection, Alma felt worse than before. Soon she would be twelve years old. Maybe things would change as she got older. Perhaps she would grow taller, and better looking, like her friends. Katherine was especially pretty. With long blonde hair and blue eyes, she was also the tallest. In fact, she reminded Alma of Dolly – who was pretty much perfect in every way. Perhaps Mami would let her grow her hair? Alma very much doubted it. Suddenly, she had an overwhelming feeling that maybe she could be honest, and tell Mami and David what had been happening at school, but by the time she got halfway across the playground she had talked herself out of it.

Mami wasn't picking her up today, so Alma was allowed to walk home on her own. All of a sudden, she felt very grown up and independent. There were children hanging around the entrance to the school. Some of them would never walk home with their parents. Tamsin was one of these. Alma had never seen Tamsin's parents. She had occasionally seen an older boy waiting for her, but she didn't know whether he was a relative.

Alma wondered what Tamsin was like at home. Would she behave the same way there? Were her parents strict? Alma couldn't imagine Tamsin being scared of anyone or anything. She wished she could be Tamsin's friend, she wanted Tamsin to like her instead of hating her. Alma remembered on several days she had said to herself that she would no longer be scared, and that she would just tell Tamsin to leave her alone. Then, as soon as she saw her, her braveness would melt away, overtaken by anxiety and fear.

***

'Happy birthday dear Alma, happy birthday to youuuuuu!' Alma looked down at her beautiful cake. It was round, had white icing, and the words *Happy Birthday, Feliz Compleanos* had been iced in red letters. A small Dolly-like figure was neatly formed on top of the cake, and twelve pink candles lit up Dolly's features. Alma blew out the candles, to a loud cheer.

'Wow,' she said, touching Dolly's face. 'It's beautiful!' She smiled in Mami and David's direction. Mami came over and ruffled Alma's hair. 'Feliz Compleanos Hija, now who would like a slice of cake?'

'Me, me, me,' came the replies. Alma was pleased that her friends had come. Yes, there were only five of them, but it was just the right number. She had never felt happier. Mami and David had brought her a new bike. It was blue and had daisies on the handle bars, with different coloured streamers hanging down from each bar.

The rest of the afternoon was spent playing games, and ended with hide and seek to ensure that Yoli was included. Alma and her friends would spend ages looking for Yoli, pretending they couldn't see her.

After the party, Alma was allowed to go out on her new bike for half an hour. She had asked David to adjust the saddle, as she couldn't reach the floor, and she was soon riding quite fast on the grassy embankment and even faster down the hills. She dismounted and started walking back up the hill, when a few kids came over to admire her birthday present and asked if they could have a go. Alma refused, saying it was new. She said her goodbyes, and rode home checking her watch.

Before bed that day, Alma had to write out some thank you cards. Mami insisted that this be done the same day, before they were forgotten about. Alma felt tired, but she quickly wrote the cards out in her best handwriting, sealing them all and putting them on the side ready to take into school on Monday.

Alma lay in darkness. The house was silent. She lifted Dolly up and squeezed her tightly. She couldn't believe she had been away from home for six years, three of them in Germany and the last three in Ireland. There had been several schools already. Mami had taken Yoli back to Honduras the previous year, and Alma had stayed with David. She had found it somewhat awkward. For the most part, she'd spent the time in her room, coming down only to eat or to watch television. She did recall David going to the park with her and her friends on a few occasions when she was younger, but mostly Alma and David just talked about school. She was frightened of his temper, and how angry he could get, especially when he was trying to ring Mami in Honduras and couldn't reach her. He would shout, 'She's never coming back! Why can't I get through!!!!? For Christ's sake!' Alma would slip away upstairs and worry, until she would hear him talking to Mami, slowly calming down. As scared as she was of David, she was even more frightened of Mami, whose temper could be much worse. Alma would never forget the beltings or slipper wacks, or the swearing. *But none of it matters as long I have you, Dolly*, she thought, clutching Dolly against her chest.

Slowly, she sank into a dreamless sleep.

CHAPTER 4
The Incident

'How come you have so many babysitting jobs?' Katherine pointed at the chart on Alma's bedroom wall.

Alma walked over to Katherine and looked at the scrawny bit of paper. 'I don't know really. David and Mami get asked, and then they ask me, and I say yes,' Alma smiled at Katherine. 'Do you want me to see if I can get you some?'

'No, I don't think Mum and Dad would let me,' Katherine sunk back onto Alma's bed. 'What do you do with all the money?'

'Well, I get twenty pounds for every job,' said Alma. She reached over to a bedside drawer and took out a flowery pot. She pulled the lid off the pot and showed it to Katherine. Inside was a roll of notes, stuffed up. 'I buy presents with it,' she said, 'and any bits that I need.'

Katherine gawped at the money, 'There's so much!'

Alma smiled, 'Come on, let's go and get Mandy.' She extended her hand to Katherine, and they both linked arms as they made their way out. 'Back later,' Alma shouted, grabbing her coat.

It was glorious outside. The girls made their way to Duke Crescent and stopped outside the block. They pressed the buzzer for Number 23 and Mandy's voice came down the intercom.

'You coming out, Mand?' echoed Alma.

'Yep be down in a sec.'

A few minutes later, they were walking into town. On the way, they stopped off at a kiosk on the parade. Alma bought a pack of beer and two bottles of wine, plus cigarettes, and then they headed up to their favourite spot on Staplemoor Hill.

It wasn't long before the alcohol took effect.

'Alma, do you fancy William?' slurred Katherine.

Mandy burst out laughing, 'No way! You do, don't you?' she shrieked.

'No, I don't! I just like him…he has gorgeous blue eyes though.'

Alma leant forward and erupted into fits of laughter.

'Would you sleep with him?' slurred Katherine.

Alma giggled, 'Might.' She pointed her finger in Mandy's face, 'Have you slept with Thomas?'

'No way.' Mandy pushed Alma's finger away.

'I don't fancy Thomas, and anyway he's into Yvonne.' Mandy had a disappointed look on her face. She lit up another cigarette and disappeared behind a fog of smoke.

'Oi, you lot!' a booming voice shouted behind them. The girls turned around and saw four boys walking towards them. William, Ed, Thomas, and Shane were often in town on Saturdays, and knew exactly where the girls would be.

'God, you frightened the life out of us,' shouted Katherine.

'Have you had enough alcohol?' William pointed at all the empty bottles. They'd brought their own bottles, and put them down by the girls' bench.

'Gotta ciggy?' Shane walked over to Mandy, hand stretched out in anticipation. Mandy chucked him the packet.

William put his arm around Alma, 'You alright then, Almita?' He bent his head down and kissed Alma's cheek. Alma instantly felt her face turn scarlet, and moved away from his grasp.

'You'll hurt his feelings,' said Shane, 'can't you tell he fancies the pants off you?' William pretended to kick Shane, and they both began play fighting and wrestling each other. It wasn't long before all the boys were rolling around on the ground.

Alma opened a bottle of wine and glugged the contents. She handed the bottle to Katherine and then looked over at William. He was handsome, quite tall, with wavy dark hair that fell down over his eyes. She watched as he stood up, and glanced over at her. She felt her heart start to flutter, and quickly looked away, pretending to engage in conversation with Katherine.

'Come on you guys, we are going to Meerax,' Katherine stood up waving her arms. Meerax was a huge department store where you could get anything and everything.

'We're coming with you,' replied Shane, wiping himself down. The girls had finished the beers now, and were almost done with the wine. Mandy had chucked the rest in the bushes before leaving. The boys' conversation had turned to where they could buy more.

Alma felt like she was floating. Everything around her seemed to be moving slowly, and voices seemed distant. Her feet were playing tricks on her. She started to laugh out loud, which in turn made the girls chuckle. Immediately, the boys started taking the mickey out of them.

'Hey, Mand,' Shane ran up to her. 'Do you know that Thomas is red hot at undoing bras?'

And why would I know that?' chirped Mandy defensively.

'Because he said he undid yours in record time,' Shane cackled. He motioned a high five to Thomas, who did not look amused.

Mandy went bright red and gave Thomas a filthy look. 'I can assure you, Shane, that wasn't my bra,' she walked off, jogging to catch up with the other two girls.

'I don't feel too good,' whimpered Katherine as she jolted into Alma suddenly.

Alma didn't feel great herself. They headed towards a small alleyway. Katherine began to run ahead, before vomiting twice and then stumbling over. Alma picked Katherine up, and Mandy steadied her. They got a tissue out of Katherine's pocket, and cleaned her coat.

'She okay?' asked Shane. All four boys had followed them into the alley. Katherine started laughing, wiping her mouth with her hand. 'Where's the beer'?' she giggled. They shook their heads, chuckling, and headed back towards town.

Later that evening, Alma steadied her hand as she pushed her key in the lock of the front door. She had sobered up a little bit, as the boys had brought everyone fish and chips. Mami, David and Yoli were sitting in the living room, watching *The A-Team*. Nobody really noticed as she walked in, so she hung her coat up and went upstairs.

'Your dinner is in the oven,' shouted Mami.

'I've had something,' Alma shouted back, closing her bedroom door.

She looked at the clock on her bedside table. Her babysitting job wasn't until seven-thirty. She lay on her bed, staring up at her Robert Smith poster. Her thoughts turned to William. Did he like her? She really liked him, but every time he got close she felt afraid of him. Her heart started racing as she imagined kissing him. She had never really kissed a boy properly. At school she would overhear girls in the toilets talking about their conquests, and one time there was a girl showing off the love bite on her neck. Alma couldn't help noticing how sore it looked – purple, blue and yellow in colour. She wondered what it would be like to have a love bite. Would it hurt? She smiled to herself and huddled up to her pillow. Feeling a bit dizzy, but content, she closed her eyes, only to re-open them and see Andrew Ridgley and George Michael looking down at her. What was it like to be famous? A gang at school were always going on about becoming celebrities. One time they had asked Alma to come and sing for them, but then changed their mind, saying they didn't want a 'spick' in their band. There had been many schools since they left Honduras, and all of them had been the same. Alma couldn't remember any school where she hadn't been treated like an outcast.

'Alma!' cried a voice from the bedroom door. Yoli had let herself in, and Alma had not heard her. 'What you doing?'

'Hi, Yoli,' Alma pulled her little sister towards her, smelling her freshly shampooed hair.

'Can you play with me?' Yoli looked up at Alma with the cutest of faces. Yoli was a very pretty girl, big brown eyes, button nose, and beautiful lips. *She looks nothing like me*, Alma thought.

'I have got to go out soon,' replied Alma.

'You are always out,' Yoli looked disappointed, 'and you smell funny.' She scrunched her nose up and pulled away from Alma, then ran out of the bedroom. Alma quickly jumped off the bed and started getting changed. She wondered whether Yoli could smell the cigarette smoke on her clothes. Feeling paranoid, she sprayed her jumper with perfume and then hung it up.

The time was seven o'clock. Alma suddenly felt tired. Perhaps she would just watch TV, with little Joe and Briony. She had babysat them for a couple of months now. Joe could be quite naughty, and Alma would have to tell him off regularly. He was four years old, and Briony was three. All in all, they were good kids. Alma hoped that they would settle down for her that night; she really wasn't in the mood for breaking up their squabbles.

'Alma!' Mami shouted from the bottom of the stairs, 'Telefono!'

Alma ran downstairs. 'Hello?'

'Hi, it's Mandy.'

'What's up?'

'What's the address you're babysitting at? We are thinking of coming over.'

Alma gave Mandy the address.

'Don't come over before nine o'clock though…just in case. I'll give a signal at the window when I'm ready.'

Thirty minutes later, Alma knocked on the Whites' door. Joe yelled delightedly when he saw Alma, and ran into her arms.

'Hey, Joe. Have you been a good boy?'

Joe nodded, and clung to Alma's waist. Briony stood next to them, with her fingers in her mouth.

'And what about you, Briony? Have you been good?'

Briony gave a big smile, and nodded her head.

Alma reached into her bag. 'Got you both a surprise,' she said, pulling out two packs of sweets. 'But first, you have to ask Mummy and Daddy if you are allowed them.'

Joe and Briony looked at Marianne. 'Please, Mummy!'

'Okay you can have them, but you have to make sure you behave for Alma tonight, agreed?' Both children nodded, and then ran into the living room perching themselves on the sofa, asking their dad to help them open the packets.

The Whites were a lovely couple, originally from Scotland. Marianne was very pretty, she had curly blonde hair and blue eyes, and was very slim. This evening she looked stunning, in a maxi length black evening gown, shaped tightly around her cleavage. The dress had a split up one side, which accentuated her shapely legs and showed off her very high black stilettos.

'Here, Alma, have a drink,' she pushed a full glass of wine into Alma's hand. 'I know you shouldn't, but what the hell?' she laughed.

'Thanks, Marianne,' said Alma taking the glass. It really wasn't a good idea, she still felt fuzzy from earlier on in the day.

Marianne ushered her into the living room. Alistair was sat watching television, a documentary of some sort. He held a glass of something up to his lips and quickly downed it, standing up afterwards and smiling at Alma, 'Hi, Alma.'

Alma noticed he was in full mess uniform. They were obviously going to an important gathering, and would no doubt be home late. Alma didn't mind – she would sleep on the sofa until they got back, and then would walk home. The army camp was very safe at night, with security barriers at entry point.

There was always good street lighting, and even though Alistair had often said that Alma would be better staying the night, Alma preferred to sleep in her own bed.

'Marianne has got you some nibbles and drinks in the kitchen,' Alistair pointed, 'just help yourself.'

'Thank you,' replied Alma, turning her attention to the kids on the sofa and sitting in-between them both. She couldn't help but notice how handsome Alistair looked. He was slightly shorter than Marianne, with dark hair, a small moustache, and perfect white teeth. Her thoughts were quickly interrupted by the doorbell. It was Marianne's sister Julie, and her husband.

After both ladies put the finishing touches to their hair and makeup, they turned to Alma, asking her what she thought.

'You both look stunning!' beamed Alma.

'Awwwhhhhh, thanks, honey,' cooed Marianne, coming over to Alma and hugging her tightly.

'Are we *going* to this event tonight?' remarked Alistair, rolling his eyes.

'Yes, darling, we are ready now,' laughed Marianne. Everyone put on their coats; the children said goodnight and then carried on eating their sweets in front of the television. *Incredible Hulk,* thought Alma, *that will keep them amused for a while.*

Alma looked out of the window. The army transport mini-bus was parked outside. She noticed other couples from blocks across the way, walking towards it. They all looked so glamourous. It was a nice evening, the sun had disappeared, but it was still light. She made her way to the kitchen and poured her wine down the sink.

It was exactly nine when Alma pulled back the curtains in the living room. She looked out and could see Katherine, Mandy and the boys across the road, smoking. Opening the window, she gave them a wave, then made her way to the front door. She pushed the buzzer to let them in. They came in the door laughing, with heavy footsteps.

'Ssshhh,' she put her finger to her mouth, 'the kids are asleep.'

'Okay okay,' said Mandy, pushing past her. The others followed, clanking carrier bags full of alcohol as they went into the kitchen.

Alma slowly opened the door to the children's bedroom. They were fast asleep. She could see Briony on the bottom bunk bed, clutching her teddy bear, her hair all tousled. Joe was on the top bunk, legs outstretched, with his pyjama top riding up his midriff. They looked so content. As Alma left the room she dimmed their light slightly, and closed the door.

William, Ed and Thomas were in the living room. They had made themselves at home on the sofa, and were flicking through the channels on the television.

'Here,' Mandy shoved a Budweiser in Alma's face.

'No, I'm alright,' Alma pushed it away.

'Don't be stupid, you have to. We have loads to get through,' she handed the bottle to Alma, who had no option to accept, and glugged back a mouthful.

'We brought snacks too,' Katherine picked up two huge bags of crisps and peanuts. They all took their shoes off, and got cosy on the large sofa. Alma perched on the armrest.

'So what time you expecting them back?' asked William, looking across at Alma.

'Not until late,' Alma replied.

'Good, shall we get a film on then?' William leapt off the sofa and headed to the bookcase, which was jam-packed with video tapes. He grinned and pulled out a case, *The Living Dead!*

Everyone grumbled their disapproval. Ultimately they decided on *Grease*, but before the end of the film they were all performing dares and forfeits if they couldn't down their drinks within a certain time.

'Yeah, Mandyyyy, you're not quick enough,' shouted Thomas. Ed puckered up his lips and staggered towards Mandy. She beamed and planted a smacker on his forehead.

'Ooooh, is that it?' yelled Ed.

'I bet it would be on the lips if it was Thomas!' shouted Katherine. Thomas seemed to blush, and Mandy stomped over to him, before grabbing his jumper and pulling him towards her. Thomas was taken aback, and when Mandy kissed him full on the lips everyone cheered.

'Right, come on, guys. Let's get these bottles and rubbish away, you better get going,' quipped Alma, getting to her feet.

'It's only midnight,' complained Ed.

'Yeah, well…it's late,' replied Alma, handing him some empty bottles.

William and Thomas both got up at the same time. They staggered to the toilet, rushing the last couple of feet to beat each other. Mandy was in the kitchen humming one of the songs from the film, and dancing around. Eventually Alma managed to get them out of the door, putting her finger up to her mouth and whispering to William to make sure the girls got back okay. He nodded. None of them took any notice of Alma as they made their way down the road, laughing and joking.

Alma felt drunk again. She looked at the crystal decanter in the drinks cabinet and smelt the contents. Without thinking, she poured some of the liquid into her glass and quickly swallowed. It burnt her throat, and felt really warm. She finished it off, and then took a little more. On the television, Jennifer Rush was belting out her hit. Alma stared at Jennifer's red mini skirt and long boots. She looked lovely, slim, and her make-up was perfect. Alma only wore make-up when absolutely necessary, like when she needed to cover spots. Jennifer Rush didn't seem to have that problem, her skin looked perfect.

Alma sang along, turning up the volume slightly. Soon, she felt herself starting to tire. She lay down on the sofa and grabbed one of the fleecy blankets, bringing her legs up and resting her head on one of the plumped up cushions.

She was awoken by a noise. At first she couldn't tell where it was coming from. She felt quite drunk, and got up to check on the children. They were fast asleep, but there was the noise again. Alma went into the hallway and listened. It was a scratching sound from outside the front door, then she heard a thud. She looked through the small peep hole in the door, and made out Alistair's head, moving up and down. He was trying to get in. Alma opened the door and he almost fell inside. Alma steadied him.

'Are you okay, Alistair?' Alma slurred.

'Hey, Alma,' beamed Alistair. 'Sorry, did I wake you?'

'No, I was awake.' Alma helped him into the living room. He stank of booze, and his bow tie was all twisted. In fact, he looked somewhat dishevelled.

'Where's Marianne?'

'They are all staying at the party,' he swayed towards the drinks cabinet.

'Okay, I will get my things,' said Alma, as she headed to the kitchen to pick up her bag and keys. She put on her shoes and went back into the living room.

'Here you go,' said Alistair, handing her a glass of something.

'Oh no, I gotta get going,' Alma studied the clock on the sideboard. It was one-thirty in the morning.

'Come on, Alma, it's early. Just one drink,' he smiled as he moved towards her, lifting her hand up to take the drink.

'Ready? After three…one, two, three!' They both threw their heads back. Alma almost retched as the liquid hit her stomach, and she screwed her face up in disgust.

'You okay?' Alistair laughed as he took her glass.

'What was that?' she looked at him.

'The finest whisky you will ever taste.' He turned back towards the drinks cabinet and poured another two glasses.

'I have to go, Alistair,' Alma fumbled with her keys. She felt very light headed all of a sudden.

'Please stay,' Alistair got the drinks and sat down on the sofa. 'Come and talk to me, we haven't really spoken properly in all the time you have been coming here.'

Alma hesitated.

'You don't have to stay long. Just one more drink, I promise,' he looked over and patted the seat next to him. Alma parked herself cautiously on the sofa.

'Have you got a boy…boyfriend?' it seemed to take Alistair an eternity to string his sentence together. Alma felt fuzzy. She stared at the television, but didn't recognise the band that was playing.

'Well?' Alistair was waiting for her to answer.

'No.'

'That's a shame, you are a very pretty girl.' Alistair moved around to look at Alma, eyeing her up. Alma felt herself go rigid.

'Come on,' he said, 'let's have a dance.' Alma looked at him, in a daze. Alistair dragged her to her feet. Within a second she was in his arms and they were dancing. Moving around slowly, she saw George Michael on the screen – 'Careless Whisper'. Alma loved this song. She closed her eyes; it wasn't a good idea. The room started to spin.

'Alma,' Alistair whispered in her ear.

He pulled back and looked at her. Alma was mesmerised. For a split second, her heart was racing, her mouth felt dry. This was wrong, so wrong, so why could she not get out of his grasp? She felt his hand slip from her waist to her bottom, and then both arms back round her middle, squeezing her towards him. She felt strange, almost ecstatic. Perhaps it was the whisky. She was floating, escaping, but towards where she didn't know.

'I liked you the first time I saw you, Alma.'

Alma held her breath.

'I think you like me too,' he buried his cheek into Alma's face, and pulled her close. 'I am going to kiss you. Don't be afraid, I promise you I won't hurt you. I would never hurt you.'

He bent down, and his lips gently touched hers. He hesitated, and then he kissed her hard. She was trembling, frozen to the spot, and clinging to him. His tongue shot in and out; it slowly danced with hers, in time and frantic. She had never been kissed before, not like that, and responded as if it was the most natural thing she had ever done. She was losing control.

Alistair pulled back, his face looked flushed.

'You are jailbait, Alma. Do you know that?' Alma didn't know what he meant, but she didn't care. He kissed her once more and Alma felt dizzy with excitement.

He stopped again and looked intensely at her, bending over to kiss her neck and face. She was floating on air. This wasn't real, was it? Perhaps she was dreaming. He fumbled with her cardigan. Alma's eyes widened.

'No, no, this is wrong!' she pulled herself from his grip and headed down the hallway. Alistair followed, pulling her back then pushing her against the wall again, kissing her frantically, cupping her breast in one hand and stroking her hair. She let out a moan. Alistair slowly removed her cardigan, and then her t-shirt. He picked her up and carried her to the spare room, where he laid her on the bed. He took her hand and brought it up to his mouth, kissing it and then bringing it down to his shirt. Alma obliged. They both lay in complete darkness, naked, and Alma felt herself shivering. Alistair wrapped himself around her, pulling the covers across both of them. It was all happening so quickly, there was no time to rationalise or think. His kisses were electrifying. He moved down to tease her nipples with his teeth. Alma moaned loudly. Then she began to panic. He was too heavy. The weight was suffocating.

'Please…stop,' she gasped.

Alistair ignored her. He slipped a finger down beneath the sheets, then two. It was painful, and Alma let out a small cry. He covered her mouth.

'I love you, Alma. I love you,' he whispered. He kissed her tummy and then the tip of her vagina. Alma felt wet. She was somewhere else, somewhere she had never been before. Her head wasn't right, this couldn't be happening.

'Are you a virgin, my darling Alma?' she heard Alistair whisper with excitement. She could feel him hard against her.

'Yes,' she seemed to blurt the word out. He grunted and kissed her harder than before, and then he was pushing inside her. She was taken aback, and grasped the bedsheets. It was painful, and she wanted him to stop. She felt like she was tearing with each push, and could feel the tears coming. Then she just lay there, motionless, and let him carry on. He was rough now, and didn't seem to care whether he was hurting her or not.

'I'm going to be sick,' she blurted.

Alistair suddenly stopped. He moved off her. Alma barely made it to the toilet in time. Her head was spinning. She tried stifling the vomit, but to no avail. It seemed like hours that she sat there, cold and shaking, crying and trying to lift herself up off the floor. She felt something wet and sticky on her thigh, and when she looked down she could see blood.

'Come on,' she heard Alistair beside her. He slowly lifted her and walked her back to the bedroom. He was stumbling. In the darkness she could just about make out his features, but she wasn't feeling good, and started looking around for her underwear. Alistair helped get Alma's clothes together, and she slowly dressed, feeling nauseous every time she bent down. Clutching her bag and searching for her keys, she began to cry. How had she let this happen? She felt hot, and ran to the toilet again, vomiting violently. As she stood up and looked at her reflection in the mirror, she felt nothing. She was numb.

'I'm sorry, Alma,' Alistair was stood outside the door. He had changed into jogging bottoms and a t-shirt now. Alma picked up her keys.

'Are you okay?' Alistair looked worried. 'Do you want me to walk you home?'

Alma looked at him, 'No it's fine.' She turned quickly and made her way down the hallway.

She was shaking as she heard the front door close quietly behind her. Making her way slowly down each flight of steps, the tears came quickly and fast. Her vision blurred, and her balance seemed out of kilt as she left the block and headed home. The journey was a blur. She was transfixed by the street lighting, the car headlights that turned the street a distorted shade of orange. It was so cold. Finally home, she crawled up the stairs and shut the door behind her. Inside her room, there was nothing but darkness.

CHAPTER 5
The Drinking

Alma stared out of the coach window. The rain was heavy, and people were running to catch shelter. The last few months had been a blur, but now she was on the way to Nanna and Clive's. Mami, David and Yoli were travelling separately. David had been unable to get the whole week off, so they were only coming for a few days.

The coach was slowing down. She could see two older men huddled beside each other, trying to light up a cigarette. Alma felt the sudden urge to smoke, she could taste the tobacco on the tip of her tongue. She felt empty, hollow, like a shell. Her face was pale and gaunt. Her eyes were sunken and dark circles had formed beneath them.

She had not seen Joe or Briony since that night, and she knew she would never see them again. The guilt and shame was unbearable. She hated herself more than ever before. A couple of days had passed before she had decided to tell Katherine and Mandy, who were completely dumbstruck, and didn't know what to say at first.

'What are you going to do?' Mandy asked.

'Have you told your mum and dad yet?' said Katherine.

'I haven't said a word to anyone about it, except to you guys, and I don't want you saying anything.' Alma stared down at her bedroom floor, 'I can never go around there again.'

'But she'll know that something is up, Alma.'

'Yeh, she'll be wondering why you can no longer babysit.'

'I know that,' snapped Alma, feeling irritated with the two of them. She couldn't possibly go around there again. She would never be able to look at Marianne, and there was no way she could ever set eyes on Alastair again. The thought gave her goose bumps.

It wasn't long before Mami and David found out. A few days later, there was a furious knocking on the bedroom door, and then Mami rushed in, grabbing Alma. She was crying hysterically.

'Why, Almita? Why didn't you tell us?'

David stood behind her. Alma couldn't tell whether he was angry, upset, or both.

'What's going on?' Alma asked.

'Why didn't you tell us about Alistair, Alma?' David said.

Alma felt her heart sink. 'How did you know?'

Katherine had betrayed her. She'd told her dad, who took David to one side and told him everything. Alma was furious with Katherine. How could she have done this? She wanted to run away, far away. She released herself from Mami's grip.

'I don't want to talk about it.'

'Alma, he has to be reported,' David said.

'¿Almita, por qué?' Mami was staring at Alma, with tears in her eyes. 'Podríamos haberte ayudado hija, Almita.' *Almita, we could have helped you.*

When they'd left, Alma could hear Mami crying loudly outside the door. David said he would ring the police. Mami cried some more, saying that this sort of thing was not supposed to happen to her daughter, and that she'd brought Alma here to have a better life. Alma rolled her eyes. She'd heard it so many times before.

The next day, David and Mami had a lengthy conversation with Alma. Sitting at the dining table, David had told Alma that they would have to report the incident. Firstly, Alistair couldn't be allowed to get away with it. Secondly, Alma was fifteen years old, so the incident involved sex with a minor.

'If not for your benefit, Alma, we have to do it for other people. If we don't report him then he'll probably do the same again.'

Alma thought hard and long about it all, and eventually agreed that she would give a statement.

Two days later, Alma was sitting across from a male and female soldier in uniform, with David sat next to her. The first part of the statement was straightforward, but then they asked for the sexual details.

'Did you consent to sexual intercourse, Alma?'

Alma cried. She couldn't answer. She felt humiliated, ashamed and angry with herself, and hated Katherine more than ever.

'Alma, are you saying he raped you?' the lady in uniform stared at Alma, with her pen poised.

Alma looked down at the desk, tears obscuring her view.

'Alma,' the woman repeated her name, and then again a third time, 'Alma.'

'I'm not sure,' Alma blurted out.

'Well, can I ask you if you know what rape means?' the woman looked intensely at Alma.

Alma flinched, she knew what rape meant, she knew it was a serious thing to be accused of. *But Alistair didn't rape me*, she thought. She had been the guilty party, perhaps she had led him on. Perhaps she had given him the impression that he *could* come on to her, the way she had danced with him for god's sake. She had kissed him back. No, she was one hundred percent to blame, and there was no doubt about it.

'Alma, please can you answer the question?'

'No, he didn't,' Alma almost whispered.

'Did he make you do something you didn't want to do?'

Alma felt confused by that question. Of course, she had not wanted it to happen. She had wanted to leave, and she would have done so if he had let her, but the truth of the matter was she had been too weak. It had been the same thing as always – she gave in to what he wanted. She could have stopped it from happening, but the easiest option was to give in, and she didn't fight it.

'I asked him to let me leave. If only he'd agreed, then none of this would have happened.' Tears stung her eyes, 'I didn't want any of this to happen. I didn't want to hurt anybody, I didn't want any of this!' Alma laid her head on the desk and sobbed into her hands.

David scraped his chair back and asked if they could take a break. The woman handed Alma a box of tissues.

'Alma, you may already be aware Alistair has also been interviewed. He has advised that you were flirting with him, and had got him up to dance. Is that your version of events?'

Alma stared blankly, trying to recall the events. Perhaps she had flirted with him. It had all become a bit of a haze now anyway. Yes, she had thought he was handsome, had she told him that? Maybe she had given him the wrong idea. No, she had not. She had not instigated this. She was not a bad person, she was a kind person. Yes, she smoked and drank, but she was a good person…wasn't she?

'I didn't want this to happen,' she replied calmly.

'Alma, can you please answer the question?'

David coughed and moved in his chair, Alma looked across at him. He stared straight ahead.

'He didn't rape me, but he wouldn't let me leave. He gave me two or three drinks which I tried to refuse. He danced with me, I didn't think I had flirted with him. I was ready to leave, I had my bag and keys ready.' The words just tumbled out in one go. Alma paused and looked up.

'I asked him to stop, but it was too late, and then as far as I remember I only just made it to the bathroom where I was violently sick.' She looked from one soldier to the other. The female soldier was writing frantically,

'Okay, Alma, we will leave it there for today.' The female soldier stood up and motioned to her colleague to do the same.

They both left the room.

David knelt beside Alma. 'You okay?'

'Not really,' Alma began crying again, but this time she didn't hold back. Tears came fast. She sobbed onto David's shoulder, and he put his arm around her, glaring towards the door.

It had been two weeks since the meeting with the soldiers. Since then, it had felt like Alma was living a terrible dream. She stared out the window as the coach pulled into the station. Nanna and Clive were waiting by the drop-off point. They gave Alma a big hug and Nanna bent down to kiss her on the cheek.

'Come on, my dear. Let's get you home.'

They walked to Clive's car and put Alma's bags into the boot. It was still raining, and the wind had now picked up.

'How was your trip?' Nanna asked, as they left the car park.

'Okay,' replied Alma. She wasn't in the mood for small talk. She just wanted to get back to the house and fall asleep.

'Sarah has been waiting for you to arrive,' Nanna chirped.

Alma smiled, half-heartedly. She remembered Sarah, from when they were little, but it had been a while since they'd seen each other.

When they arrived home, Alma settled down into a chair beside the open fire. Nanna made up a mug of hot chocolate, and then gave Clive a very deliberate look. He went out to the kitchen, leaving the two of them together in the lounge.

'Alma,' Nanna whispered, 'we are all here for you, no matter what.' She smiled at Alma, her grey hair flickering in the light. 'There are things that happen to us in our lives, things that we cannot control or understand at the time.' Nanna drew herself closer and held onto Alma's free hand. 'He will be punished, Alma.'

Alma looked away, removing her hand from Nanna's grasp.

'It's all my fault,' she looked at Nanna, 'I guess I'm not a very nice person.'

Nanna stood up. 'Don't say that, Alma. None of it is your fault.'

All of a sudden, there was a knock on the back door.

'Come in,' shouted Nanna, walking towards the kitchen.

'Alma!' Sarah wailed, 'I have been waiting for you to arrive! How long are you staying for?' She crossed the room and bent down, giving Alma a big squeeze, almost spilling the hot chocolate.

'Hi, Sarah, you look great,' smiled Alma, 'I'll be here for about six months, so have to get to school whilst I am here.'

'Oh brill, I missed you. There's a party for Ralph's eighteenth next Saturday…he will be really happy you are back.' Sarah grinned, and rubbed her hands together, 'Better go, gotta help mum with the food shop.' She gave Alma another squeeze and bid Nanna goodbye.

Alma's gaze was back on the fire. There was not a chance she would be going to the party. She knew that.

***

The next few days were chaotic. Relatives and friends appeared, seemingly from out of nowhere. Time seemed to disappear, and Alma found it hard to keep up the pretence that she was happy to see everyone. David, Mami and Yoli arrived soon after, yet Alma found herself feeling moody and low and irritated by everyone, even Yoli.

The following day David and Alma visited Ferry Hill secondary school. Alma took an instant dislike to it. She just wanted to get back to Ireland, to see her old friends, except Katherine, of course. How could she have done this to her? None of this would be happening right now, if it wasn't for Katherine.

'So we look forward to seeing you on Monday then, Alma.'

She looked up, the headmaster towered over her. Alma smiled at him and followed David out of the office, staying a few paces behind him all the way back to the car. She sat in silence all the way home. She felt tired, perhaps she would go home and sleep for the rest of the day.

Ferry Hill was frustrating. All the subjects she had chosen were different to the ones in Ireland, she kept thinking it was all a waste of time. She would be back in Ireland before the end of the year, and soon after that she would be taking her exams. But now, how would she even pass anything? Once again, she found herself the loner. Everyone else knew everyone, she found it hard to fit in, and it was a constant battle. Sarah would meet her at break times, with a few other girls. It was soon known that Alma could speak Spanish, so she would be asked on numerous occasions to translate things, and invariably it would be quite humorous. It was like they had never heard a foreign language before.

The word about Ralph's party soon spread. 'So, Alma, have you got your glad rags ready for Saturday?' asked Sarah.

'Errr... well... the thing is...' started Alma. looking at Sarah and noticing her facial expression change. 'I don't think I will be going.'

'What do you mean?' quipped Sarah, 'I've told everyone you are going! It's a good way to get to know people better.'

'I haven't got anything to wear,' answered Alma, hoping for a second that this would throw a spanner in the works.

'Well we can go into town Saturday morning and get you something. I still have to get some bits anyway,' replied Sarah excitedly.

Alma wasn't in the mood to argue.

'You got any ciggies?'

'Only got one left,' Sarah reached into her coat pocket. She linked arms with Alma, pulling her behind the school wheelie bins. Looking around to make sure the coast was clear, Sarah lit up the last Marlborough and passed it to Alma, who inhaled deeply and slowly. She instantly felt calmer and more relaxed.

The next day was Saturday. Alma had just finished getting dressed, when there was a knock on the door.

'You ready?' Sarah stood in the front doorway.

'Yep,' replied Alma, slipping her coat on. She'd already decided that she wouldn't find anything to wear. Then she could make her excuses again. She really didn't want to go to this party. But Sarah quickly set about changing her mind.

'Hey Alma, what about this?' Sarah was holding up a black and white polka dot ra-ra skirt. Alma loved it instantly.

'Try it on,' Sarah shoved the skirt up to Alma's frame. Alma took the skirt and started looking for a top. She pulled one off the rail, black with a white slogan on the front that read *Frankie says Relax*.

'Perfect,' said Sarah.

Alma also brought some black shoes with small heels, natural coloured tights, and some jewellery. By the end of the spree, she felt quite excited. They had some lunch at the local Wimpy, and then made their way to the supermarket to get some cigarettes and alcohol. Sarah looked much older, but it was touch and go whether they would ask for ID.

'Right, I will be round at seven,' Sarah was trying to stop the bottles clanking in the carrier bag, eventually handing Alma two bottles to put under her coat.

'Okay see you then,' replied Alma, putting the key in the front door whilst steadying herself, with the two bottles, and all the bags she was carrying. A few hours later, she tried on her outfit for Nanna.

'Well, what do you think?'

Nanna beamed at her, 'Oh, Alma, you look beautiful! Will you not be cold though?'

'No, I've got my coat and tights on,' Alma pinched the flesh coloured tights.

'You will be walking home with others, won't you? Clive, doesn't she look lovely?'

Clive looked at Alma from over the top of his newspaper. 'Very nice,' he said.

'Have you got money?' Nanna enquired.

'We don't need money, Nanna, all the food and drink are supplied.'

'I hope there isn't going to be any alcohol there.'

'Only for the over-age ones, Nanna,' Alma smiled, thinking about the bottles in her room upstairs. She suddenly remembered she hadn't eaten anything since lunch time. Walking into the kitchen, she grabbed a couple of biscuits from the cupboard. She couldn't afford to be putting weight on, not now she was on track to reach six-and-a-half stone.

'Alma! Sarah's here.'

Sarah looked absolutely gorgeous. She was wearing a red ra-ra skirt, a silky blouse, and high heels. Her hair was up, and she wore massive hoop earrings.

'Looking good, girl,' Sarah hugged Alma. 'Can't believe how thin you are, Alma. You will waste away soon if you're not careful.'

'I love your outfit,' Alma looked Sarah up and down.

'All set then?' Sarah opened her coat to show Alma the carrier bag containing the bottles.

'Yep just quickly need to nip upstairs and get my coat,' Alma winked at Sarah and ran upstairs, leaving her talking to Nanna and Clive.

The party was at a hall, about five minutes away from the Fighting Cocks pub, and a ten-minute walk from Nanna and Clive's house. Ralph was the brother of one of Sarah's good friends. Alma had known him on and off, but hadn't seen him since she had got back.

There was quite a crowd when Alma and Sarah turned up.

'Hey, birthday boy,' shouted Sarah as she grabbed Ralph from behind. He swung round, looking surprised, and hugged Sarah.

'Hi, Alma, I didn't know you were back!' he held out his arms and Alma hugged him. The girls handed him his birthday cards and gave him the bottles of drink. He walked over to a large table, where there was enough drink to sink a ship. Ralph's mum and two older sisters were serving everyone, cautious to serve only soft drinks to the under-age individuals.

It didn't take long before Sarah had plied Alma with various drinks. Already tipsy, Alma felt relaxed. The music blared. Ralph was stood at the edge of the dance floor, laughing with a few friends, and pointing to one guy shouting, 'When will I, will I be famous?' into his pretend microphone.

Alma slipped her vodka and coke. She couldn't help but laugh. The girls from her class had joined her.

'Ralph is so hot,' chuckled Ella, one of the girls.

'Yeah, well, he's too old for you,' said another, named Emma.

'No he's not, he's only two years older than me!'

Alma looked across at Ralph. Was he hot? She thought he was okay looking. Tall, with blonde hair, Alma thought he dressed nicely too, and he had a nice physique…but she didn't think he was hot.

'Do you think he's hot, Alma?' Emma asked, catching Alma by surprise.

'He's alright,' replied Alma.

'Has Sarah told you he likes you?' Emma smiled.

Alma looked at both girls, 'No?'

'Oh yeah, rumour has it that he was going to kill Sarah if you didn't come.'

'But he didn't know I was back?'

'Oh don't be so naïve,' said Emma, 'That's what he wants you to think.'

Sarah walked over to the girls. Madonna came on and the hall erupted. Alma and Sarah looked towards the dance floor, some of the antics were hilarious.

'Is it true about Ralph liking me?' shouted Alma, trying to make herself heard over the noise.

'Yup,' Sarah nodded. 'He's always liked you, even when he was younger.'

'But he's eighteen,' blared Alma, suddenly feeling extremely drunk.

'So?' Sarah shrugged, she could no longer contain herself, and started moving to the beat.

'Well, I am not interested,' Alma knocked back her drink.

'You're mad,' shouted Sarah staring hard at her. 'Look at you. You're gorgeous, have a figure to die for, and one of the most popular guys has the hots for you…but you're not interested?' Sarah finished her drink. She glared at Alma, looking unimpressed.

Alma grabbed Sarah and pulled her onto the dance floor. Emma and Jo joined them. They all pranced about moving their hips and sticking out their chests provocatively, laughing uncontrollably. When the song died out, the tempo changed, and 'Careless Whisper' came on. Alma froze. She moved quickly towards the toilets. Girls were rushing out, hoping that they would get asked to dance, fixing their makeup and hair and checking their outfits.

'You okay?' Sarah had followed Alma into the bathroom.

Alma looked around, checking no-one else was in there with them. She stared at her drunken reflection in the mirror. Her lips were bright red, eyes big, the dark circles didn't look so bad, but then again she was wearing quite a lot of makeup.

'I hate this song. Do you know what I was doing when I last heard it?' Alma wobbled and held onto the sink for support. She was slurring.

'What?' Sarah sounded drunk too.

'I was sleeping with a married man,' Alma blurted out.

'What do you mean?'

Alma told Sarah about the incident with Alistair. She started to cry. 'You see, Sarah, I'm a slagggg. Ralph would never want anything to do with me if he knew.' Alma stumbled into one of the cubicles, slamming the door behind her.

'Alma,' said Sarah, banging on the door. 'You are the last person I would call a slag! Oh my god, is that why you are back here for so long this time?'

Alma came out holding a handful of toilet roll, 'I let him, Sarah. I let him. He has got a fucking wife and children! That makes me an awful person.'

'No, Alma,' Sarah was holding Alma's arms tightly. 'He was the grown up, you are fifteen, fifteen for fucks sake. He took advantage of you, the dirty git! What's happening with him, has he been arrested? Does his wife know?'

Alma stared into the mirror. For a second, she thought she looked beautiful, but then she noticed her big lips and wide nose. She hated herself. She needed another drink.

'Come on,' Alma led Sarah out of the toilets. Girls were coming in now, giggling and drunk, discussing their prospective conquests for later on.

'Oi, I've been looking for you,' there was a voice behind them. Alma turned to see Ralph. He smiled at her, 'Do you wanna dance?'

'Of course she does,' Sarah pushed Alma towards Ralph, and he led her to the dance floor.

Ralph held Alma tightly around the waist. Suddenly, they were close, very close. Alma looked over at Emma, who was dancing with a dark-haired guy. She gave Alma a thumbs up sign, and had a satisfied grin on her face.

Alma could smell Ralph's aftershave. His heart was beating fast, as was hers. She rested her head on his chest. She closed her eyes…and immediately saw Alistair's face. Her legs started to buckle. Ralph put his arms out and caught her.

'Woah, are you okay?'

Alma composed herself. She nodded.

'Thank you for coming tonight,' shouted Ralph. 'Oh, and thank you for my card. I'm eighteen today,' he laughed.

'I do know,' replied Alma, smiling, but at the same time looking for her exit.

Bronski Beat came on, 'Smalltown Boy'. *Thank god*, thought Alma. She released herself from Ralph's grasp, leaving him stood there, but he was soon next to Alma at the table. Ralph's mum looked at her.

'Are you eighteen, love?'

'She's okay, Mum,' Ralph gestured, putting his arm around Alma and getting her another drink. Alma gulped it down greedily. She grabbed another, and downed that too. With every gulp, her head felt calmer. Her body took over. She was dancing again, frantically, loving every minute. She didn't care where she was, the tempo was all she heard. She was six feet tall, everyone loved her, she was thin and beautiful. She was in the best possible place, hoisting her skirt higher and higher up her thigh. She didn't want the night to end…but it did.

They walked home in a group. Alma had sobered up towards the end of the night, and now her feet were killing her. She felt hungry. Sarah passed Alma a cigarette, but Ralph promptly took it off her. 'Don't Alma, you don't need that,' he looked at Sarah disapprovingly. They all stopped at the corner of Alma and Sarah's road.

'Can I see you tomorrow?' Ralph looked at Alma.

'Errr, I don't know what I'm doing,' Alma felt panicky. She didn't want to see Ralph, she just wanted to get home.

'Well, shall we meet at Don's Fish and Chips place, at two o'clock?'

Alma hesitated. She didn't answer.

'I'll wait there for you, if you show you show, if you don't I will be really upset,' Ralph put his hands to his heart, pretending to be heartbroken.

'I had better go,' she moved towards Sarah, who was smoking and talking to the others.

'I will be there, Alma, two o'clock, two o'clock!' Ralph held Alma's arm.

***

'Oh, Alma, I don't want you to go home!'

'It's gone super quickly,' Alma remarked.

They were sitting in Sarah's back garden, watching Poncho, Sarah's cat. It had been five months since Ralph's party. Much to Sarah's disappointment, Alma hadn't gone to see Ralph the day after. In fact, she'd barely ventured out at all since she arrived in England. She'd only seen Ralph a few times since that night, and now there were rumours of him and Emma seeing each other. Alma had decided she didn't care. She wasn't ready for a boyfriend. Besides, she could hardly believe she'd be back in Ireland the following day. There had been no contact with anyone since leaving.

Poncho dived into the bushes. He came out with a disappointed look on his face.

'When will you be back here?' asked Sarah.

'I don't know.'

'Will you be okay when you get back home?'

'I really don't know,' Alma leant back and looked up at the blue sky, not a cloud in sight. She thought about Katherine and her other friends. She wasn't sure about how it would be, going back, but she wanted things to go back to normal, and she missed Mami, David, and Yoli.

'I will write to you,' Sarah smiled.

'Okay, swap addresses later,' Alma smiled back.

David arrived later on that day. He looked tired, and went to bed early, in preparation for the journey ahead. Lying on her bed, Alma closed her eyes and breathed in deeply. She hadn't managed to reach her target weight, despite trying hard, and even skipping meals. She had decided already that she would carry on when she got back to Ireland. David had agreed that she could start running with him in the early mornings. As she lay there, she pondered on how she would resolve things with Katherine when she returned to Ireland. She wanted to understand why Katherine had done it. What had possessed her to tell her parents?

Alma tossed and turned and eventually fell asleep very late, only to be woken by David's alarm across the landing. It was time to head back home.

CHAPTER 6
Lost

It was lovely to be back in familiar surroundings. Yoli and Mami were in the kitchen as Alma walked through the door. There was that same aroma, the polish that Mami would use on the wooden furniture, and that same room spray.

'Almaaaaa,' shouted Yoli, running towards her. She had definitely grown, her facial features had changed. Alma squeezed her, suddenly feeling quite emotional.

Mami turned around and smiled that familiar smile. 'It's lovely to have you home,' she looked Alma up and down, 'you look thin though. Did Nanna and Clive not feed you?'

Alma mumbled a response.

'Are you home to stay now?' Yoli asked eagerly.

Alma nodded.

'I'll show you my new dolly,' Yoli ran into her bedroom, bringing out her new toy. She beamed with excitement as she handed it to Alma

'Yolanda, let Alma have a rest please,' Mami brought over her drink.

Yoli took the dolly back, her smile disappearing.

'No it's okay,' Alma said, 'let me have a look.' She took the doll from Yoli's hands and examined it. 'She's very pretty. Have you given her a name yet, Yoli?'

'Yes, she's called Abigale.'

Alma gave the dolly a hug and then grabbed Yoli and squeezed her tightly. She had missed her so much.

That afternoon Alma was awoken by the phone. She opened her eyes, it was still daylight. She could hear David talking to someone. His voice was stern but official, so she guessed that it was something to do with work. After a while, he put the phone down, and she heard him say something to Mami about going to the office. He sounded annoyed. David did not return until the early hours of the morning. Alma heard him mulling around, clanking glasses. It sounded like he was drinking. Soon, Alma fell back to sleep.

In the morning, she found out that someone from David's office had left, and stolen some important documents. David had been tasked with ensuring that the documents didn't fall into the wrong hands. Mami seemed worried.

'Mami, please try not to stress,' Alma sat at the dining table, warming her hands around her hot mug of tea. 'I am sure David will be alright.'

'I hope so, he could lose his job over this,' Mami looked down, stirring her bowl of cereal.

'I have to go,' Alma stood up and quickly washed her cup.

'Alma, I am also worried about you,' Mami said.

'Don't worry, Mami, I am okay.' She squeezed Mami's hand.

***

'God she's back, look at her!'

'Who does she think she is? Bloody slut.'

Alma was nearly at the bottom of the hill, walking towards the school bus, when she heard the shouts behind her. She turned around and saw Mandy and Katherine. She hardly recognised them.

'What the fuck are you looking at?' Katherine almost spat the words out.

Alma carried on walking, feeling a bit shocked. She heard their footsteps getting faster, until they were running. It all happened so quickly. Suddenly, she was knocked clean off her feet. She lay on the pavement, in a daze.

'Take her fucking school bag, Mand,' shouted Katherine, as she grabbed Alma by the hair and dragged her up.

'Do you know how much stick I've had to take because of you?' Katherine's face was almost touching Alma's. 'You are nothing but a fucking slag, and you deserved everything you got. Even my mum and dad think you deserved it.'

Katherine punched her hard in the stomach. She dropped Alma to the floor and started kicking her. A group of kids started to circle them, and Alma could hear them jeering, taunting and laughing. As she lay on the ground, Mandy put her foot on the back of Alma's neck, whilst Katherine got on top of her and started to push her head against the pavement. Alma tried hard to release herself, but Katherine was too strong.

'Go on Kath, punch her, give it to the stupid bitch,' shouted Mandy.

'What the hell did I see in you as a friend?' Alma could feel Katherine's breath on her face. She stank of alcohol. Alma swung her fist around and managed to grab Katherine's jumper, but as she did so, Mandy leaned over and punched her in the face. Alma fell back against the pavement. There was blood on her tongue and lips.

A loud voice suddenly cut through the crowd, 'That's enough! Let me through!' It was the school bus escort. 'I said that's enough, let me through.'

Katherine climbed to her feet. She smirked at Alma, 'She shouldn't be such a bitch then.' She aimed another kick at Alma's thigh, and leant down close to Alma's face, 'You're dead.'

Alma watched, dazed, as Mandy and Katherine walked away. The escort waved everyone away from the scene. She bent down next to Alma.

'Alma, are you okay, or do you want to go back home?'

Alma struggled to her feet. Her tights were ripped and she had blood all over her school blouse. The escort handed her a tissue.

'I want to go to school,' Alma said, and moved awkwardly towards the bus.

'Okay, but you will have to sit at the front with me.' They both walked slowly down the hill. Alma could see faces pressed against the back of the coach window, staring at her.

The journey was long and uncomfortable. Alma was in a lot of pain. She tried to understand why Katherine had been so angry with her, but it didn't make sense. She knew it would be difficult coming back to Ireland, but she hadn't expected that. When she got to school, on the instructions of the bus escort, she made her way to the Head's office. Mrs Wilmot was elegant in her navy suit and crisp white blouse. She wore a large butterfly brooch just below her suit collar, and a blue and white scarf was tied neatly around her neck.

'Welcome back, Alma,' Mrs Wilmot held the door open. 'Please, come in.'

Alma sat down on a hard-backed wooden chair. Mrs Wilmot sat opposite her.

'So, Alma, your bus escort has filled me in on this morning's events,' she looked across at Alma and smiled. Her teeth were perfect and very white. 'Now, whilst this didn't happen on the school premises, with your permission I would still like to address the individuals involved here,' she tapped her fountain pen on the desk, waiting for Alma to reply.

'It's fine, Miss, it was just a bit of a misunderstanding, that's all.' Alma couldn't look at Mrs Wilmot. She felt a shooting pain in her lips, but tried to smile.

'Well it doesn't look like a misunderstanding from where I am sitting, Alma. Can you tell me what it was about?'

'No, not really,' Alma looked at her sheepishly.

'Katherine has been in a lot of trouble recently. It would really help me if you could at least tell me what happened…'

'To be honest, Miss, I really don't know why she did what she did. It was a shock for me as we were really good friends before...' she paused.

'Before you went away?'

Alma nodded. She looked down at the floor. Her head was starting to throb.

'I will be speaking to her and Mandy today, and I will also be speaking to their parents. This is unacceptable behaviour, and it won't be tolerated, I hope you understand,' she looked at Alma for reassurance.

Alma nodded. This was going to be disastrous. Mrs Wilmot didn't realise that she was only making things worse.

'I would also like you to get checked over by first aid, you don't look all that good.' Her face was sympathetic. She stood up, and Alma followed her out of the room.

'I wanted to say that we are very happy to have you back here at Drummond School, Alma. You have been through a lot, and we want you to know that if you need anything or if you want to talk, my door is always open.'

'Thank you, Miss.'

The medical staff wanted to send Alma home, but she refused. She just wanted to get on with her lessons, and her study material for her exams had not even been given to her yet. In one lesson that day she was in the same classroom as Katherine. Alma felt nauseous seeing her again, but luckily Katherine didn't even acknowledge her. *I should be angry with you*, Alma thought to herself, as she sat in the library at lunch time, *you dropped me in it, for god's sake*.

As Alma left the library, she saw Thomas, William and Yvonne heading her way.

'Hi Alma,' smiled William. 'God what happened to you?' he pointed at her face.

'Got into a bit of fight.'

'What on your first day back? Who with?'

'Oh, it doesn't matter,' Alma shrugged her shoulders.

'You okay? You've lost loads of weight.'

'Have I?' Alma was delighted that someone had noticed.

'Heard it was Katherine Miller,' Yvonne folded her arms

'Katherine!?' exclaimed William. 'But you were best friends, I don't understand.'

'Yeah, well, neither do I,' said Alma. 'To tell you the truth I don't really know what's got into her.'

'Well she's in with Nikki, Michelle and that lot, so that's not good for a start,' Yvonne said.

'What's wrong with Nikki and Michelle?' Alma was curious, as she didn't really know of them, but she remembered Nikki from before she'd left.

'Nikki is on the verge of being expelled, she got caught with aerosol cans and glue. Katherine was caught doing the same, so yeah they're already in a lot of trouble.'

'Blimey,' remarked Thomas, completely oblivious to all of what Yvonne had just shared.

Alma finished the day with double science. Her head was still throbbing, and it was all she could do to concentrate. When she came out, William was waiting by the door.

'Hope you don't mind me waiting,' he shuffled uncomfortably on the spot.

'Going to your bus?'

'Yes,' replied Alma.

'I'll walk with you.'

As they walked, Alma glanced across at William. Somehow, his eyes seemed bluer than before. He was still as good looking as ever.

'I just wanted to say how sorry I am about everything that happened Alma…' He paused, '…you know, before you went away.'

'It's fine.'

'I've heard all sorts of rumours, and so many horrible things have been said about you. I was angry and really had to restrain myself from saying stuff. To be honest I don't know what I would have said, as I don't know what happened at the end of the day.'

He looked over at Alma.

'It doesn't matter. There will always be rumours, whether it's about me or you or whoever. I just want to get my exams out of the way and then I'm done with it all. Do you fancy going out Saturday afternoon?'

'Well, we are all meeting at Yvonne's at six-thirty. It's Ed's sixteenth. Do you wanna come?'

'That's really sweet, and thanks, but I don't think I will be partying for a while. Not looking like this, anyway.'

They both laughed. Alma gave him a hug and got on the bus. She made her way to the front and sat down. Behind her, voices started up immediately.

'Bitch, Bitch, Biiiiiiiitttttttccccchhhh.'

'Slut, Slut, Sluuuuuuuuuuttttt.'

Katherine was sat with other two girls on the back seat. They stood up and yelled more insults at Alma, until the escort got onto the bus and sat down next to her. During the journey, there was further commotion, and Alma could hear everyone at the back joking and laughing. Eventually the escort got up and confiscated the offending article – a magazine containing topless photos of Samantha Fox. The boy who it belonged to sat there utterly distraught.

When the bus stopped, the escort asked her to wait until everyone else had got off. As the girls walked past they sniggered and threw screwed up paper and paper clips at Alma.

Alma knew what she was facing when she got off the bus. Her mouth was dry and her hands were shaking. She would need to fight back, but she was terrified.

'Alma, please go straight home,' warned the escort. 'Don't be distracted by them.'

Ahead of Alma, the girls were walking up the hill. They weren't looking back. She breathed a sigh of relief.

'Do you want us to walk you home?' a voice said from the other side of the road. Alma turned and saw two girls, stood together, trying to light a cigarette.

'Err, no I'm okay thanks,' Alma said, trying to muster the last of any pride she had left.

'What? You gonna get the shit kicked out of you again?' the taller of the girls walked over to her.

'Don't think we can watch that again,' laughed the shorter girl. 'I'm Kim and this is Suzy.'

'Wanna drag?' Suzy handed her the cigarette.

'No, I'm okay,' declined Alma. 'I'm Alma, by the way.'

'Oh don't worry we know who you are, you're the talk of the school, that's what you are,' they both laughed.

'Well, here they come,' said Suzy, looking back up the hill. 'They were only waiting for the bus to pull away, cows.'

Alma looked and saw the girls walking back down the hill. Nikki was with them. Alma instantly felt sick. Her brain was yelling for her to run, but she stood frozen to the spot.

'Hey, Suzy.' Nikki went up to the tall girl, and kissed her on the cheek. She whispered something in her ear, and they both laughed. 'Surprised you haven't ran away yet,' she turned to face Alma. 'Katherine is dying to finish where she left off.'

Katherine walked over to Alma whilst Nikki went around the back of her. 'Did you drop me in it with Wilmott?' she jeered.

'No, I didn't,' Alma almost whispered.

Katherine pushed Alma violently, only for Nikki to push her back the other way.

'You are a fucking lying bitch,' Katherine's eyes seemed to bulge. Her face was twisted with hatred. Another shove, this time almost knocking Alma over. Nikki virtually caught her, before pushing her back twice as hard.

'Shouldn't this be one vs one?' a voice chimed in.

Katherine looked round at Kim. 'What the fuck's it got to do with you?'

'Well, it isn't very fair, two against one, is it?' Suzy had joined in.

Katherine looked round at Nikki before storming up to Suzy. 'Why do you want some then?' Katherine pushed her hard.

'Hey hey,' Nikki rushed over, getting in-between them both, 'Leave her Kath, she's okay.' She wrapped her arms round Suzy's shoulders, 'You're right, Suzy, it's not my fight. Just get on with it, Kath, I'm starving.' She laughed and pushed Katherine in Alma's direction.

Alma looked at Katherine. This was it. Katherine came towards her with a determined look on her face. For a moment, Alma almost stumbled. She saw the first punch coming, and managed to move out the way, but Katherine was quick. She jumped on top of Alma, pushing her to the ground. Alma felt her hair being yanked, and nails digging into her skin. Katherine had her knees on Alma's arms, preventing her from moving. Using her legs, Alma pushed up, wriggling free and grabbing a lock of Katherine's hair. Katherine yelped in pain and rolled away. Alma grabbed onto her, moving her hands towards Katherine's throat. She squeezed. Katherine brought her hands up, trying to get Alma to release her grip, but she was losing strength. Alma squeezed even tighter. Katherine's legs were moving up and down now on the pavement, like she was riding a bicycle.

Something thumped into Alma's back. She was thrown sideways onto the pavement.

'What the hell are you doing?' Nikki and Mandy were bending over Katherine, checking she was okay. Nikki turned back to Alma, 'You stupid bitch!' She walloped Alma in the face. Alma fell back across the concrete, with her ears ringing.

'Stop it Nikki!' shouted Suzy, 'leave her alone!' Suzy rushed over and pulled Nikki away. Meanwhile, Katherine was on her feet. She glared at Alma.

'You're fucking dead, bitch.'

Nikki put her hand on Katherine's shoulder. 'Leave it, it's not worth it.' She lit a cigarette and passed it over to Katherine, who put it in her mouth. They walked back up the hill, leaving Alma with Kim and Suzy.

'Jeez, you nearly choked her,' Kim and Suzy started walking with Alma.

Alma looked at her hands, they were shaking violently. She took another few steps and then vomited down her uniform.

'Oh god, come on, let's get you home,' Kim picked up Alma's school bag and grabbed some tissues out of her pocket.

When Alma got home, Mami had cried, as usual. David was furious, and was ready to go and pay all the parents a visit.

Yoli looked sad. 'Does it hurt?' she said to Alma, as they were sat on the sofa. Alma was holding a bag of frozen peas to her face.

'A little, but I'll be okay.'

'Are Mami and Daddy going to call the police?'

'No, Yoli, there's no need for the police.'

'Why did they want to hurt you?' Yoli carried on her investigation.

'Sometimes people do silly things,' replied Alma, hoping that would satisfy her curiosity.

'But it's not nice to hurt someone, is it?'

'No Yoli, it isn't, you are right,' Alma ruffled Yoli's hair. She was growing up so quickly.

Mami and David would not let Alma go to school for the rest of the week, and they made her go to the doctor's surgery too. The doctor only told her what she already knew – she would need to refrain from any physical activities for a while, and rest.

Alma tried to make up for the lack of activity by studying, but she couldn't concentrate. On top of that, Mami was constantly fussing. In the end Alma pretended that she needed to go to the shop, just to get away for a while. Before she left, she rummaged in the back of one of her drawers and found a packet of cigarettes and a lighter. She lit up on the way to the shops, and when she got home she went straight to her bedroom, opening the window and lighting up again. A sudden pang in the pit of her stomach made her wince, an overwhelming sense of sadness that she could not control. She dragged harder on the cigarette and smoked it down to a tiny butt. Her hands were shaking as her heart thudded against her chest. Her breathing suddenly became erratic, she felt like she was going to swallow her tongue. As she held onto the chest of drawers, the room felt like it was closing in. Alma opened her mouth to shout but nothing came out. What was happening to her? She fell to her knees and began to sob uncontrollably. She didn't know how long she was on the floor, but when there were no more tears left her breathing steadied, and she began to calm a little. She closed her eyes and began to imagine green fields full of sunflowers, and bright sunshine, then deep blue waters – calm and glistening in the sunlight.

'Please, God, let me be okay,' she whispered.

The phone rang for Alma a couple of times that day, but she didn't want to speak to anyone. Mami had made meals, but Alma couldn't eat. She wanted to exercise, but as soon as she started moving her legs, she froze with panic. Immediately she rushed back to her room and climbed under the covers, trying to calm her breathing. Panic had taken over again, her heart was racing uncontrollably.

***

'Alma, we are going to call the doctor,' David was stood over Alma's bed. 'You haven't been to school for weeks now.'

Mami sat at the end of the bed, looking tired.

'Just leave me alone, I want to sleep.'

David and Mami sighed, looked at each other and then left the room. Later that day, David made the call.

The doctor diagnosed Alma with anxiety and depression. He told her that she was having panic attacks, and prescribed her with tablets. She wouldn't be able to go to school for at least another seven to ten days.

It was decided that the school would send her homework and study material. The study material stayed in the corner of Alma's room. She didn't touch it. Over the next week, she felt herself going mad. She would feel ecstatic, then extremely sad. She would have terrible dreams, and wander around the house. She could stare at the television for hours, not seeing anything. Alma started to question who she was. What was she doing there? What was her purpose? There wasn't a purpose, she concluded. There was just emptiness. Nothing mattered anymore. Towards the end of the week, Alma had an out of body experience. The television was blaring. Everyone was talking and laughing.

Alma could see herself, in a white nightdress and dressing gown, with gaunt features, and matted hair. She was in a room full of people, but she wasn't present. She was a ghost, a shell without expression. And in that moment she knew, more than anything else in the world, that she wanted to die.

CHAPTER 7
The Clock Tower

Alma brought her hands to her face, trying to block out the light. There were loud bleeping noises, and when she opened her eyes she could see two nurses and a man wearing a white coat.

She was lying in a hospital bed. Next to her was a trolley and on the trolley was a stethoscope, a plastic bowl, and a bottle of liquid.

'Alma,' the man touched her arm gently.

She looked down and saw a tube running from her arm. The tube fed into a bag hanging from the trolley.

'How are you feeling?' the man smiled. He had a kind face.

Alma nodded, feeling her dry mouth and crusty lips as she ran her tongue along them.

'Where am I?'

'You are at the emergency unit, on camp.'

'Why, what happened?' her mind was racing.

'Well, you were quite poorly, hopefully we have you back on track.'

Suddenly, Mami rushed through the door. Her eyes were very red and swollen. 'Almita, Almita! Thank god you are awake.' She ran over to Alma and smothered her, kissing her head. 'Mi hija, you've woken up.'

Alma smiled weakly. The nurse approached Mami.

'Sorry, miss, I'm going to have to ask you to come back a bit later. We need to ask Alma some questions.'

Mami wiped her eyes, 'Okay, okay.' She kissed Alma's fingers. 'I'll be back soon, Almita.'

Alma watched Mami leave the room. The doctor stood at the end of the bed, looking at her. He was holding a clipboard and pen expectantly.

'Alma, I need to understand why you tried to do this to yourself.'

Alma ran her finger across her lips. They felt bone dry.

'I notice that you were recently prescribed some new medication, is that right?'

She nodded weakly.

'Do you remember how many of the tablets you took?'

'All of them,' she whispered

'Did you take anything else other than those?'

'No,' she snivelled.

'Would you like to tell me why you felt you needed to do this to yourself?' he stared hard, tilting his head to one side.

She hesitated before answering, 'No, not really.'

'Your parents have mentioned briefly what happened over the last six to seven months, and I think it would be a good idea if we referred you to a counsellor…so you can have a one to one talk with someone. How would you feel about that?'

Alma looked up at him, 'I don't want to talk to anyone.'

'Well, you will have plenty of time to think about it. In the meantime you will be moved to the general hospital until you are well enough to leave.'

He smiled at her, bringing the clipboard to his stomach and placing his pen in his top pocket.

It was a total of eleven days before Alma was back home. She counted the days religiously. Mami and David were to give Alma her daily medication, and she knew they were under instructions to keep a close eye on her. *Suicide watch*, she thought to herself. She hadn't even been able to do that job right. The knot was always there, in the pit of her stomach. To make it worse, she couldn't even have a cigarette or a drink. Mami and David were always watching, and the medication warned about side effects.

A few days after she got home, Alma went to see a counsellor. Her name was Judith, and she was lovely. On her first visit Alma found herself in floods of tears as she told Judith about what had happened, and when she first arrived in the UK.

'Alma, I believe you are suffering from clinical depression. I want you to understand that it isn't your fault. It's an illness. It's basically an intense state of unhappiness experienced over a prolonged period of time.'

Alma stared at her, 'But why me? Why is it happening to me?'

'Well, some people don't have enough serotonin or dopamine. This is called a chemical imbalance in the brain. Dopamine provides what you and I would call the happy chemical that normal people have automatically.'

Alma looked down at the floor, trying to comprehend what the counsellor was saying to her.

'Sometimes events from the past can trigger certain thoughts,' she opened up a folder and looked at Alma. 'I want to ask you a few things, Alma. Is that okay?'

Alma nodded.

'For more than two weeks have you felt sad, down, or miserable most of the time or lost interest or pleasure in most of your usual activities?' she looked across at Alma.

'Yes, all of those.'

'Have you stopped going out?'

'Yes.'

'Are you not getting things done, for example your schoolwork?'

Alma nodded again

'How about your family and friends, Alma, are you withdrawing from them in any way?'

More nodding. More questions.

'Are you relying on alcohol or any other substances?'

Alma felt herself getting more and more agitated, as all her answers seemed to be forming a pattern. Judy asked her if she felt she was a failure. Did she blame herself for things? Did she feel worthless, ugly or as if life wasn't worth living?

'So how long will I feel like this?' Alma fidgeted in her chair.

'Well, Alma, firstly we will see how your new medication works, we need to give this at least six weeks to get into your system.'

'Six weeks?' she asked, horrified.

'Yes, but in the meantime, we are going to work closely together to put a plan of action into place.'

Judy closed her file and moved over to her desk, where she picked up a document. She handed this to Alma. It outlined a six week schedule of what they would be doing. Unable to concentrate on the content, Alma placed it in her lap, feeling despondent.

'Alma, it is important that you learn to love yourself.'

Oh my god that would be the day, thought Alma. She suddenly felt as if this whole visit had been a waste of time.

'Please don't give up, Alma. You have your whole life ahead of you, so much to experience, so much you haven't done yet.'

'Can I go now?' Alma stood up

'Yes, of course.'

As she left the building, she saw David's car parked outside waiting for her.

***

After a couple of weeks in bed, sleeping for hours on and off and hardly eating, Alma mustered the energy to complete some of her school work. She thought that perhaps the tablets were finally taking effect. She attended her weekly counselling sessions and even began to exercise again, slowly at first, indoors on her own, and over the coming weeks she started running with David most mornings, then gradually she would be running twice a day. Judy had told her to get as much exercise as possible, as it was good for producing serotonin.

After a while, it was time to go back to school. She had been in touch with Kim and Suzy, and they had visited her following her return home from hospital. She found out that Nikki was so in love with Suzy that any problems Nikki had with Alma were soon forgotten about. Katherine and Mandy on the other hand were still chipping away. Their crude remarks were getting boring, but Alma was still fearful that a heated argument could break out at any moment, and avoided them as much as possible.

As her exams loomed, Alma became more and more anxious. She hadn't studied as much as she should have done, in fact she was very cross about how much time she had wasted. She felt like a disappointment. When the exams finally arrived, Alma struggled. Some questions she was unable to answer, and had pretty much guessed, which she later beat herself up about.

Kim had told Alma and Suzy that they were going to go out and celebrate the end of exams. The girls didn't argue with Kim, she was definitely the extrovert out of the three, and whatever she suggested was normally great fun. To Alma's surprise, Mami and David were fine with this, and for Alma to stay at Kim's. What they didn't know was that the girls were going to a place called The Clock Tower, in town. It was a pub that Kim and Suzy had been frequenting on a regular basis. 'It's the place to meet a squaddie,' they had told Alma.

'Bloody hell, it's packed in here,' Kim pointed towards the bar. 'Come on,' she pulled Alma through the crowd, with Suzy following close behind.

'Hi, girls, what you having?' shouted a very tall guy with a Geordie accent, looking down at all three of them.

'Nah it's okay,' Kim shouted back.

'Come on, you'll never get served,' he was waving his money in the air.

'Yes, mate?' one of the bartenders had spotted him.

'My normal please, mate, and three blue angels for these beautiful ladies,' he smiled Kim's way, and she turned around to look at Alma and Suzy, grinning from ear to ear. 'What the hell are blue angels?' she asked.

'Christ knows,' shouted Suzy

'Who cares?' laughed Alma

'So where you girls from?' the man shouted in Kim's ear.

'We're from camp.'

Three other guys joined them, and others were getting ratty because they couldn't get to the bar.

'We're gonna move somewhere less crowded,' shouted Kim, motioning to Suzy and Alma to move away.

'Catch up with you later maybe?' The man winked at Kim, she smiled at him awkwardly. They moved to another part of the pub, it was less busy in the upstairs section. The girls downed their drinks.

'Oh my god, what the hell were they?' Suzy looked at her empty glass.

'Let's get another lot,' Kim laughed, leading them straight to the bar. The whole building seemed to be packed full of squaddies.

'What do you think, Alma?' Kim was ordering another round of drinks.

'Yeah, it's really good, atmosphere is brill…can't say much about the music though.'

Alma listened, she didn't recognise what was being played.

'Right after three. Ready...' Kim handed out another round of blue angels.

'Christ that's like drinking some sort of cleaning product,' the girls laughed, screwing up their faces.

'Hey ladies, looking gorgeous tonight!' came a loud voice behind them. They turned around to see a group of squaddies. 'Can we get you some drinks?'

Alma noticed the shorter one almost instantly. He was stocky, and his shirt fitted tightly, emphasising his physique. He smiled at her, and she quickly looked away to face the bar, so he couldn't see her embarrassment.

'Can I buy you a drink?' his money was out before Alma could answer.

'Thanks, I'll have a Budweiser,' she felt herself blush.

'I'm Titch,' he held out his hand.

She shook it, 'Alma.'

'Do they call you Titch cos you're short?' she asked, smiling.

'Well something like that,' he laughed

'No it's cos his dick is tiny,' said one of his mates cackling and nudging Titch in the ribs.

'Ignore him, Alma.'

'Hi, I'm Paddy,' said the big guy.

'This is Alma and she is a nice girl so bugger off,' Titch shoved Paddy away in jest.

Alma looked across at Kim and Suzy, who were both engrossed in chat with the lads. They were from the nearby barracks, between eighteen and twenty-one years of age. Paddy was the eldest.

'So who's your old man then, Alma?' Titch swigged back on his beer.

'Why?'

'Oh well, you know, just curious,' his smile was infectious.

'David Jennings.'

Titch nearly choked on his beer and took a couple of steps back. 'What? Warrant Officer Jennings?' he looked shocked.

Alma nodded

'Blimey O' Reilly! Oi, guys you'll never guess who Alma's old man is? Only Officer Jennings!'

'Bloody hell, Titch, you better mind your Ps and Qs mate.' They all laughed, as Paddy ordered another round of drinks for everyone.

The bar was filling up quickly now. Alma looked around and saw a few girls across the way. They were dolled up to the nines, with tight mini-skirts and lowcut tops, and heels higher than Alma had ever worn. Suddenly, she felt underdressed, and wished she had made more of an effort. She looked down at her tight-fitting black trousers, black vest and black mesh top. Her pointed black boots only had two-inch heels, which didn't give her much height at all.

'I haven't seen you here before,' Titch distracted her.

'No, it's my first time,' replied Alma.

'You have the most amazing eyes and lips, has anyone else ever told you that?' he was looking at Alma's lips longingly.

'Is that your best chat up line?' Alma laughed.

'Well you can't blame me for trying,' Titch smiled cheekily. 'Come on, let's dance,' he stood up and held his hand out.

'What? To this?' Alma paused, listening to the music.

'Come on,' Titch grabbed her hand.

Kim and Suzy came to the rescue. 'Alma, we're going to the bathroom. You coming?'

Alma nodded, she released herself gently from Titch's grip, and followed them into the loo. Kim quickly dashed into a cubicle, and then there were vomiting sounds.

'Kim, are you okay in there?' Suzy banged on the toilet door.

'Err yeah, just been sick.' There was an almighty crashing noise from within the cubicle, 'Ohhhh shit, I have just broken the toilet roll holder!' Kim stumbled out of the door, clinging onto Suzy for support.

'Jesus, Kim.'

'I feel fucked,' Kim walked over to the mirror.

'Why didn't you guys tell me my bloody mascara had ran?' Alma pointed at her eyes. 'I look like shit!' She tried to shift the black mark from under her eye, steadying herself by holding on to the sink with one hand.

'So are you getting off with Titch then?' Kim giggled into the mirror.

'I think he's nice,' Suzy chirped.

'Yeah I really really like him, but I dunno....he knows David.'

'Bloody hell, Alma, all the soldiers will know your dad. There's no getting away from that.'

As they came out of the toilet, Titch grabbed Alma's arms and led her downstairs and outside. He lit a cigarette.

'Give us a drag,' Alma reached out.

'Only if you are a good girl,' he teased

Titch took a deep drag before handing the cigarette over. Then, he came up close to Alma, putting his arm around her waist and prizing her lips open before blowing the smoke into her mouth. He kissed her, his tongue exploring every part of her mouth. He pulled away and took her hand. They walked for a couple of minutes then went down a dark alleyway.

Titch put his arms around Alma. He pushed her against the wall and kissed her hard. His hands were clutching her bum cheeks tightly, then pulling her vest out of her trousers and undoing her bra. He pulled her top and bra up and squeezed her breasts gently, then sucked hard on her nipples, teasing them with his teeth.

Alma could hardly breathe. In her drunken state she longed for him to kiss her again, and she moaned, feeling him hard against her. She reached down and fumbled with his belt, managing to undo it, then his zip. He kissed her more urgently, now moaning as she released him, making swift up and down movements, feeling her hand becoming wet.

'Let's go somewhere,' he whispered in a hoarse voice. Alma nodded as they kissed each other hungrily.

Back inside the pub, Titch whispered something to Paddy and then to Kim. They left shortly after. Standing outside, waiting for a taxi to show up, Alma shivered. Titch wrapped his jacket around her shoulders, kissing her gently. They got into a cab and Titch muttered something to the driver. Alma didn't know where they were going, but she didn't care. She was floating, she felt so happy.

When they got there, Titch led her down a corridor, and then they went into a room. It was dark, with bunk beds, and a sink in the corner. Titch threw his jacket down and turned towards Alma, who was quite unsteady on her feet.

He kissed her gently, then harder. He started taking her clothes off. Alma followed his lead, but struggled to get his shirt off. When she finally did, she gasped. He was perfect, and so defined. She kissed his chest and heard him moan, and then he picked her up and placed her on the bed. Her top came off easily, and her bra followed. He was looking at her, studying her body, kissing her tummy.

'Are you on the pill, Alma?' the question took her by surprise.

'No,' she whispered, hoping that wouldn't put him off.

His tongue was probing her belly button. He took her trousers and boots off slowly, kissing her legs and then back up to her black panties. He teased her, kissing her inner thighs and then coming back up to kiss her lips.

'You're gorgeous,' he paused and looked into her eyes.

Alma was in a daze. The room was dimly lit, but as she kissed Titch she could see tattoos on both of his upper arms. He was so well proportioned, she was falling in love with him there and then.

He gently removed her underwear and spread her legs. She trembled in anticipation, holding her breath.

Titch brought his mouth down, kissing her vagina lips so lightly that she could hardly feel him. She wanted him so badly and arched her body. His tongue flicked over the top of her clitoris, making her gasp. He sucked his fingers and gently inserted one and then two, god she was in heaven. His tongue was moving quickly up and down, making her wetter by the minute. She couldn't stand it any longer.

'Please,' she cried, grappling, trying to reach him, 'please Titch, fuck me, fuck me now.' Her breasts were rigid, nipples erect, getting harder and harder every second. Then he was finally inside her, pushing gently at first, only to become rougher. She could feel his excitement.

'Please don't stop,' she cried.

He was deep now, thrusting harder. She gasped, feeling pain then ecstasy. This had to be heaven, surely. He suddenly felt heavier, his breathing getting faster and faster, kissing her, biting her lips, their tongues entwined. He filled up the whole of her mouth as they moved together, as close as possible, perfectly timed. He was so deep inside her, she could feel him increasing in speed. He moaned deeply, kissing her breasts and moving her legs apart even more. His face felt hot and his eyes were closed. *Let this never end,* thought Alma, *please let us be together forever.*

Suddenly, Titch withdrew and ejaculated fiercely over her stomach, crying out. He shook frantically, jerking and eventually resting on top of her. He took deep breaths and kissed her head before rolling onto his side.

She stroked his head, listening to both of them breathing heavily.

'You okay?' he broke the silence.

'I didn't want you to stop,' she leaned over and kissed him.

'I know, I'm sorry,' he kissed her back.

Alma's head was spinning. She desperately needed some water.

'Where are we, by the way?'

'At the barracks.'

'Oh my god.'

'Don't worry, loads of girls come back here.' Alma's head was suddenly filled with images of girls being ferried in and out of the barracks, like it was the most natural thing in the world.

'Shit, I left Kim and Suzy. They'll be wondering where I am.'

'It's okay, Paddy knows you're here.'

'Christ, did you tell everyone?' Alma suddenly felt alarmed.

'No, just Paddy,' he smiled. He pushed himself up on one elbow and faced her. 'I really like you, Alma,' he kissed her on the lips.

'I like you too,' she felt goose bumps up and down her arms. 'I cannot actually believe I am here with you,' she looked into his eyes and started to giggle.

'Me neither,' he found her lips again, and their tongues met in anticipation.

'I'd better get going,' Alma pulled back.

'Please stay,' he touched her breasts, looking longingly at her. 'I'll get you a cab, as long as you're out by five o'clock no one will know.'

Alma didn't need much persuasion, she hadn't wanted to leave anyway. She nodded, smiling, and ran her hands over his arm.

'Did these hurt?' she looked down at one of Titch's tattoos. It was a half-naked woman, holding what looked like a rifle.

'A little,' he followed her gaze. 'Got 'em done bit by bit, you know?'

She stared at the tattoo.

'You haven't got any, have you?' he surveyed her body.

'God no, don't think I could stomach it,' she laughed drunkenly.

'Ralph and Oliver's tattoo parlour is the best. I'll take you there one day, you'll be fine.'

Alma imagined how Mami and David would react if she got one. They'd probably hit the roof.

'You've got a great body, Alma.'

'So have you! You must have to work out so much. Look at your six pack,' she ran her fingers over his front, smiling.

'Yeah, well, you know how it is…have to make sure that I stay in shape for the ladies,' he pulled his legs up as Alma swiped at him, both of them rolling around laughing. Suddenly, he moved his mouth to hers, and the same feelings overtook her. They made love again, slower this time, moving as one until Titch climaxed once again.

After that, they fell asleep. Alma didn't sleep for long. When she woke, she heard the birds outside the barracks, and knew it was time to leave. She unravelled herself from the sheets, without waking Titch, and carefully dressed, before leaving the barracks.

Alma slept until nearly lunch time that day, and was awoken by Mami knocking on her door.

'Alma, dinner is on the table, and you have to take your tablet!'

Alma pulled her head up from the sheets. Eating was the last thing she wanted to do, she felt terrible. The realisation of the previous night's events came rushing back. She felt sore and bruised. She didn't even know Titch's first name. Oh god, she had spent the night with him and she didn't even know his real name. She reached out for the slip of paper on her bedside table. *Titch 865437.* She read it over and over again. Her heart fluttered. He was a lot older than her, at least six or seven years. Mami and David would be livid. She would have keep this under wraps, especially if she was going to start seeing him on a regular basis.

Later that day Alma nervously dialled the number from a payphone, only to be told that Lance Corporal Mason was not available. The person answering obviously knew who she was referring to when she asked for 'Titch'. It made her feel stupid.

'Lance Corporal Mason,' she muttered to herself. What the hell was his first name? She desperately wanted to see him again. She couldn't concentrate on anything else.

Alma, Kim, and Suzy got together after their night out, to discuss the events.

'So, what happened to you two?' Alma sat on the end of Kim's bed.

'Do you know what? I haven't got a fucking clue,' laughed Suzy. 'I woke up in some girl's house with a crowd I didn't even know. They'd put me to bed upstairs, as I'd passed out in the toilet. All I know is that one minute we were playing cards and then I woke up in this strange bed.'

'Bloody hell, Suzy. How the hell did you get home?'

'Taxi,' she smiled. 'Only when I got back to Kim's she wasn't there, was she?!' Suzy gave Kim a dirty look.

'Yeah well at least my sister let you in, better than freezing your butt off outside, and anyway I was busy,' she broke into a fit of giggles.

'Okay I know where you were, Kim, you dirty cow. What I wanna know is where did Almita get to?' they both turned to Alma, waiting for her reply. She hesitated and felt the colour rise to her cheeks.

'At the barracks,' she almost whispered.

'NO WAY!' Suzy and Kim laughed and stared at her with wide eyes. 'Did you stay with him?'

'Yes,' Alma started giggling.

'Whoop whoop, look at you, girl! Fair play to you,' Kim high-fived Alma.

'What about Paddy? Are you seeing him again?'

Suzy collapsed in hysterics, 'You mean is she seeing Paddy *and* James again?'

'What?' blurted Alma. 'Oh my god, you didn't?'

Kim looked away smiling, not at all embarrassed. She leant back on her bed, 'God, what a night. Come on, let's get out for a ciggy.'

***

'Hello…' Alma could hear background noise but nothing else. 'Hello, is Lance Corporal Mason there please?' The line went dead.

Alma held the handset for a few seconds, before placing it back on the receiver. She wondered whether she had the right number.

She had tried three times now, but still nothing. Leaving the phone box, she could see Kim chatting up the lad behind the counter in the nearby off licence. Surely he knew she wasn't eighteen.

Kim came out with vodka and wine, she had a victorious smile on her face, 'Got it.'

Alma laughed.

'Right back to mine, Suzy is coming round at seven-thirty.'

Alma picked up her bag of overnight stuff. Kim's parents were away, her sister was having friends round, and Alma and Suzy were staying round again…or at least that's what their parents thought. The plan was to get ready at Kim's then head into town, where there was a drink offer on at The Clock Tower.

'Does this look too tarty?' Kim came out of the bathroom.

'Crikey, is that short enough?' Alma stared in disbelief.

'It looks cool,' exclaimed Suzy, who was also wearing a short dress, although not as short as Kim's. 'Alma, you've gotta get out of those tight trousers, all you wear is black!'

'How about trying a few things on?' Kim opened her wardrobe. It was packed with so many outfits, all different colours. They picked out a pair of high heels for Alma and a mini-skirt, and the girls completed Alma's look by curling her long dark hair and applying far too much makeup. She barely recognised herself when she looked in the mirror.

'Wow, you look great,' Suzy smiled.

'I could quite fancy you myself,' laughed Kim. 'One thing's for sure, Titch is not going to be able to keep his hands off you.'

Alma stared at her reflection in the mirror, that couldn't be her staring back, surely?

'Cab's here!' shouted Kim's sister.

At The Clock Tower, the drinks offer was working a treat.

There was an enormous queue to get in. After standing in the cold for a while, they made their way to the bar. Alma felt eyes following them as they walked past. She concentrated hard on making it in her heels, having had quite a bit to drink already.

Once they'd bought more drinks, they stood at the edge of the dance floor. There were bodies everywhere. It hadn't taken Kim long to start chatting to some bloke. Alma sipped on her vodka and coke. There was no sign of Titch or any of that crowd yet. Alma wasn't even sure he would be there, since she hadn't had the opportunity to speak to him since that night. Suzy and Alma moved onto the dance floor, leaving Kim talking to her new friend. It wasn't long before Alma felt a bit more comfortable in her new footwear. The tempo of the music overwhelmed her, and she moved her hips to the rhythm. She could sense guys watching them on the sidelines. They were on show, and she loved the attention.

A man tapped Alma on the shoulder. 'Can I buy you a drink? he shouted.

'No, thank you,' Alma shook her head so he understood her over the noise.

He pulled a disappointed face, then turned to Suzy, who was by now dancing with someone. She too ignored his advances, and he walked off into the crowd looking annoyed. Suzy and Alma glanced at each other and shrugged their shoulders.

They made their way back to Kim, who had now got a table with a group of guys.

'Suzy, Alma, this is Tim.'

'Nice to meet you girls,' Tim lent across. 'This is Squish, Ferret and Mick.' Suzy and Alma laughed at their nicknames.

'Right, let's get some drinks then.' Tim went to the bar and ordered a huge selection of drinks, with Ferret accompanying him. Suzy was staring at Ferret, her mouth almost salivating.

'God, he's gorge,' she shouted in Alma's ear.

'Yep, not bad,' Alma nodded with approval.

Her eyes made their way to the other end of the bar. She stared hard…was that him? Yes, she had spotted him. There was no mistaking Titch. He wore a black short sleeved shirt and jeans. Just seeing him, her heart skipped a beat. She was transfixed.

'Here you go,' Tim had brought the whole bar by the looks of it. He was carrying a tray and so was Ferret.

'Thanks,' the girls took their drinks. Alma downed hers quickly, before looking back to the bar. There was a girl standing next to Titch. His hand was caressing her bare back. Alma could see her tossing her head back in laughter as he whispered something. She was beautiful, taller than Alma, and she had an amazing figure and long, curly blonde hair. Alma felt an overwhelming ache in her chest. She watched him lean into the girl, and then they kissed. Alma couldn't watch. She felt sick. Standing up, she made an excuse to go to the toilets, pushing past everyone. She would not cry, she would not allow herself. Why, oh why, had she been so stupid? He wasn't interested in her. She was a stupid fifteen-year-old kid, not experienced in any way whatsoever. Of course he hadn't taken her calls, he had no intention of doing so. She felt so humiliated. What a fool she had been.

Looking in the mirror, she fixed her make-up, putting on even more red lipstick. She walked over to the other side of the bar. She couldn't help but look…but Titch and the girl had gone, probably back to the barracks. She felt herself raging with jealousy. She wanted to confront him. He couldn't treat her like that, she wasn't his plaything to use whenever he felt like it.

How could he do this to me? Alma thought. The torture was too much. She ordered two more drinks. Her hands were shaking. Picking up the first drink, her head felt hazy, and her focus wasn't what it should have been.

'You alright over here on your own?' a voice said.

Alma looked up. She recognised the man from somewhere, but she couldn't figure out where.

'It's Alma, isn't it?' he sat down on the stool next to her, waving at the girl behind the bar. 'I'll have a bud please, love, and a vodka and coke.'

She looked at him, how did he know what she was drinking?

'I'm Peebo,' he stuck out his hand. Alma shook it, wishing for him to go away. 'Real name Jonny Peebles, just in case you were wondering,' he smiled, bringing the Budweiser to his lips. 'I was here the other night with Paddy and that lot.'

'Okay.'

'But then again everyone had a bit too much to drink that night, so you probably wouldn't remember…' he smiled and then looked over her shoulder. 'Paddy, Titch, over here!'

Alma spun round. She could see Titch staring at her with a confused look on his face.

'I didn't realise you were here,' he said, looking uncomfortable. Two girls had come over with Titch and Paddy. One of them was the blonde whom Alma had seen earlier.

'So, Alma, can I interest you in a dance?' Jonny Peebles said hopefully.

'Sure, why not?' Alma climbed off the stool and steadied herself.

They headed to the dance floor. Alma was determined to enjoy herself. She felt like she was floating, and even though she was fuzzy, she could still hear the music. Her and Jonny pretended to be the best dancers possible, and to be honest he wasn't a bad mover. He was taller than Titch, quite skinny, but there was something about him that she hadn't noticed before. Paddy and Kim were also on the dance floor, rekindling their friendship from the other night. Paddy's hands were riding up Kim's dress, and she quickly slapped them away, making Alma laugh.

The music changed, and Alma gestured to Jonny that she was going to the ladies. As she came out, she saw Titch waiting outside with a beer in his hand.

'Alma, what the fuck are you doing?' he shouted over the music.

'What?' She steadied herself against the wall.

'What the hell are you doing with Peebo?'

'What the fuck's it got to do with you?' She pushed past him, but he swung her round, grabbing her hand. He pulled her down the stairs. Alma almost lost her balance trying to keep up with him. They stood outside while Titch lit a cigarette.

'Don't fuck me about,' he said angrily.

'What d'ya mean?'

Titch didn't respond to that. He took her hand and walked up the nearby alleyway. Alma followed, in a daze. She was shivering, but she didn't feel cold. Then, Titch kissed her. He kissed her hard, putting his hand up her dress and in between her legs.

'Please don't fuck me about,' he groaned. They kissed urgently, Alma closed her eyes, thinking she would faint in that moment of passion. She was drunk but she knew where she was. She was where she wanted to be, and with the person she wanted to be with.

Titch's breathing was heavy. 'I want you so bad, do you know that?' he murmured.

Alma suddenly came to her senses, opening her eyes. 'No, stop,' she pushed him off. She pulled her dress down and started to walk away.

'What the hell are you doing?'

'Shouldn't you be fucking your Irish girlfriend?' she shouted back, as she stumbled back up the alleyway. Titch caught up with her.

'What does that mean?' he looked confused.

'Oh don't bloody act the fool, I saw you with her. You couldn't keep your fucking hands off her.'

He looked into her eyes, 'She's not you, Alma.'

'You didn't take my calls,' Alma's voice quivered. 'You didn't take any of my fucking calls.'

'I'm sorry,' he looked genuinely upset, 'I saw you tonight with Peebo and knew I'd made a mistake.' Titch leaned closer to her and cupped her face.

'Please come back with me tonight?'

Alma's heart melted. She needed him, and she wanted him so badly. Hesitating, Titch kissed her again. He took her by the hand, and together they walked back down the alleyway.

CHAPTER 8
Let Me Stay

The day had arrived. Alma held the brown envelope in her hand, sitting on the edge of her bed. Her hands trembled as she began to open it.

An A4 sheet of paper showed lots of black writing. She quickly folded it, getting up nervously and walking over to her bedroom window. She closed her eyes for a brief moment and took a deep breath.

English Language	*O'level grade B*
English Literature	*O'level grade C*
Art	*O'level grade A*
Physical Education	*O'level grade B*
Pitman Typing Elementary	*Pass*
French	*CSE grade 1*
Biology	*CSE grade 5*
Maths	*CSE grade 5*
Home Economics	*CSE grade 3*

As Alma looked down the list, she felt a wave of disappointment. She was annoyed that she hadn't done better, especially in maths and biology.

'Well?' said David, standing in her bedroom doorway.

'Not very good,' Alma passed him the results, afraid of his reaction.

'Alma, these are good results considering how much time you've had off,' he waved the piece of paper and turned around to go and show Mami. She heard a yell of delight, and then Mami rushed into the room, suffocating Alma with a huge hug.

'Estoy muy orgulloso de ti!' *I'm so proud of you!*

***

Kim and Suzy were not happy with their results either.

'Well, I'm buggered,' Kim lit up a cigarette. 'Not one O'level for me. Oh well. who gives a shit?' she pretended to kick something on the ground.

'What did your mum and dad say?'

'They were okay, as long as I did my best then they're fine with it,' she looked a bit frustrated.

'Well I have just scraped getting into sixth form,' Suzy piped up. 'What are you doing, Alma? Are you gonna go sixth form?'

'Dunno yet.'

'Your mum and dad must be well proud of you, you swat!' Kim shoved Alma playfully.

'Yeah, I guess they are…I should have done better though,' Alma thought back to Mami and David's reaction.

'Anyway, I've got to tell you something,' Kim said, hesitantly.

'Are you okay?' Alma looked at Suzy.

'I've caught an STD.'

'A what?' Suzy looked puzzled.

'An STD, a sexually transmitted disease.'

'Oh my god! Who from?' Alma gasped.

'Dunno,' Kim looked cross. She turned away and Alma thought she could see tears in her eyes.

'Have you been to the docs?'

'Yep went with my sister. Luckily she's not telling mum and dad, but she gave me a bloody lecture.'

'Well, have you got some medication? It's not serious, is it?'

'I will have it for the rest of my life. It's called genital herpes,' Kim stubbed out the fag. 'Some kind of genital sore…it's contagious too.'

'Oh, Kim, that sounds awful,' Alma moved over to hug her. Kim stood rigid.

'Yeah, well, the prick who gave it to me obviously didn't give a shit, did he?'

The girls headed home, it was getting late. Alma thought about Titch, and how they had not used any contraception. She had been bloody stupid. She was glad to get indoors.

***

'Alma Jennings, please.' The receptionist looked around the waiting room.

Alma stood up. The receptionist directed her into a small room, at the end of the corridor. 'Doctor Phillips will be with you shortly,' she said.

Alma looked around at the posters on the wall. One of them showed a picture of lungs, before and after smoking. She was dying for a cigarette.

'Hello, it's Alma, isn't it?' The doctor had come in behind her, making Alma jump.

'Yes, that's me.'

'Well, Alma, I'm Doctor Phillips. How may I help you today?'

'I would like to go on the pill,' she said shyly.

'Okay,' he leaned back in his chair, reading the notes in front of him.

'You've just turned sixteen, is that right?'

Alma nodded.

'Do your parents know about this?' he looked up.

'No, and I would like to keep it that way,' she shuffled in her seat uncomfortably.

'Do you have a regular partner?' he was jotting down notes as he spoke.

Alma didn't really know whether she could call Titch a regular partner. They had only slept together a few times, but he was the one who had suggested that she go on the pill, and of course she thought it was a good idea.

'Yes, I do.'

'Right,' he said, jotting some more notes down. He tore off a strip of pink paper and handed it to her. 'Here you go. Take this to the pharmacy. It's a prescription for the birth control pill.'

'Thank you.'

'What are you currently using as contraceptive, Alma?'

Alma had to think quickly. 'Condoms,' she lied.

'Good,' he looked down again, 'is there anything else?'

'No, that's it,' she smiled sweetly.

After picking up the tablets, she phoned Titch to tell him the good news. He sounded pleased. They were meeting up the following day. Titch was treating her to her first tattoo, as a birthday present. He still thought she was seventeen. She had to remember that, as a couple of times she had almost dropped herself in it.

The tattoo was one of the most painful experiences Alma had ever gone through. She had chosen a butterfly to go on her lower back. At first she had yelled, and then had to ask the tattooist to stop so she could have a drink of water. Titch found the whole saga very funny, and held Alma's hand throughout. It took a while for it to heal. Alma ensured she kept it clean and changed the dressing frequently, beaming with delight as she looked at it in the mirror. It was beautiful.

'That's so cool,' Kim touched Alma's back, 'did it hurt?'

'Of course it did,' Alma pulled her top down.

'Do your mum and dad know?'

'Christ, don't be stupid, they'd flip!'

Kim pulled her top up and pointed to the tattoo under her left breast. It was a dragon, and quite big too.

'I didn't know you had one,' Alma took a closer look.

'Yeah got it done when I was thirteen, really bloody painful.'

'OOOOH god I couldn't do it,' shivered Suzy, 'I'm crap with pain, doesn't appeal to me in the slightest!'

'You wuss, we'll drag you down there when you've had a few too many. You won't feel anything then!'

'So tonight, we going to Lacey's yeah?' Kim sounded really excited. She had met a Belgian solider there, and had been harping on about him ever since.

'You gonna get Titch and his mates to come down, Alma?'

'I'll try.'

'You guys both staying at mine again, yeah?'

'Of course,' they both smiled back at her, knowing full well they probably wouldn't.

Lacey's was an actual club, much bigger than The Clock Tower. It was popular with Belgian and English squaddies, and a frequent hang out for both Irish and English girls, who competed with each other. Kim said the music was better too.

Alma had managed to lose another few pounds. The dress that Mami and David bought her for her birthday fitted perfectly. It was red and very short, slightly padded on the shoulders and slit low at the back, showing off her butterfly. Wearing it, she felt sexy, and couldn't wait for Titch to see her.

'My round,' shouted Alma, pulling money from her purse. They were soon joined by Kim's Belgian bloke, and a few of his friends. Alma made it clear she wasn't single, looking around in case she caught a glimpse of Titch. But come midnight, there was still no sign of him.

'Alma!'

She wheeled around, and saw William. He was with Ed, Yvonne, Thomas, and a couple of other girls she didn't know.

'I didn't recognise you at first,' William was drunk. He gave Alma a big hug. 'Did you hear about Kath...Katherine?' he was slightly wobbly, and Alma held out her hand to steady him. 'She's in hospital.'

'Why, what's happened to her?' asked Alma.

'I'm gonna get...another drink,' he fell into Ed, and both of them headed to the bar.

Alma spoke to Yvonne about Katherine.

'Overdose,' Yvonne said.

'Flippin ek, when did all this happen?'

Yvonne shrugged her shoulders. 'Everyone's pointing the finger at Nikki. She's a bad influence, that girl.'

Come one-thirty, Titch still wasn't there. He wasn't coming. Alma was starting to feel unwell. Her vision was playing tricks on her. Holding her pint of water, she felt herself going dizzy. She felt the room starting to spin. Before she could stop herself she vomited down the side of the tables, and then again. People backed away, horrified. Alma looked at them, without seeing any of their faces. She could hardly lift her head up. She tumbled to the floor, and the room went black.

***

Alma opened her eyes and tried to make sense of her surroundings. She could taste bile in the back of her throat.

Mami was looking at her. Alma could see she wasn't at all happy, she knew that look and instantly felt ashamed. All around her was hospital equipment.

David was talking to one of the nurses.

'What's happening to you, Alma?' Mami was stood beside her. 'My daughter is nothing but a tramp!'

Alma tried to speak, but her mouth was dry as sand.

'You are a disgrace,' Mami continued. 'I've ruined you by bringing you up here.' Her voice was trembling, and her eyes began to well up. 'All I ever wanted was the best for you, the life that I never had. I thought bringing you here would give you opportunities and a better life. This is how you repay me, you are out with your slutty friends…this isn't the way I brought you up, Almita. I am sorry to say it, but I don't like the person you are becoming.' She pulled a tissue out of her pocket and dried her eyes.

'David has heard you've been staying at the barracks… rumours that you have been sleeping around. ¡Dios Mío Alma que vergüenzaí, I didn't believe it you know. I said to myself, no not mi hija, not my Almita…but I guess I know the truth now. How could you do this to me?'

Mami stood up. She turned her back on Alma and walked out of the room, wiping her eyes. Alma watched her leave, feeling sick to her stomach.

One of the nurses made her way over to Alma and smiled, pulling the curtain around the bed.

'Alma, the doctor would like to talk to you. He should be with you in a few moments.' She scribbled on the clipboard at the end of Alma's bed, 'Would you like some water?'

'No, thank you,' Alma didn't think she could stomach anything.

The nurse left, and then Alma could hear someone approaching. The doctor pulled back the curtain. He had brought Mami and David with him.

'Alma, can I check that you are still taking your medication? I know that your parents have said they are giving this to you in the mornings, but I need you to confirm this.'

Alma looked at both Mami and David before answering. 'Yes.'

'Great, can I also check…have you been consuming large quantities of alcohol whilst you have been taking this medication?' he looked at Alma, and then at Mami and David, who were waiting for a response.

Alma thought about how much she had been drinking. Yes, it was a lot. She knew that, especially the previous night. She hadn't really thought about the tablets, but Mami and David had told her enough times that she couldn't drink while taking them.

'Yes,' she bowed her head. She didn't really know what else to say.

'Okay, well I just need to remind you that it is very important you don't consume any alcohol whilst on this medication, Alma. Alcohol acts as a depressant, so it will make you feel lousy, I don't think I need to tell you this, considering what has just happened,' he almost tutted and Alma felt embarrassed.

'I need you to understand this. If you choose to use alcohol whilst taking these tablets then you could face some very serious consequences next time.'

Alma nodded, but didn't say a word. The way Mami was looking at her, there was no way she was going to try and deny anything. Shortly after, everyone left. Alma lay there with her eyes closed. She wondered where Titch was. As far as she could remember, he hadn't been there, but then she couldn't be a hundred percent on that. She tried hard to think, but nothing came to mind.

Giving up, she slowly got up to go to the toilet. She felt unsteady on her feet. Across the ward, she could see someone being wheeled in with two nurses each side of the trolley. When she got back, there was a voice behind her.

'So you've been overdoing things too then?'

Alma turned around. Katherine was standing near the curtain. She looked thin and pale, almost ashen, and had black circles around both of her eyes.

'Katherine!' Alma blurted out her name. 'God, are you okay?'

'I'll live,' she tried to smile but couldn't, 'what you in for?'

'Drinking too much,' Alma rolled her eyes.

'Yeah well you always did like a drink!' Katherine managed a chuckle.

There was an awkward silence.

'Katherine, listen about everything that's happened…'

'Let's just forget it. I was fucked up, okay?'

Alma looked at the floor wishing she hadn't said anything. She got back into her bed. Katherine forced a smile, 'I'll see you later, Alma.'

Alma was discharged the following day. She'd missed the deadline for sixth form, and now she'd been grounded too. No more visits to Kim's, and no seeing Suzy either. She missed Titch so much. David had spoken to him and had read him the riot act. Under no uncertain terms would he be able to make contact with Alma again. That was the hardest thing for her. She felt sick with anxiety at not being able to see him again.

It wasn't a good atmosphere at home. Alma spent a lot of time in her room. Yoli was annoying, and Alma had no time for her.

She was numb. As soon as she came home from hospital, David broke more bad news. They were due another posting, this time back to England, and it would be happening in the next six weeks. Alma stared blankly into space. She wasn't going. She was sixteen now and didn't need to go with them. She felt so resentful, especially to Mami and David. How dare they. They couldn't do this to her. She was in love with Titch and he was in love with her. There was absolutely nothing Mami and David could do about it. They would be together – Alma was sure of it. But he still wouldn't take her calls. A couple of days before, she had got a taxi to the barracks and asked to see him, but that hadn't worked either.

Heartbroken, she sneaked round to Suzy's house, taking some of Suzy's parents' booze to calm her down.

'Alma, you are gonna be in bigger trouble if you are caught round here,' Suzy tried to sound calm.

'I don't bloody care,' Alma blurted out.

'Are you gonna go back to England?'

'No,' she sobbed.

'Don't be ridiculous, you'll have to go. How can you possibly stay here with nowhere to live and no job?'

'I love Titch, Suzy. I love him, there's no way I can be without him,' Alma wiped the tears away and sighed deeply.

'You'll meet someone else,' Suzy held her hand tightly.

'Not like him.'

'Have you spoken to him?'

'I've tried, he won't talk to me.'

'Well, after David's talk with him you can't blame him, right?'

Later that evening, Alma sat opposite Mami and David. She'd called a meeting, and she was going to speak her mind.

'I'm not going back to England.'

'What do you mean?'

'I am going to get a job and stay here. I'm sixteen now, so it's okay for me to do that.'

Mami looked at David. He stood up and walked over to Alma. 'Alma, listen, you are not staying here.'

Alma stood up defiantly. She could see Mami's face becoming furious.

'Yes, I am. There's nothing you can do to stop me.'

Mami exploded, 'You think you know best, don't you, Alma? Is this because of that Tony Mason?'

It took a moment before Alma realised she was talking about Titch.

'When will you learn, Alma? He's not interested in you, he never was.'

Alma felt herself flinch. 'Don't say that, you don't know him!'

Mami started laughing, a wicked laugh, almost teasing Alma. 'Please don't make me laugh. You have no idea, do you? You don't know what love is. Guys like that use girls like you...STUPID girls like you.'

She moved closer to Alma, 'What? Do you think you are special? He probably sleeps with a different girl every night.'

'Shut up, shut up.'

'Don't be so bloody naïve, Alma.' Mami stormed out. Alma stood in silence, hating her mother more and more by the second. She went into her bedroom and slammed the door. She cried into her pillow. Would she never see Titch again? He would meet someone else and forget all about her. Her heart ached, this couldn't be happening. Alma couldn't bear it. *Why, God, did you make me come here?* she thought. Maybe Mami was right, maybe she would have been better off staying with her family in Honduras. She hated it here, the only person that made her happy was Titch, and now that had been taken away too.

Alma didn't sleep well that night. She mulled things over and over in her mind. She had nothing now, no friends, no boyfriend, no family that she could talk to. Soon she would be somewhere new, and would have to start over yet again. How much longer could she carry on doing this? *Not much longer*, she thought to herself, *not much longer*. She sat up and took her tablet. Then she opened her drawer and took out some paper and a pen. She was going to write to Titch, and hand deliver the letter to the barracks. He would have to reply once she told him how much she loved him. Surely he would see that Mami and David couldn't do anything to stop them seeing each other, not now that she was old enough. They could get a place together, maybe get married. She would be a military wife, and they would travel all over the world. Her mood lifted slightly. She would keep it to herself, no-one would know, just her and Titch. She began to write:

Dear Titch

I pray to God that this reaches you. I have missed you so much you will not believe.

I am writing because we have a posting back to England in the next six weeks, but I have decided not to go. I want to stay with you and thought I could get a job and if ok with you maybe find somewhere to live....

I know you feel the same way and I know if it hadn't been for David speaking to you then we would still be together. I love you so much and long to hug and kiss you. God I cannot breathe without you.

I have tried calling, even visiting you at the barracks, but I totally understand why you won't see me.

Please write back to me at the address shown, I will pick your letter up from Suzy's when it arrives but please hurry as we haven't got long.

I love you so much.

Alma xxxxxxxxxxxxxxxxxxxxxxxxxxxxxxxxxxxxxxxxxxxxxxxxxxxxx

She wrote Suzy's address on a separate bit of paper, and slipped it in between the folded page. She sealed the envelope and delivered it to the barracks later on that day. The guard on duty promised her that he would make sure Titch received it.

Now all she needed to be was patient. She knew he would reply, she felt it in her heart.

CHAPTER 9
The Truth Hurts

William had been led into the apartment, and Alma could hear Mami talking to him and ushering him into the living room. He had rang earlier, saying he would pop round, after Alma had got a bit emotional on the phone. Mami had commented on what a nice boy he was. This had surprised Alma, as she hadn't said anything nice about Alma's friends since the hospital saga.

'Almita, William is here,' she stood outside Alma's room whilst Alma finished brushing her hair, tying it up scruffily into a ponytail.

Alma went into the living room and hugged William.

'You okay?' he looked at her.

Alma nodded, putting her coat on. 'Where we going?'

'Don't mind, up to you.'

The bus dropped them in town, and they headed for the nearest kiosk.

'Coffee or an alcoholic beverage?' William asked cheekily.

'I think I'd better stick to coffee,' laughed Alma, as they both grabbed a couple of chairs outside. The waitress was there before they even had a chance to sit down.

William ordered two coffees. People were mulling around and Alma could hear the familiar mixture of English and Irish voices.

'So, what's been happening?'

Alma looked across at William, who was leaning forward and had both hands on the table. She closed her eyes and put her head back.

'I think I have serious issues, Will.'

'Yeah, well, tell me something I don't know.' They both burst out laughing.

Alma told William about her trips to the hospital, her medication for the depression and anxiety, and finally about Titch.

'Do you love him?' he looked at her curiously.

'Like you wouldn't believe,' she felt that crushing ache in her chest again.

'So, what's happening about your posting?'

'I'm not going,' she quipped, 'been looking for a job.'

'What's your mum and dad said?'

'Oh god, they are totally against me staying, told me I am going back to England simple as.' Alma sipped her coffee, 'Mami has threatened me, saying that they are going to send me back to Honduras, but I've heard it all before.'

'Have you heard from Titch?' She looked up at him, then back down into her coffee cup.

'No.'

'Do you think you will?'

'Yes,' she said, sounding slightly desperate. She could hear it in her own voice, and started to feel her eyes water. William picked up on this, and quickly changed the subject.

'Right, come on let's drink this and head up to Yvonne's. I said we'd pop over there.'

They spent most of the afternoon watching Yvonne and a group of others playing hockey, with William and Alma joining in for short bursts. Alma tried to avoid any cigarettes or alcohol, and somehow she felt a little better. On a couple of occasions, however, her mind went back to Titch, and she felt that same overwhelming ache inside her chest. She had gone to Suzy's virtually every day since she sent the letter, but still no reply. It had been eleven days now, and she was beginning to wonder whether she would hear from him.

Later that evening, all of them headed off to get some food. Alma had a curry, and regretted eating it so quickly.

'Come on, Alma. We're gonna get some booze and watch a couple of movies before we head out later.'

'Nah, I'm gonna head back. Think I've had enough excitement for one day,' Alma hugged them all in turn. They looked disappointed.

'Do you want me to walk you to the bus stop?' William was always so thoughtful.

'No, you're alright, Will. I'll ring you tomorrow,' Alma motioned a wave and headed in the opposite direction.

The bus home was full. Alma had to stand, and when it came to a halt she breathed a sigh of relief. *Suzy must be sick of the sight of me by now*, she thought. She knocked on the door. Suzy answered.

'Anything?' she waited in anticipation.

'Yeah, arrived this morning,' Suzy held the door open for Alma to come in.

Oh my god, he'd replied. She knew he would, she knew it, he loved her as much as she loved him.

They headed to Suzy's bedroom. Suzy handed her the envelope. Alma stared at it.

'Well…are you gonna open it?' Suzy's voice was impatient.

'I'll read it at home,' Alma put the envelope in her coat pocket. Her heart was racing, and her palms were sweaty. 'Suzy, thank you so much,' she wrapped her arms around her, 'I really appreciate it.' Alma began to well up.

'I just hope it's what you want to hear, Alma.'

'Thank you. I'll let you know what he says!'

Alma almost ran home. She sat on the bed, and opened the seal of the envelope, her hands shaking.

Dear Alma…

Met someone else.

Alma stared at the page. The words became a blur.

Go back to England Alma.

She stifled a sob, but then she couldn't contain herself. Alma burst into tears, beating her fists against the bed. This couldn't be happening. She wanted to die. She held the letter to her chest as she sobbed and sobbed.

'No, Titch, you love me. I know you do, please you can't do this, you can't.'

She paced the room like a caged lion, her mind racing.

'USE STUPID GIRLS LIKE YOU,' the words haunted her, realisation slowly catching up. The blonde girl that she had seen him with…where had he been the night he hadn't shown? Alma blew her nose and took a sip of water. Taking a deep breath, she looked again at the letter, trying to keep calm and comprehend the words.

Dear Alma

Thank you for your letter

I needed to clear a few things up with you.

We had a great time but the truth is, it was a bit of fun, I was never in love with you.

Your dad lectured me and I was really angry when I found out your real age, why would you lie like that? I trusted you, I would never have been involved with you if I'd known.

I have met someone else and we are very happy, you will meet someone when you return to England, I'm sure of it.

I wish you all the luck, you're a nice girl

Regards,

Tony

She looked at his name at the bottom of the letter – Tony – in squiggly writing. For a second she thought it wasn't from him.

This wasn't the same guy she knew. Their love making, his kisses, their passion, had all of that not meant anything to him? Had she imagined all of it? Maybe she had been too drunk. Perhaps he hadn't had the same feelings as her. Was she going completely mad? Crying once more, she stared at the letter over and over. Had she missed something? Was there anything in the content that perhaps had a hidden meaning? No...nothing. She imagined him with his new girlfriend and quickly closed her mind to it. She hadn't given one thought to him meeting someone else. What was she like? Was she skinny and blonde like the last one? Alma went over to her bedroom mirror. She recoiled, hating her reflection. She couldn't blame him, could she? She needed a drink. She needed something to numb the pain. Then she remembered the doctor's words at the hospital.

A short time later, she was back at Suzy's house. Kim was there too.

'Oh god, what's happened?' Kim pulled Alma in, and they shut the bedroom door behind them.

Alma handed Kim the letter, and both her and Suzy read it.

'What a lousy wanker!' Kim looked angry.

'Oh, babe, come here,' Suzy squeezed Alma tightly, and the tears flowed once more. They all had a group hug and sat on the bed.

'Everyone was right,' Alma cried. 'Why couldn't I see it for myself?'

'Listen, listen, we are all the bloody same, we are always the last to see it. Anyway, even if we'd told you, you wouldn't have listened. Same goes for me and Suz, right?' Kim looked at Suzy, who nodded her head in agreement.

'They're all bastards, just after one thing. Trick is not to get too involved or attached, then you don't get hurt, know what I mean?'

Alma thought about Kim and her conquests. She seemed to go from one guy to another, but she had never seen her cry over any of them. As for Suzy, Alma only knew of a couple of guys she'd slept with. Alma thought she was more interested in Nikki than any bloke. Was it just her? Why did she feel the way she did? She'd never felt like this before.

'Here,' Suzy had brought in three beakers full of wine. Alma hesitated, but only for a few seconds. Instantly she felt calmer, It was just what she needed, she'd missed that feeling so much.

'You know what, Alma, I wouldn't give that twat another thought. Paddy was the same, I'm sure he was the one that gave me that herpes thing and he's probably giving it to other girls too,' Kim swigged her drink.

'All men are wasters, we just need to use them like they use us, right?' the girls cackled loudly.

They chatted until late. The girls persuaded her to rip the letter up and bin it, but when Alma reached home she still hadn't been able to get rid of the pain. She cried herself to sleep.

'Alma…Alma.'

She opened her eyes, David was gently nudging her.

'I've been knocking,' he put down her glass of water and tablet on her bedside table.

'How are you feeling?' he folded his arms.

How was she feeling? Numb, hurt, angry, resentful and jealous. Alma swallowed her pill with water and sat up.

'Fine,' she said.

'Listen, Alma, your mum wants to have a chat with you,' David lent up against the wall.

Alma looked up at him and put her head back against her pillow. 'Oh god, not if she's going to nag.'

'She just wants to talk to you, we need to resolve all this. We're not getting anywhere shouting and arguing all the time,' he looked exasperated.

'Don't worry, David. I am going back to England, you were both right.'

David looked totally shocked.

'Really, it's fine. I'll come with you.'

David composed himself. 'Okay, well, Mami will come speak to you soon.'

Minutes later Mami popped her head round the door. Alma noticed how tired Mami looked. She had lost weight.

Mami sat down on the bed next to Alma. She looked nervous.

'Almita, I wanted to talk to you about your father.'

Alma stared at her.

'I haven't told you…but I've been in touch with Maria, who has met up with him, and passed on the letters and photographs that I sent over.'

Alma's head was spinning. What the hell was happening?

'He's very proud of you, Alma.'

'What do you mean he's very proud? I haven't heard from him since we left, and suddenly he's interested?'

'It was my fault,' Mami said. 'I didn't give him any contact details, so he wouldn't have been able to reach you even if he'd wanted to, I have been wanting to tell you for a long time, but couldn't find the right moment. I know moving away from Honduras and leaving your father was hard for you, but I need to let you know what happened, so it makes sense.'

Alma looked up to the ceiling and closed her eyes. She didn't want to listen to this, not right now, but Mami was not letting up.

'We came here to have a better life. Things were extremely hard in Honduras and when I had to work in Belize to make extra money it got tough for me. Your father and I had problems and I tried so very hard to make things work, but he had made up his mind.'

Alma looked at Mami. 'Made up his mind? What do you mean?'

Mami shuffled uncomfortably. 'He met someone else. He was going to make a new life with her…' she paused, as if running through the events in her head.

Alma tried to take in what Mami was saying. Papi had left Mami for someone else. How could he? Why?

'Papi left you?'

Mami nodded and held Alma's hand.

'I loved your father very much, Alma. He was working his way through the ranks of the army…his family wanted him to settle down with someone who had an education and a good family background. I couldn't compete with her. She was a teacher, her family had money. I was a seamstress and could hardly feed us, it was inevitable that he would marry her.'

'But…but you had me!' exclaimed Alma. 'Didn't Papi love me?' All of a sudden, she felt extremely sad. She thought back to the Cola-Cola factory, the strange woman at that house, and the parrot.

'Listen to me, your father loves you very much. He was heartbroken when you left, he didn't sign any of the papers to let you out of the country. David had to help me pay for a lawyer to sort it all out. We had problems at the airport in England, remember?'

Alma cast her mind back, but she couldn't really remember.

'Me and your father were not on good terms, for many years.

When I worked in Belize I met David. He seemed like a nice man.' Mami smiled and then got up and walked towards the window.

'I'm sorry for what I said about Tony. I just care about you so much, and I said things in the heat of the moment.' Mami wiped her eyes, 'I hate seeing you suffer the way you have been. I know I have been very strict with you, but it's only because I love you. I've only ever wanted the best for you. You do understand that, don't you?'

Alma closed her eyes. None of it made sense. What did it matter if Mami was a seamstress? He couldn't possibly have loved them. Suddenly, she felt extremely angry.

'I was wondering whether you would like to go and visit the family?'

'When?'

'Well any time, you've finished school now. I could arrange it with Maria and you could see your father whilst you were there. He would be so happy to see you.'

Alma knew it would make Mami happy if she went, but she didn't feel any inclination to go. What would she even say to him?

'Maybe later. I want to see about getting back to England and sorting a job out first,' Alma waved her hands in the air, as if these things were going to be too big a task.

'Okay, you take your time. There's no rush, perhaps you could write to your father in the meantime,' she headed to the door, looking round and smiling at Alma, who was left bewildered.

A couple of minutes later Mami returned with an envelope, containing photographs of Papi.

Alma stared at him. He looked smart and important in his uniform. In one photo he was shaking someone's hand, and there were a couple of flags in the background. On the back of the photo it read *El presidente Jimmy Carter – 28 de jenero 1979.*

Alma brought the photo nearer. Papi stood proud, and it suddenly reminded her of the photograph of him and Mami in the big frame.

She cast her mind back, trying to remember things about him, but there wasn't much she could recall. Then she looked up from the photographs. He had left Mami for someone else, just like Titch had left her. She had to be strong, like Mami. She would need to start again in England, but she would get a decent job and make the effort to meet new friends. *I can do it,* Alma resolved. She placed the photographs in her bedside drawer.

***

'I'm gonna miss you, Alma.'

William leaned over and kissed her on the cheek. Everyone else cheered loudly. Alma could see people in the restaurant looking round and staring. Her friends had arranged a surprise farewell dinner.

'I'm gonna miss you too,' Alma was blushing

'You had better write,' shouted Kim from across the table.

'Of course I will. I have all your addresses and you guys can come and stay,' Alma looked round at everyone at the table.

'You can come back here and visit too,' said Suzy, with a mouthful of food.

'Well you better send me an invite then,' Alma pointed her fork at Suzy.

'Yeah, well we are off to Cyprus next month,' chirped Yvonne.

'Christ, why can't we get a bloody posting to Cyprus?' whined Thomas.

'Maybe we should all go on holiday together.'

'Oh my god, how cool would that be?' Kim laughed

Watching them all, Alma felt an overwhelming sense of sadness. Even though she'd promised to make the most of it, she'd rather have done anything than go to England.

They shared two taxis back to camp, and it was gone midnight when they arrived. They bundled out of the taxi noisily. Alma tried to quieten them all down, but they were too drunk to take any notice.

'Ssssshhhh, you guys, it's late!'

'I need a pee,' Kim dragged Suzy over to the nearest bushes.

'Oh my god, I can't believe you're doing that,' Alma grabbed William's arm and started walking away, shaking her head.

'Hey, wait up!! WAIT!!!' Alma could hear high heels clunking behind them. 'We love you, Alma,' Suzy rushed up and planted a smacker on Alma's lips.

'We fuckin luuuvvvv you,' Kim missed and kissed Alma's forehead, making them all giggle.

'Right, I'm gonna get home,' William shivered. He hugged Alma tightly. 'Have a great trip back,' he whispered in her ear. 'Make sure you write…and you've got my number so no excuses.'

'I will, as soon as I'm settled, I promise.' Alma kissed him on the cheek, feeling tearful. She watched him walking away, wobbling slightly, with his hands in his pockets. And then he was gone.

'God, Alma, he loves you,' Kim had linked arms with her.

Suzy joined in, 'Yeh, Alma, he does.'

'Oh god, you two, shut up.' It was a slow painful trip up the hill, with all of them bursting into fits of giggles. By the time Alma had got home and into bed it was gone one in the morning. She thought about where she was heading. David had received a promotion, and him and Mami seemed very excited about the move. Yoli had expressed excitement about starting her new school, something Alma had never done. She thought about Titch again, and their time together. It was still raw. She could still feel him kissing her. She closed her eyes and imagined his aftershave, his face, and his body against hers. What was he doing now? She imagined him sleeping and then she thought about him making love to the blonde girl. She opened her eyes, staring into darkness, becoming overwhelmed with sadness once more. She suddenly felt worthless again. Why couldn't he have loved her the way she'd loved him? She hadn't been good enough or pretty enough for him. She was too short, not slim enough, and her breasts were not large enough. *STOP*, her brain was yelling at her, *STOP.*

Alma looked at the clock beside her bed. She said a prayer:

'God, please be there for me, give me the strength to carry on.'

After a few repetitions, she felt a little better, and eventually she drifted into an uneasy sleep.

Alma's final days disappeared quickly. Before she knew it, she was on her way to say goodbye to Suzy and Kim. As she walked the familiar route, she could see Katherine's block and wondered what had happened to her. There were rumours that she'd been posted to Scotland, but nobody seemed to know the truth.

Reaching Suzy's block, she pressed the buzzer to the flat.

'Yeah?' came Suzy's voice.

'It's me!'

The buzzer sounded, and Alma made her way up.

'You alright?' Alma hugged Suzy.

'Yeah, can't believe you are leaving today.'

Kim was laid on Suzy's bed, reading *Smash Hits*, and looked up as the girls walked in. 'Bloody hell, Alma, you're leaving us today!' She swung her legs round and almost threw herself at Alma.

'Will always remember that first time we spoke when you got your second beating of the day,' Kim had a stupid smirk on her face.

'Yeah, you silly cow, and you wouldn't accept any help.'

'Well, what were you gonna do exactly?' Alma laughed

'I could have persuaded Nikki to speak to Katherine,' Suzy gloated.

'What's going on with you and Nikki anyway?'

'Oh you know…this and that.'

'No, actually I don't know.'

'We like each other, but that's it.'

'What, no relationship?' Kim said.

'Not like that, Nikki wants to but I'm not comfortable with it.'

'Christ, it's not the done thing anyway, is it? You know…lesbos and all that!'

'What's wrong with that?' Suzy sounded cross.

'No, I don't mean you, I just mean….' Kim had dropped herself in it.

'Listen, if you like someone then I don't think there's anything wrong with it. You obviously have feelings for each other,' Alma said.

'Shit, Mum and Dad would disown me anyway, so there is no point in even discussing it,' Suzy was getting agitated. She looked at Alma, 'What time you leaving?'

'We're catching the ferry at three this afternoon, this time tomorrow we'll be back in England,' Alma tried to sound enthusiastic.

'Have you heard from Will again?'

'Yeah, spoke to him and Yvonne yesterday.'

'Oh shit, forgot to say I got you some copy photos,' Suzy walked over to her dressing table. She handed the bag over, there were a couple of packets of photos and the girls started looking through them. It wasn't long before they were in fits of giggles.

'Jeez, Alma, I can't believe what you used to wear.'

'Where?' Alma snatched the photo. Younger Alma stared back. Her complexion was like a ghost, and her hair was jet black. She was all in black, surprise surprise.

'Look, compared to this one,' Suzy handed Alma another photo. She was wearing a tight-fitting black dress and high heels, her hair was dark, but long and wavy. Wearing heavy makeup, she didn't look like the same person.

'Oh my god, look at this one!' It was Kim and four blokes sat at a table, with what looked like a hundred drink bottles surrounding them.

'What's wrong with it?' Kim looked serious, trying not to laugh.

'You look like a hooker!'

There was a knock on the bedroom door. Suzy's mum brought in a small tray with a square cake. On the top it read *GOOD LUCK ALMA* and had white daisies around the letters.

'You shouldn't have,' Alma choked up.

'Well we did, so let's cut it up and have it with a cuppa,' Suzy beamed

Finally, it was time to leave. Alma felt a weight in her chest as she walked out of the door. She turned to say goodbye, welling up.

'No, come on, we will walk you back,' Kim insisted.

They all made their way back to Alma's. As they approached, the lorry was already outside loading up the boxes. Suddenly, it was real. She was leaving.

All three of them burst into tears.

'Listen, Alma, you better write,' Suzy squeezed her tightly.

Alma nodded, wiping her face.

'Yeah, we're soul sisters, never to be separated,' Kim shoved Alma, laughing.

'I love you guys,' she grabbed them both and they hugged for what seemed like eternity. Deep down, she knew it would probably be the last time.

Making her way back indoors, Alma heard someone shout her name. She turned around, and saw Katherine walking towards her. She looked so much better, very skinny and still pale, but much happier.

'Hi, Alma!'

'Hi?' Alma said, surprised to see her.

'Look, I know you are leaving today and I just wanted to come over and say how sorry I am for what I did to you.'

'Don't worry about it.'

'No, Alma, I was a horrible person, a bully. I needed help and I got it just in time.'

'I knew that wasn't you, don't worry,' Alma looked at her sympathetically. 'I'm just happy you're okay.'

'Nikki spoke to Suzy for me, to find out when you were going. I just couldn't let you go without saying sorry.'

'Well, thank you.'

'I didn't know if I should give you my address, but just in case you wanted to write, here it is. You can always rip it up and throw it away…'

Alma took the folded piece of paper.

'Oh, and although I cannot remember exactly what I said about what happened before you went away, I just want to let you know

I didn't mean any of it. I should have been there for you and I wasn't,' she suddenly burst into tears.

Alma gave her a hug, 'It's in the past. We'll write, okay? And then we can arrange to meet up again.'

Katherine wiped her eyes. She smiled, 'I err…just got myself in such a mess, you know?'

Alma felt sorry for her, she still looked like she was struggling. 'It's in the past, okay?' She held onto Katherine's arm reassuringly.

'Thank you,' Katherine said.

'For what?'

'For being so forgiving.'

'Oh my god, Katherine, how long were we friends for? Really, forget about it. You need to make sure you get yourself fully recovered.'

They chatted a little longer, before Alma had to make a move, telling Katherine that she would definitely write to her.

'Right, got everything?' David asked

'Yep,' Alma held onto Yoli's hand as they made their way to the car.

'Look, there's Emily,' shouted Yoli, waving to her friend. 'Byeeee Emily!'

'You gonna miss your friends, Yoli?'

'Yes, but I'm going to make new friends at my new school, so that's okay,' Yoli looked up at Alma as they both belted up in the back of the car.

As they drove down the hill and past all the blocks, Alma looked out. There were a lot of memories here, good and bad, but mostly good. She would never forget Ireland, not for one minute.

CHAPTER 10
Breathe

The house in Oakley Close was lovely. Alma and David had walked countless times around the camp, trying to familiarise themselves with their surroundings, but it was a lot to take in. On one occasion, Yoli had ridden her bike round with them. When they ventured to the local shop, Alma saw plenty of younger children with their parents, but barely anyone who looked her age. Yoli had already made friends, and Alma felt somewhat resentful that her little sister could manage so well in these situations, something she would never be any good at.

Standing in the shop, she noticed an advert in the shop window:

Office junior required for busy insurance brokers in town centre, no experience required as full training will be provided. Duties to include: administration, filing, answering the telephone. If interested please call Hannah Miles on 04261 653876, completed application will be required.

Alma walked up to the cashier. 'Excuse me, have you got a pen I could borrow? Do you have the application for the job at the insurance brokers here?'

The cashier rummaged around near the till. 'I think they'll send you the application form,' she said. 'You just have to ring them.'

'Oh, okay, thanks.'

Yoli was beside her, stretching on her tiptoes. 'What you doing?'

'I'm writing some job details down.'

'Why?'

'Well, because I need to get a job.'

'Why?'

Alma stopped writing and looked straight ahead of her. 'Because I need my own money, that's why.'

'So you don't need to take Mummy and Daddy's anymore?'

Alma smiled, 'Yes, that's right.'

'I have my own money at home if you need some. It's in my piggy bank.'

'That's okay, Yoli. You keep your money, you may need to buy something with it,' Alma ruffled Yoli's hair and went to meet David by the doors.

'Alma is getting a job,' Yoli announced.

'Is she now?' David looked sideways at Alma.

'Yeah just taken some advert details down, I'll give them a ring when I get home.'

The three of them walked back home, stopping a couple of times for Yoli to do her laces.

Later that afternoon, Alma called the insurance brokers.

'Hello, please may I speak to Hannah Miles?'

'Yes, can I ask who is calling and what it's about?'

'It's to do with the office junior role that I have seen advertised.'

'Hold the line please.'

After a moment, another voice said, 'This is Hannah Miles speaking.'

Alma's interview was booked for the following week. The application would be sent out in the post, along with bus details and directions. She would be seeing a Mr Saddler. Alma guessed that he was the owner of the company, since they were named Saddlers & Co. Alma shook when she finally placed the telephone receiver back in its place.

'Well?' Mami was untying her apron.

'Got an interview next week!'

'That's great,' Mami walked over and gave Alma a hug.

'I haven't got a clue what I'm gonna wear though…'

'You'll find something, if not you still have time to buy a suit.'

Alma cringed. She'd never worn a suit and didn't have anything like that in her wardrobe. In the end she settled for a crisp white blouse and a black knee length skirt. She teamed this with a grey cardigan. It looked a little like a school uniform, but it would have to do.

'David, what do you think Mr Saddler will ask me in my interview?'

All of them were sat at the dining table.

'Well, he will probably ask you why you want the job, he will obviously look at your job application to see what qualifications you have.'

'What if I can't answer any of his questions?'

'You will be fine, Alma. Just remember to breathe and relax. I would also advise to have a few questions of your own to ask him.'

Once back in her room, she thought long and hard about what she would ask Mr Saddler, and tried to imagine what his replies would be.

The day of her interview arrived faster than she expected. True to her word, Hannah had posted the application form together with bus details and directions. Alma arrived forty-five minutes early. Feeling embarrassed, she waited in the café a few doors down. Her legs were wobbly. Ten minutes before the interview, she got up and walked into the reception of the Saddler building.

Mr Saddler was short and round. He had ginger hair, and cleared his throat after every second sentence. His eyes were blue, deep-set, and piercing.

'So, Alma, you are from Temple Barracks?'

'I've been there a few weeks now.'

'I see you've lived in Ireland…and Germany too?'

'Yes, I spent a year or so in Germany.'

Mr Saddler cleared his throat again. 'Ah, Alma, wie geht es dir?'

Alma smiled at him, 'Gut, danke.'

They both laughed, and she felt herself start to relax.

'So, why don't you tell me why you would like the job?'

Alma was ready for that one, she'd practiced and practiced.

'Well I have finished school now and I wanted to get into an office environment. I think everybody needs insurance in one way or another, so I would like to know more about the subject...' she waited.

Mr Saddler was looking closely at her application form. 'Sexorat,' he said. *Oh no, please don't let him ask me about those*, Alma thought.

'You suffer from anxiety and depression?'

That was it, she was finished. There was no way she was getting the job now.

'Yes.'

'And how are you coping with that?'

Alma thought for a moment. She had been coping really well. With the exception of feeling nervous about the interview, she had felt so much better lately.

'I've been feeling fine,' she lifted her head up and tried to sound confident.

He nodded and seemed to forget about it, going on to discuss interests and then explaining more about the role.

'Right, thank you very much for coming today, Alma. I will keep your application and we will be in touch in due course,' he stood up.

What about the questions? He hadn't asked her if she had any questions.

'Err…Mr Saddler, is it okay if I ask you a few questions?/

Mr Saddler looked surprised. 'Of course,' he said, and sat back down, smiling at her.

Alma had pre-prepared for this moment. She started by asking him how long the business had been established. Then she asked roughly when she would hear back. Were there good prospects with the job? Did she have a good chance of getting the role? She was sweating and trembling so much by the end that she hadn't noticed his stare.

'I have a few other candidates to see, but I will let you know in writing by the end of the week.' He smiled as he got up from his chair and shook her hand. 'It was lovely to meet you, Alma.'

The days passed, and on the Saturday Alma received a letter from Saddlers, advising her she had been successful. She would start in two weeks' time. Absolutely delighted, she read through the letter three times.

Naturally, Mami and David were thrilled.

'Right, you will have to get yourself a bank account now,' David was writing something down, he tore the slip of paper off and handed it to her. 'I would recommend this bank. Make yourself an appointment as quickly as possible, as you will need an account to pay your salary into. Oh, and well done, I knew you could do it,' he smiled at her proudly.

Then it happened. On the Friday before she was due to start her job, Alma was walking Yoli back from school. As they crossed the road, she felt herself go dizzy. It was only slight, at first, but then the whole road span round, and she fell to the floor, feeling nauseous. Yoli ran back into the house crying. Alma tried hard to get back to her feet, but she couldn't. She just lay helpless, on her side, waiting for help. Mami and David helped her inside and called a doctor.

The doctor told Alma that she was suffering from vertigo, and possibly an ear infection too, both of which were affecting her balance. He prescribed her tablets, and told her that it was likely to come back at some stage, but there was also a small chance that she'd never have another episode. She'd need to stay in bed for three days minimum though, meaning there was no way she could start work on Monday.

Alma felt despondent. She couldn't be sick on her first day. *Bloody hell, I'll get the sack before I've even started.* Why did these things keep happening to her? She resolved to try everything she possibly could, to get there on Monday.

On Monday, the alarm went off at six-thirty. Alma was already awake. She moved her head slowly, still feeling dizzy, and trying not to move too quickly. She glanced over at her clothes, and felt a wave of dizziness again. She was too ill to go to work on her first day. Christ, she would be the first person to lose a job without even turning up for it. She was so disappointed in herself. Alma buried her head in the pillow, feeling disgusted. Some time later, she woke with a start. David was knocking on her door.

'Alma, I have spoken with Mr Saddler and he hopes you get better soon. He hopes to see you later this week, once you're fully recovered,' he looked at Alma sympathetically.

'He really said that?'

'Yes, he totally understands and said that these things happen, so now you can relax and recover without worrying, okay?'

As David left the room, Alma felt warm inside. Mami was right, David was a good man, even though he did have a bad temper.

Later that week, with Alma feeling better, she ventured into the office. Mr Saddler greeted her warmly.

'Alma, this is Ross, he will be showing you the ropes.'

Ross was tall and thin with blonde hair. His fringe was too long, and he constantly fidgeted with it, brushing it sideways and trying to tuck it behind his ear. Mr Saddler went around the whole office, introducing Alma to everyone. There were about eight employees in total, so not a huge company.

Ross started by showing her the computer system, and Alma wrote notes frantically. The office was really busy with customers coming and going all the time, it seemed non-stop, and by the end of the day Alma almost fell asleep on the bus.

She ranted on about her first day to Mami and David over dinner.

'So you think you'll like it then?' asked David.

'Yes, the people seem really nice,' Alma stabbed her chicken thigh with her fork.

'Are you gonna be rich now?' Yoli beamed.

'I hope so,' Alma laughed.

'Can you take me out on my bike?'

'No, Yoli, it's nearly your bed time,' Mami pointed at the kitchen clock.

'But it's only....the long hand is on the six and the little hand is on the six...so it's half past six?' Yoli stared at her pink Disney watch.

'Wow, when did you get so good at telling the time?'

'I am really good. Alice in my class can't even tell the time and she's eight, the same age as me,' Yoli seemed very cocky all of a sudden.

'Come on, I'll take you out for half an hour, 'Alma looked at Mami, who nodded in approval.

'Yay!' Yoli ran to get her shoes on.

Standing at the bus stop the following morning, Alma noticed a girl dressed all in white. *Maybe she's a cook or maybe she works in a hospital*, Alma thought. The girl glanced over at Alma and smiled.

'Hi, you new to the barracks?'

'Yeah, only got here about a month or so ago.'

The girl pointed an open cigarette packet in Alma's direction. 'Want one?'

'Oh, no thanks,' Alma said politely.

'I'm Julie, but just call me Jules,' she stepped forward to shake Alma's hand.

'I'm Alma. How long have you been here?'

'Too bloody long,' Jules took a deep drag and slowly exhaled. The smoke lingered in the air.

'Are you on your way to work?' Alma pointed at her white outfit.

'Oh yeah, work at the kitchen in Billy's just three days a week, then the other two nights I work at The Lime Bar.'

The bus pulled in. Jules sat behind Alma.

'Where do you work, Alma?'

'I have just started a new job in town... in fact today is my second day – Saddlers and Co.'

'Nah don't know it.'

'Where are you on camp? I'm in Oakley Close.'

'Oh yeah that's two roads up, I'm on Nordell Road. Although I'm hoping I won't be there too much longer,' Jules stared out of the window.

'Why, where you going?'

'Don't get on with the parents, you know? The sooner I'm out the better...what about you, anyway? Where are you from? You look Mexican or something.'

Mexican? Alma thought. Wow, she'd never heard that one before. The girls were about the same age. Jules was saving up for driving lessons, and stayed away from home as many nights as possible. She seemed very bitter about her home life.

'Anyway this is me, better go,' she wriggled to the end of her seat and with that she was gone, waving goodbye to Alma as she stepped off.

Alma walked slowly to work. Someway back, she could hear a siren. As she turned into the road, a man standing in a doorway winked at her. He was dressed in dark clothes, and looked a bit older than she was.

'Morning,' he said.

Alma smiled, 'Morning.'

'What you doing later?'

Alma gave him a quick look. She laughed, and then carried on walking.

'I know you like me really,' he shouted at her back.

Ross looked up as Alma walked into the office. He looked like he'd been there all night. His hair was scruffy and hung down his face.

'Hi,' he smiled at Alma.

'You okay?'

'I've got a meeting this morning, are you gonna be alright if I leave you some bits to do?'

'Of course. Do you want a coffee?'

Ross smiled, 'God yeah that would be great, haven't had a chance to have one yet.'

Alma hung her coat up. As she walked through to the small office kitchen, she could see Mr Saddler in his office, deep in conversation with Ben, another employee at the company. Alma had only met Ben once, but he seemed nice.

Ross was stressed. He kept pushing his fringe behind his ear and muttering to himself. They went through a few things, and Alma tried frantically to keep up by writing notes so she wouldn't forget. Before she knew it, Ross had grabbed his suit jacket and briefcase, and was out the back door. He'd hardly touched his coffee.

'Alma, just shout if you need any help okay?' Laura said. Ever since Alma started, Laura had been incredibly kind, helping her get to grips with everything.

'Thank you, I think I am going to need it!' Alma felt panicky all of a sudden. She looked through her notes, but somehow they made no sense.

Ross was gone almost all morning. Luckily Laura was on hand to help, and by the time Ross got back Alma had filed all of the queries that Ross had left her.

'What you doing for lunch?' Laura glanced sideways at Alma.

'Nothing.'

'Do you wanna come with me and Ben to The George?'

'If that's okay with you.'

'Of course!'

Ten minutes later, Alma was sitting at a pub table, opposite Ben and Laura. The waiter took their order.

'Lager shandy and two glasses of wine please. Oh…is that okay with you, Alma?'

'Yeah that's fine,' one glass of wine wouldn't hurt.

'Are we eating?' Ben held up the pub menu.

'Oh no not for me, I've got lunch back at the office,' Alma said, suddenly remembering she hadn't touched any of her lunch.

The waiter went away.

'So, how you finding it then, Alma?'

'Not too bad, gonna take me a while to get to grips with the system but better than I thought.'

'Well old Saddler must have liked you, he interviewed loads of people for the job.'

'Yeah well Alma was the prettiest,' Laura laughed taking a huge mouthful of food.

'Well I should hope so,' chuckled Ben, 'considering most of them were male.'

'How you getting on with Ross?' Ben's tone of voice changed.

'Yeah, he's nice.'

'He's a dick that's what he is.'

Laura interjected. 'Oh shut up, Ben.' She turned to Alma, 'Him and Ross don't really see eye to eye.'

'Nope, but it's such a small office that I guess we just tolerate each other. He's such a fucking know it all,' Ben swigged back most of his shandy. 'He's right up Saddler's arse, you know the type?' He looked at Alma as he finished his beer, then stood up and scraped back his chair, 'One more for the road, yeah?'

'Ben, just a spritzer for me this time,' Laura shouted.

'Here, I have some money,' Alma rustled in her bag.

'Nah you're alright, Alma, you get 'em next time.'

Alma watched as Ben and Laura finished their food. Ben lived a couple of minutes from the office, he rented with another guy, so he only had to walk in. Laura lived a good half hour away and got the bus in. She was in the middle of taking driving lessons, and her mum and dad had promised to get her a car for her twenty first birthday. She'd already shown Alma her tattoos – two on her back and one on her ankle. It turned out Alma was the youngest in the office.

'You're the baby,' Laura put her arm round Alma lovingly.

'You got any, Laura?' Ben mimicked holding a cigarette.

'Yep.'

They headed outside. Alma could see two guys heading toward them, she instantly recognised one of them. It was the same guy from that morning. He smiled at her cheekily.

'Hello again, we must stop meeting like this.' He shook hands with Ben.

'Alright, mate, what's happening, you weren't there the other night?'

Laura and Alma made their way to one of the tables in the garden. Laura put her hand in her pocket and came out with something that looked like a cigarette, but then she started rolling it.

'Is that a joint?' Alma asked.

Ben had joined them, 'Hurry up, Laura, we've only got ten minutes.'

'Gis a chance,' she lit up and took a deep drag.

'God that's better,' Ben seemed to relax a bit. 'Here you go,' he passed it to Alma.

She held up her hands, 'I'm okay, thanks.'

Ben laughed, 'Nah, come on. Just give it a try. It takes the edge off, I promise.'

Alma slowly put the joint up to her mouth, and took a short drag. Immediately her head was filled with clouds. She wanted to laugh, but she didn't know why. Then she took another drag, and immediately started giggling.

'Don't tell me this is your first joint?' Ben looked bemused.

'Oh my god, Alma's a weed virgin!' They teased her, and she blushed, trying to make out that it wasn't her first time, these were just different to the ones she'd had in Ireland.

'Shit we'd better get back, otherwise Saddler will be on the war path.'

Ross spoke double Dutch that afternoon, and Alma felt incredibly tired. She started to regret smoking the joint, and when the end of the day arrived she was relieved. Walking to the bus station, it was cold and drizzly. She pulled her hood up around her face.

Suddenly, there was a loud shout from behind her. 'Oi, Alma!'

Alma turned to see a long silver car, parked up on the pavement. She went over and looked in the open passenger window. The man grinned.

'Me again,' he said.

'Hi.'

'Come on, Alma, get in.'

She looked at him. 'No, it's okay, I'll get the bus.'

'You're getting wet. I'll take you home, it will be much quicker.'

Alma hesitated. The rain got harder. Sighing, she pulled open the car door and got in next to him.

He smiled, 'So, where to, my lady?'

'Err...Temple Barracks please. Do you know where that is?' she looked across at him.

He nodded, putting his foot down on the accelerator.

'An army girl then?' Alma could feel his stare on her. She wished he would keep his eyes on the road.

'Is it your dad in the army?'

'Yes.'

'Is he an officer?' he was teasing her, she could tell by his voice.

'Yes he is?'

'Oh shit I was only joking when I said that! Better get you back safe and sound then.'

'Listen, I feel really stupid. Thank you for the lift, but I don't even know you,' Alma shuffled uncomfortably in her seat.

'What do you wanna know?'

'Well you could be a mass murderer…'

'Yeah and you've just got in the car with me so that was a bit silly, wasn't it?'

Alma glared at him.

'My name is Luke Giles. I own a few businesses here and a couple of properties too. This morning you walked past one of my businesses, LG Motor Parts. I have two brothers and one sister, no wife, no kids, and my mum lives around five miles from my house. I like nice things, including money and clothes…anything else you want to know?'

'No that's fine,' Alma felt silly. She clung to her bag, wishing she hadn't asked.

'One thing I'd like to know, and I think I am entitled to ask…' he glanced over again, 'can I take you out Saturday night?'

Alma hesitated. She felt like she was twelve years old again.

'Just a meal and maybe we can go to a club afterwards,' he said, 'so you can get to know me a bit better.'

Alma stayed silent. She thought about it. How was she supposed to get to know anyone if she didn't make the effort? Luke seemed like a nice guy. He was a bit arrogant, but if she was really honest with herself she found that quite attractive. It wouldn't hurt to go out with him just the once.

'Hello, is anyone there?' Luke touched her hand, making her flinch.

'Okay.'

'What?' he seemed shocked.

'Yes that's fine, what time were you thinking?'

'I will come and get you at seven-thirty.'

Alma made Luke drop her off a few houses down. She didn't want him knowing exactly where she lived. As she got out the car, he winked.

'See you Saturday, if not before.'

She watched the car turn around and head back towards the entrance barrier of the camp.

***

'Laura, what do you know about Luke Giles?'

Laura picked up her coffee cup and brought it to her lips. 'Why?'

'I'm going out with him tomorrow night,' Alma kept typing, as if the conversation wasn't taking place.

'Oh my god, Alma, are you serious? He's gotta be ten years older than you at least, I suppose it's okay if you like older men…'

Alma looked round at her, 'I'm having second thoughts now.'

'I think he's a bit of a ladies' man, if you know what I mean.'

'Oh really?' Alma felt like she'd made a big mistake. 'It's just as friends though, you know? It's hard to meet anyone, other than you guys I don't speak to anyone around here.'

'You can always come out with me, Ben and the girls from here. We sometimes get together on Fridays after work.'

'Thank you,' Alma looked down at the ground, still feeling stupid.

'Ben will know more about Luke, anyway. He hangs around with him and his brothers. Do you want me to mention it?'

'Oh god, no, don't. I don't want the whole world knowing!'

Laura laughed, 'I know one thing though, he's loaded, so he'll be able to show you a good time.'

At seven thirty-five the following evening, Alma was pacing the living room. She didn't want to seem too eager, but she felt nervous. She was wearing her signature black dress, not too short, with a long coat covering her up nicely. A car pulled up a few doors down. Alma went outside to greet him.

'Hello, gorgeous.'

Luke got out. He was wearing a dark suit, with a crisp white shirt, and when he opened the door for Alma she smelt his aftershave.

'Where are we going?' she asked.

'Well, firstly we are going to a good friend's restaurant.'

Alma did up her seatbelt. She felt tingly inside. Luke had perfectly manicured hands, and on one finger he wore a gold signet ring. She could see a bracelet peeking out from under his sleeve.

'Are you okay?' he asked.

'I'm fine…just nervous, I suppose.'

Luke smiled, 'Don't be nervous, I'm not gonna eat you…well maybe later.' He winked, and Alma felt herself relax slightly.

***

'White or red?'

'White, please.'

'We'll have a bottle of your best white and best red, please,' Luke handed the menu to the waiter. 'We'll have a few minutes to order if that's okay.'

Over dinner, Luke told Alma about his business ventures, of which he had many. He also spoke about his mother a lot, which Alma liked. They were originally from the West Indies, and things had been hard for him growing up.

'I always had a fear of being poor…so when I was little I decided I would do everything I could to prevent that from happening.'

'How old are you?' Alma said, taking him by surprise.

'Do you wanna take a guess?'

'Well I'd say early twenties.'

'Are you to trying to flatter me? I am twenty-seven, actually.'

'Are you really?' Alma's eyes widened. He was ten years older than her.

'What about you? Let me see, I would say…twentyish.'

'I'm seventeen next month.'

Luke leaned back in his chair, looking dumbstruck.

'So basically, you are sixteen? And you are sat here with an old-aged man?'

Alma laughed nervously, not knowing how to respond. Shortly after, a man approached the table. He tapped Luke on the shoulder and shook his hand.

'This is Ken,' Luke introduced him. 'Ken, meet Alma.'

Ken put his hand out to Alma. She shook it, and he kissed her fingers.

'Very nice to meet you, Alma. However, what are you doing out with this ugly bloke?'

They all laughed. It turned out that Ken was the owner of the restaurant, which Alma thought was quite convenient. After a bottle of white wine, Alma felt herself starting to relax. She couldn't remember the last time she'd had such fun.

As they left the restaurant, Alma wrapped her arm around Luke's, 'Can we go dancing?'

Luke grinned, 'Yep, I know just the place.'

When they arrived at the club, the bouncers let them straight in the door. *More of Luke's connections,* thought Alma. There was already a table marked 'reserved', just for them, but Alma didn't want to sit down.

'Let's dance,' she said.

'Drinks first,' Luke motioned to a scantily clad waitress, who made her way over.

'Three bottles of champagne on ice, please.'

Alma was a bit taken aback. Why did they need three bottles? She sat close to Luke, staring at him and making him smile.

'Are you drunk?' She leant forward and kissed him gently on the lips. He hesitated and then kissed her back, quickly, urgently, before pulling away as the champagne arrived.

'To getting to know each other,' their glasses clinked.

Luke leaned in close. 'Are you having a good time?' he whispered.

'The best,' Alma kissed his cheek, 'But I wanna dance...'

She put her glass down on the table and led him to the dance floor.

Luke was a really good mover, Alma felt ecstatic. She was living the dream. Nobody else moved the way she did. Everyone was looking at her. The men on the floor adored her. She moved towards the middle of the floor and danced behind a man in blue jeans, holding onto his waist. He looked around at her, surprised. Suddenly, she felt herself being pushed back, where someone caught her.

'Come on, think you have done enough dancing for one night,' Luke took her hand and tried to drag her off the dance floor.

'Get your fucking hands off me!!! Get off, you don't fucking own me.' Alma struggled, but she couldn't get out of his grasp.

Luke shoved her onto the seat at their table, where she reached for the champagne bottle.

'Here, I'll do it,' Luke poured her another drink. She downed it, and then motioned for more. Luke reluctantly obeyed. Soon, others had joined them at the table. Ken was with them.

'Think we had better get you home, young lady,' Luke said.

'No, please, can we go dancing?'

Luke handed her a glass of water. Alma downed that too, and then hesitated as Luke kissed her on the neck. It turned her on. There was more alcohol after that, and then Alma lost track of where she was. There was definitely a car journey, then somewhere else, more drink, more kissing, maybe even sex…it was a blur.

'Alma, you're home,' Luke was trying to get her out of the taxi. 'Come on, try and act sober, otherwise your parents are gonna flip. Which is your house?'

'DUNNO!!!' she yelled

'Ssshhh quiet, you'll wake everyone up.'

'I don't wanna go home, let me stay with you. I love you, I really love you.'

'What number house are you?'

The next morning, the sun shone through her bedroom window. Alma could feel it on her face, but that wasn't what she wanted. She sat upright and then bolted to the toilet, trying to be as quiet as possible, before vomiting three times. Christ, she felt like shit. Collecting an unused toilet roll, she headed back to bed. Her bedroom floor was covered in clothes and shoes, and the contents of her handbag were strewn across the carpet. God, what a night. She hadn't had that much fun in ages.

On Monday, Luke popped into the office. He said hello to Ben, and casually walked around the room, pretending to be interested in car insurance. Stopping in front of Alma, he handed her a note. Alma looked at him questioningly.

'See you soon,' he said, with a wink, and walked out.

Sitting next to Alma, Laura whispered, 'Jammy cow.'

Alma didn't read the note until lunch time, but when she did she felt her heart start to flutter.

Sat night, pick you up seven pm at yours.

Dress sexy, 24-hour party so make sure you make

your excuses to stay out all night.

Saturday night came round quickly. Alma wore a red dress this time, shorter than the black one, and very tight fitting. Mami looked disapprovingly as she came down the stairs.

'Alma, that dress is far too short, it's freezing outside!'

Alma took her coat from the peg and put it on, 'It's fine, Mami, I've got this over it.'

Luke picked up her from outside the house. He took her bag and put it in the boot of the car.

'You look stunning, Alma.'

She smiled, 'Thanks. Where are we going?'

'It's a surprise.'

As they drove, Luke filled Alma in about what happened the previous weekend. Alma didn't remember any of it.

'God you are a bloody nightmare, Alma. I didn't think I was gonna get you off that dance floor without a fight breaking out.'

'Was I that bad?' she looked at him, feeling guilty

'Yes you really were,' he chuckled.

Luke pulled into a narrow lane, then followed a gravel driveway up to an enormous house. All of the lights were off, but Alma didn't need light to know that this was the biggest house she'd ever seen.

Luke got out of the car and opened the passenger door.

'Where are we?'

'Do you like it?'

'It's beautiful!'

'Come on, I'll show you around.'

There were at least four reception rooms in the house. Upstairs, Alma counted five bedrooms, and the bathrooms were the biggest she'd ever seen. There was a games room, a cinema, a bar and a swimming pool.

'Is this your place?' Alma looked at Luke, almost worried about what his answer would be.

'Yeh…still paying for it, mind you.'

'It's stunning.'

'Well thank you. Come on, let's get a drink…but I think we should ration you tonight,' he smiled and Alma felt her face go hot.

They stayed up for a couple of hours, sitting in front of the crackling open fire. It reminded Alma of Nanna and Clive's fireplace.

'Why don't you have a girlfriend?'

'Maybe I just haven't met the right person…I might ask you the same, anyway. Why haven't you got a boyfriend? You are a lovely looking girl…boobs to die for.'

Alma gasped, and gave him a playful shove.

'I guess I've just had enough of relationships,' she sipped her wine, thinking about Titch.

'What, at sixteen? How many have you had?'

Alma looked at Luke over the rim of her glass, 'Not many.' She wasn't going to admit it was just the one.

At around ten o'clock, a car pulled up outside the house. Luke told Alma that they were meeting some of his friends at The Lime Bar, in town. Alma thought that the name sounded familiar, but she couldn't recall where she'd heard it.

Once they arrived, the champagne came in buckets. Alma took her time, she really didn't want a repetition of the previous weekend. As the night progressed though, she felt herself slipping back into that same euphoric state. Then, suddenly, Luke was waving to someone from across the bar.

'Jules, over here!'

A girl made her way over to them. She was completely topless, like all the other waitresses, with the exception of a silver petal covering each nipple. Alma stared at her.

'Jules.'

'Alma...I didn't recognise you.'

The Lime Bar, now Alma remembered. Jules wore a tiny frilly ra-ra skirt, and 5-inch heels, but that was pretty much all she was wearing. She looked beautiful, with full make up and big hair.

'Another three bottles please, Jules, and where do you two know each other from?' Luke looked curiously at them both.

'Bus stop!' The girls almost said it in sync, and both burst out laughing.

'Oh bloody hell, keep forgetting you are at the barracks, well that's probably because you're never there,' Luke smacked Jule's bum so hard she almost dropped her tray.

Later that evening, they all went to Luke's house. Immediately everyone was stripping off and jumping in the swimming pool. Alma straddled Luke against the side of the pool, nodding her head to the background music.

'I am so happy I met you,' Luke said, kissing her softly.

'Me too,' she whispered.

Someone caught Alma around the waist. Alma turned around, drunkenly. It was Jules. She kissed Alma, forcing her mouth open. Their tongues intertwined, and their nipples pressed hard against each other.

'Here, open your mouth, Alma. Put your tongue out,' Jules took a small blue pill and placed it on Alma's tongue. She held out a glass of wine and teased Alma's cleavage with the stem. Alma closed her eyes and swallowed.

***

The bedroom was dark, the bed bigger than anything she'd slept in. Luke bounded in, knocking against the doorway entrance, nearly splattering the bottle of drink over the carpet. He climbed clumsily onto the bed and grappled at Alma.

Was Jules there or was it someone else? It didn't really matter, everything was so beautiful. Alma was floating on a pink cloud. The stench of cigarette caught her nostrils, she reached out and took a deep drag.

Alma rode Luke hard and fast. He moaned loudly and held onto her waist, pushing himself deeper inside her. He was so deep, she felt the pain and yelped. There was someone kissing the back of her neck, female lips, soft and sensual. Luke played with Alma, making her wet. He pretended he wanted to break free, but both girls held him down. Alma felt light headed. She couldn't hold for much longer. Then, suddenly, her hair was pulled back with force. Luke entered her, this time from behind. She screamed and pushed herself back against him. She was in charge, moving closer and closer, feeling him so deep. He loved it, slapping her backside time and time again. She was soon enveloped in cleavage, almost suffocating her, she sucked hard and could hear cries of ecstacy.

Then Luke moved faster and faster, and Alma clung to the bed sheets. He came, and the hot liquid splattered onto her bum. Alma collapsed in a heap, but the girl hadn't finished with her. She spread Alma's legs, and her tongue found her clit. She was in heaven. 'Please don't stop,' she gasped. She was hungry for it. 'Don't stop, lick harder, harder you bitch!' The time was coming.

She exploded, and then again. Alma had never felt this way ever, what had just happened? Please, God, what had just happened?

All three of them were sweaty and delirious, and lay there breathing heavily.

···

Alma awoke slowly, feeling the bed moving. She opened her eyes and could see Luke making love to the other girl. Moans of pleasure could be heard. Alma couldn't move. She was there, but she wasn't. As she blinked, she felt tears rolling down her cheeks. She managed to muster enough energy to move from the bedroom to the kitchen. Ken was standing by the oven, naked.

'Hi, Alma, do you wanna coffee?'

'Errr no thanks I'll just get some water…' In her own nakedness, Alma suddenly felt self-conscious. God, where were her clothes?

'Ken, please could you write this address down, I need to call a cab.'

'Sure.'

Another man walked into the room. He smiled at Alma, then walked over and kissed Ken, before making himself a coffee.

By the time she got home, the birds were singing. Alma was just glad to be back in her own bed. She still felt intoxicated. But she needed more, she needed to forget what had just happened. Pulling open the cabinet door, she grabbed a bottle of vodka. She took the bottle to her room and sat on the bed, swigging from the neck. Immediately, she felt calm, and her breathing steadied. It was another experience that she wouldn't be in a hurry to repeat. Laura had told Alma that Luke wasn't a one-woman guy, but she hadn't listened. Why hadn't she listened? Alma fell back on the pillow, and quickly dropped off into an intoxicated sleep.

CHAPTER 11
Nineteen

Laura passed the last of the boxes to Alma. They were flipping heavy, what the hell did she have in them?

'Here, let me take that.'

'Thanks, Ben,' Alma was grateful. She took some lighter items from the back of the van. Her head was thumping so hard, but she didn't even know why. She hadn't drunk for a few days now, and she should have been excited. After all, today was moving day. They were finally getting their own flat.

It was all Laura's idea. They'd been sitting in The George, when she'd turned to Alma and said, 'I need to leave home, Alma. How about you and me renting somewhere together?'

At first Alma thought she was kidding but soon realised from Laura's face that she was deadly serious.

'Well?'

'When?'

'As soon as.'

Alma looked into her wine glass. She hadn't even considered leaving home, not really. She'd thought about having her own place one day, but that had seemed a long way away.

'I only have a bit of money saved, wouldn't we need quite a lot for a deposit?'

'I have some savings,' Laura smiled as she got up to go to the bar.

'But you're getting a car, aren't you?'

'I'm getting that for my birthday, remember?'

As Laura stood at the bar waiting to be served, Alma thought about the idea of moving in together. The more she thought, the more appealing it seemed. No more worrying about disturbing anyone when coming home late. They could have parties and no-one would say anything.

Later that afternoon, Alma had spoken with Mami and David about it. Although Mami was upset at first, she soon came round. As David pointed out, Alma was nineteen now. It was the right time. The girls had spent the following couple of weekends looking at flats, and both fell in love with a two-bedroom apartment, approximately ten minutes from work. It was full of character, a bit old fashioned, but the landlord had agreed that they could decorate and make it their own.

Eventually all the paperwork was drawn up, and on the day of signing and picking up the keys Alma thought she would explode with excitement.

'God, I think we should call it a day,' Laura fell back onto the sofa, both legs flying up in the air.

'Let's toast our new home,' Alma walked into the kitchen, and grabbed two wine glasses and a bottle. Perhaps having a drink would make her feel a bit better. When she came back into the room, Laura gave her a big hug.

'Thank you, Alma. I would never have been brave enough to do this without you.'

'Awwww of course you would. I can't actually believe we are here, in our own home.'

'I know! Christ, imagine the fun we are gonna have. Eeeeeeek I am sooooooo excited,' both girls clinked their glasses and put their feet up on the coffee table.

'So tomorrow we'll finish up, and then Saturday is the flat warming.'

'Okay, but no smoking in the flat,' Alma looked at Laura as she began to roll up a joint.

'Oh, what about in the kitchen under the extractor fan?'

'No, Laura, it will stink the place out, just go outside the front door.'

Laura reluctantly stood up and put her shoes on, making her way to the front door, pretending to be hard done by. 'I hope you're not gonna be Miss Bossy Boots,' she grinned, as she shut the door behind her.

By the end of the following day the flat was ready. The girls had worked so hard cleaning and going to the tip to get rid of packaging and rubbish. Ben had been a godsend. He'd borrowed his friend's van and assisted where the heavy stuff was involved.

The three of them ordered an Indian takeaway and went to the local video store to pick out a film for that night.

'I'm going to get the booze for later and for tomorrow night, might as well get it now whilst I still have the van,' Ben grabbed his keys. 'You girls gonna be okay for money? You know, with your rent and all that?'

'Oh shut up, who are you? Our dad?' they all laughed as Laura shoved him out the front door.

'I suppose he's right, we better watch our spending.'

'Oh, Alma it's only a flat warming, we probably won't be able to eat for a month afterwards, but we'll manage,' Laura giggled, convincing Alma to see the funny side. 'Tell you what, we'll sit down and work out all our outgoings then we can look at putting something aside for treats, what do ya say?'

'Yeah cause I dunno how long my little heap out there is gonna last,' Alma looked out of the window at her red Mini. It was her baby. She'd bought it off Mr Saddler, but the money had come out of her salary each month. Finally, it had been paid off, and the Mini was hers. Her Garfield cat was sat high on the back shelf, looking out at the world, and there were two fluffy red and black cushions in the back.

'Bloody hell, Alma, it's such a low mileage car. It will last you for ages yet and it's not like we have miles to travel to work.'

'What car have you decided on?'

'Well my mum and dad have a budget of a couple of grand, so will probably go for Fiesta or something. Gonna have a look at a few cars next weekend, if you wanna come with us.'

'I can't next weekend, I have to take Yoli to a party and I said I would take Mum out on Sunday.' The girls looked up as they heard the door, it was their takeaway.

'God I'm starving,' Laura scurried to the door.

The next day Alma woke up feeling ill. She threw up most of her takeaway, even though she'd barely drank anything at all. Walking round the supermarket, Laura was as bright as a button. Alma wondered how she always managed to avoid hangovers.

'I'm gonna get a bottle of water and wait outside,' she said to Laura.

'Are you okay? You look really pale,' Laura waved a bag of hot chicken at Alma. The smell was enough to make her vomit on the spot. She quickly covered her mouth and ran out of the supermarket, heaving in the fresh air. When they got home, Alma made her excuses and went straight to her room. Soon though, she was vomiting into the toilet. Laura stood in the bathroom doorway, 'God, Alma, I think you may have some sort of tummy bug.'

Alma went back to her room and lay on the bed. Laura followed.

'Here's some water, do you want me to make you a bit of dried toast?'

'No, I couldn't stomach it. I'm gonna sleep it off.' Alma turned onto her side. Even the thought of booze was off-putting at that moment.

When Alma woke up later, her mouth felt bone dry. She took a glass of water off the bedside table. As she did so, she knocked a pack of tablets to the floor. Bending down to pick them up, her head swam. Contraceptive pills, but she didn't know which day she was on. There were two packs open, both with unused tablets. She opened the drawer and saw another unused pack. Placing the tablets back on the table, she laid her head against the pillow. Her period was late. She needed to do something about it. She picked up the Friday and Saturday pills and took both in one go.

The word spread quickly about their flat warming party. First all the older people arrived, family members, even Mr Saddler and his wife came. Lorraine Saddler was a petite lady, with rosy cheeks, and dressed quite posh. Alma and Laura were taken aback by all the cards and presents they received. And to top it off, they had enough booze to sink a ship. Yoli played with Mr Saddler's granddaughter, running around the house like lunatics.

'Alma, can me and Leyla play outside?' Yoli had her cute face on.

'Yes but stay at the front, don't go wandering off.'

'Come on, Leyla.'

The two girls looked so grown up now. Leyla was ten, a couple of years younger than Yoli. They both took their plates of food and sat on the grass. Alma wondered how and when Yoli had suddenly become so big.

By half past nine the older people had started making their excuses to leave, making way for the younger crowd. Luke and his brother, and most of their friends turned up. Ben and his mates came too. Jules brought her new girlfriend, who was stunning. They also had three other girls with them, none of whom Alma recognised.

Luke brought a huge bunch of flowers and a bottle of champagne.

'Hey, gorgeous, congratulations on your new home. I brought you something,' he planted a smacker on Alma's cheek, handing her the flowers, and digging in his trouser pocket, before hanging Alma a little box.

'Open it.' He took the flowers from her.

Alma prised open the box. Inside was a silver locket. Her eyes widened.

'It's beautiful!'

She slowly lifted the locket from the case, and a small heart glistened in the light.

'You need to open the heart,' he seemed really excited.

Inside there was a photo of her and Luke, heads together and both smiling.

'When did you take that one?' she looked up at him.

'I've got loads,' he smiled, squeezing her tightly.

Luke placed the bottle of champagne on the kitchen table and walked over to Laura, congratulating her and hugging her.

Alma looked at the necklace. It was beautiful. Another one of Luke's expensive gifts, another one to make up for the absences and unreturned calls, something Alma was now used to. They were not in a relationship. He would be with her when he wanted to be with her. Laura had warned her so many times that he would break her heart.

Alma looked across at him, he wasn't a bad person really. He helped a lot of people, he was very generous with his money. Mami and David liked him, but didn't think he was good for Alma. David called him 'The Showman'. Even Ben, his friend, had warned Alma that Luke would never settle down.

'Well it didn't take you girls long to make this into a cosy little place,' Alma was startled by Ken.

'Yeah we worked pretty hard, it feels a bit more like ours now.'

'Another little gift from his lordship?' Ken pointed his glass at the necklace.

'Oh, yeah, you know what he's like,' Alma quickly put the necklace back inside the box.

'He's very fond of you, Alma.'

'I know,' Alma blushed.

'No I mean, he's very fond of you.'

Luke had noticed them talking. He came over.

'Alright, Kenny?'

Both shook hands and started chatting.

Alma picked up her glass of wine and walked off into the lounge. She was trying to watch the amount of alcohol she drank, because even the smell made her stomach turn.

Later that night, as the last of the guests were leaving, Luke asked Alma if he could stay.

'No, I think it's better if you don't,' Alma said. She didn't want to put Laura out.

'Come on you know you want me to,' he grabbed her around the waist, kissing her neck.

'No, Luke, I'm tired.'

'Pretty pretty please?' he kissed the other side of her neck. Alma felt herself shiver, but she was adamant.

'I said no,' she pulled away and headed towards the kitchen, where Laura was clearing up.

'Come on, Luke, our taxi's here,' Ken grabbed Luke by the arm, handing him his coat.

Luke smiled and swayed a little. He walked over to Alma and kissed her on the cheek. 'I'll call you,' he said.

After they'd left, Laura turned to Alma and gave her a hug. 'Well done on being strong, girl. We are gonna find you a nice guy, someone who knows how to treat a girl properly.'

'I don't want to meet anyone,' Alma dried the plate vigorously.

Laura stopped washing and turned to Alma.

'Are you okay?'

'No, not really.'

'Wanna talk about it?'

'I've just been feeling shit lately'

'Yeah well I had noticed, you still feeling sick?'

'A bit, even my wine is making me retch.'

'Bloody hell, never thought I'd hear you say that,' Laura laughed as she grabbed another tea towel and helped Alma dry up.

'Laura, can I ask your advice on something?'

'Try me.'

'Well I've always been crap at remembering to take tablets and all that, but I've really messed up my contraceptive pills these last few months.'

'What?'

'My period is late, it may just be the worry and stress of the move and it's not the first time I've been late.'

'How late?'

'About a week…or ten days, can't really be sure.'

'Oh my god, Alma, and you're only just telling me? We've just rented this place together and you didn't think to tell me?'

'I'm sure it's okay, its only two weeks.'

'What you gonna do if you're pregnant?'

'I'm not!'

'But what if you are!?'

Alma considered it, 'Haven't thought that far ahead yet.'

'Is it Luke's?'

Alma ignored that. She carried on drying up.

'Alma, let's say you are…is it Luke's?'

'Yes.'

'Does he know?'

'No! You're the only person I've told.'

'You've been drinking so much, Alma, have you thought about what damage that could have caused the baby?'

'Laura, I'm not pregnant okay, just leave it.' They both carried on clearing up in silence. Alma thought about her drinking. She would stop for a while. When she did get her period, she would be extra careful with taking her pill going forward. God, what if she didn't get her period? She couldn't have a baby. What the hell would Luke say?

'Oh god, what if I am?'

'I think you need to go to the doctors.'

By week five Laura convinced Alma to go to the doctors to have a test done. Her breasts were tender, and she had cried non-stop in the bath the night before.

The test didn't take long. Alma was told to wait outside in reception. Her heart was pounding faster and louder by the minute. Her tongue was on the roof of her mouth, she felt like she would swallow it. *Please God, don't let me be pregnant. Please, I'll do anything, just don't let me be pregnant.* Her right leg was shaking like a leaf.

'Alma, would you like to come through?'

Her legs were jelly. She stood up straight and followed the lady back into the room she had just left.

'Your test results are positive, Alma.'

POSITIVE, POSITIVE, POSITIVE…NO NO NO NO!!!!

'I'd guess you are about seven to eight weeks, possibly nine weeks, pregnant.'

'Nine weeks? But I can't be, I can't be.'

'Are you okay? Do you need me to call anyone?'

Alma stared at the lady. She wasn't seeing her. She felt cold, numb, empty.

'Alma? Do you need me to call anyone for you?'

'Errr no, no thank you.'

'I guess you weren't expecting this?'

'No, I can't believe it. Can we do another test?'

'We can, Alma, but the results are pretty conclusive.'

The rest of the visit was a blur. Alma drove home dazed and confused. This could not be happening to her. Not this, not a baby, not now. Laura was in complete shock when Alma told her the news.

'You are going to have to tell him, Alma.'

'I know, I will, but not yet though.'

'Jesus, you are nineteen for god's sake. You've got your whole life ahead of you, what were you thinking? And with him, Christ, him of all people.'

Alma burst into tears. She didn't hold back, and Laura threw her arms around her.

'Oh god, I'm sorry, I'm so sorry. I'm a stupid bitch for saying those things, please don't cry, this must be so hard for you, Alma, I'm sorry.'

Over the next few days, Alma couldn't concentrate on anything else. She made stupid mistakes at work, and found it hard to communicate. She'd arranged to meet Luke after work on Thursday, but she hadn't told him what it was about.

Mr Saddler poked his head round the door, 'Alma, can I see you in my office please?' Alma went in and sat down. She felt sick. What had she done now?

'I just wanted to check you were okay, Alma. You haven't been yourself lately.'

'Oh I'm fine, just feeling a bit tired, that's all... haven't been sleeping very well recently,' Alma lied through her teeth.

'Well if you need anything you know you can always come and talk to me, okay?' Mr Saddler smiled at Alma. Even though she couldn't tell him, Alma felt grateful for his support.

'Thank you, Mr Saddler, I appreciate that.'

When she got back into the office, everyone else was packing up to go home. Laura looked at her, 'Do you want me to come with you to meet him?'

'No, it's okay, I'll be fine.'

'Okay, good luck. I'll be at home worrying, so hurry up and get back, love you and be strong,' she squeezed Alma's arm.

Alma got to the pub before Luke. She took a seat outside and waited. Shortly after, Luke arrived.

'I got you a beer, I didn't know what you wanted,' she pointed at the pint on the table.

He kissed her cheek and sat down, taking his dark glasses off.

'I've missed you like crazy,' he put out his hand and she held it, feeling sick at what she had to tell him.

'You okay?'

'No, not really,' she sipped her water and placed it down slowly.

'What's wrong? You haven't fallen out with Laura already have you?' he smirked as he said it.

He was so handsome, his smile still gave her goosebumps.

'No, nothing like that...I've got something to discuss with you.'

Luke let go of her hand. He leaned back in his chair, looking concerned.

'What's up?'

'Well, I'm…I'm errr…'

'What, Alma?'

'…I'm pregnant, Luke.' Alma looked at his face, she needed to see what he really felt. There was no expression, just a blank look. His lips were pursed, in a way that might have meant he was angry.

'How? I thought you were on the pill?'

'I was, or I am. I just…'

'What, you accidentally forgot to take them?' He picked up his drink and looked away, deep in thought.

'What do you want me to say, Alma? Do you want me to marry you, play happy families, is that what you want? Did you do this on purpose?'

'No, no of course I didn't. I would never do that, I've just been drinking a lot and I've missed quite a few days.'

'So you basically didn't care, you didn't think to let me know there could be a possibility that you may get pregnant. God, how irresponsible can you get?' Luke was very angry now, a couple on the other table were looking over as his voice rose. 'Who else knows? Do your mum and dad know?'

'No, I've only told Laura.'

'Christ, Alma, I cannot believe you are telling me this. This is the last thing I wanted to hear.'

Alma scraped her chair back and stood up to leave. 'I wanted to tell you, as it's your baby as much as it is mine…'

'Is it mine?' Luke got to his feet. He towered over her.

'You know it is,' Alma felt tears coming. How dare he? How dare he accuse her of sleeping around, she hadn't slept with anyone else, and he knew it. She clutched her bag and pushed past him, but Luke grabbed her arm and swung her round to face him.

'We have to talk about this, we need to discuss what we're going to do.'

'I'm not talking to you until you've calmed down, Luke. Let go, you're hurting me!'

The couple were staring over at them now and Alma felt bad for making such a scene. She smiled over at them and then at Luke who slowly let go of her arm. Alma walked quickly away from the pub, leaving him standing there.

She drove slowly back to the flat. She hadn't known what to expect from Luke, but it was out there now, and she knew how he felt. He wanted nothing to do with it. For the first time, she stopped to think about the baby growing inside her. Putting her hand on her flat stomach, Alma imagined it moving, another human being inside her. She couldn't believe it.

Laura ran out to meet her.

'Oh my god, I've been worried sick, you okay? What did he say?'

'He got angry.'

'What? Why?'

They walked into the flat, Laura made Alma a cup of tea and they both sat on the sofa.

'He asked me if it was his baby.'

'Christ, what an arrogant git, who does he think he is?'

'Well I suppose he had to ask the question, how does he know I haven't slept with anyone else?'

'Oh my god, there you go again, sticking up for him. I think you love this moron, I really do.'

'I know I do, Laura. Part of me thinks I shouldn't and I get this niggly doubt inside, but I can't help the way I feel.'

'You deserve so much better. Are you going to tell your mum and dad?'

'I don't know yet…' Alma thought about Mami. She would be horrified.

'You're not saying you'll get rid of it, are you?'

'I'm not saying anything, but I can't rule it out. I'm nineteen…'

'Shut up, there's mums at sixteen. You would be great, imagine a little girl or boy running round. I could babysit and we could go on holidays together,' Laura hugged Alma and kissed her on the forehead. 'Just don't make any rash decisions, okay?'

The phone rang, and Laura answered.

'Hello? Oh, hi, Luke. Yes she's here, hold on…' Laura mimed *shit* to Alma and passed her the phone.

'Hello.'

'Hi, we need to talk. Can I come round?'

'Not tonight, Luke. I just wanna have a bath and get an early night.'

'Alma, I need to talk to you. I'm sorry about earlier, please…I can be round in ten minutes.' Alma looked up at Laura, who was biting her lower lip nervously.

'Okay, see you then.' She heard the receiver go dead and gave a deep sigh. God, what a nightmare.

'I'll go round to Ben's, give me a call there when the coast is clear, okay?' Laura shoved her shoes on and grabbed her anorak. 'Is it okay if I take the car?'

'Sure, keys are on the worktop.'

'Love you, remember be strong and don't put up with any of his crap.'

When Luke arrived, he hugged her tightly. 'Can we talk about this as adults and not get into another shouting and slanging match?'

Alma nodded in agreement, 'It's as much a shock to me as it is to you, Luke. I was scared to tell you.'

'I know, and I was a complete prick about it. I've had a chance to think about it and I think the best thing is to get you to a clinic I know in London. You're only early days, aren't you? So from what I've been told it's only a one night stay, and then you'll be out,' he smiled at Alma. 'I have a friend…his girlfriend went there, apparently the place is really nice, and she was really looked after. It wasn't the right time for them either.'

She stared at him whilst he rambled on and on about how he could fix the appointment, and would get her there and pick her up the following day.

'What if I want to keep the baby?'

'What?'

'What if I want to keep it?'

'You're nineteen, Alma, you can't have a baby at your age. Later on perhaps, when you are ready you will meet someone you really love, someone who can make you happy. I have so many things I need to do. We've had great times, but I'm way too old for you, even your mum and dad probably think so…'

'But you're not too old to fuck me?' she lifted her chin up and dared him to answer.

'Alma, please,' he moved towards her, but she side stepped him.

'Please can you leave?'

She walked over to the front door and opened it so he could go.

'Alma, come on.'

'Just get out!' Alma shoved him out in the cold, and slammed the door behind him. She rushed to the fridge and poured herself a glass of wine. It was gone within seconds. Alma refilled the glass and held it to her lips. *This isn't the answer*. She opened a bottle of lemonade and poured half the wine down the sink, then grabbed the phone.

It was hard avoiding Luke over the next few days. There was so much to organise and think about. Laura had tried talking to Alma, but she had made up her mind. She had already spoken with her doctor, and they had referred her to the local hospital the following week.

Later that week, when Alma finished work, Luke was waiting outside. He looked dishevelled.

'Why haven't you returned my calls?'

'I've been busy,' Alma quickly brushed past him.

'Have you decided what you're doing?'

'You don't need to worry yourself, I'm sorting it.'

'What do you mean?'

Alma sped up, not wanting to talk to him.

'Alma, wait.'

'Just leave me alone. I'm getting rid of the baby, you don't have to worry about anything.'

'Alma, let me help you, please.'

'No, I'll do this on my own, I don't need you there holding my hand, I don't want to see you again. Just leave me alone.'

Luke stopped walking and watched Alma get into her car.

She didn't need him, she didn't need anybody. She had gotten herself into this mess and she was going to sort it. Her hands shook as she started the engine, and as she put her seat belt on she noticed Luke walking away. Suddenly, she felt sad. What the hell was wrong with her? Why did she only get involved in relationships that didn't ever work out? Her mind went back to Titch. He was the same, he didn't love her, he used her just like Luke had. After this, there would be no more men.

***

'Alma, you are going to go to sleep in a minute or so. The lights will dim. Can you hear me?'

She was drifting, the lights were getting darker. *Please, God, forgive me for what I'm about to do, I never wanted this to happen. I'm not ready to be a mum, please…my baby, my baby…please forgive me…*

From the next bed, Alma could hear sobbing. She turned her head and she could see a girl in the bed next to her, crying. Alma wasn't fully awake yet. It was a dimly lit room, with at least five or six beds. Some of the other girls were still sleeping and a couple were stirring.

'Nooooooo nooooooo I don't want to…' another girl from the other side of the room was shouting out.

'Sam, come on, drink some water please.' The nurse had come into the room, then a second nurse with a tray arrived. 'Hi, Alma, how are you feeling?' her hand was cold on Alma's forehead. She gave Alma two small tablets and handed her a plastic cup of water.

'Would you like some soup? It's tomato or mushroom, which would you prefer?'

Alma swallowed her tablets, her mouth was dry.

'Err…tomato please.'

'How are you feeling?'

'Okay, I guess.'

'You are quite hot so keep drinking this water and I'll be back with your soup.' The nurse smiled and walked to the next bed.

Alma sat herself up. She felt dizzy. Then the realisation of everything hit her. It was done. No more baby, no more worry. She began to cry, then sobbed uncontrollably. The same nurse came over to her and wrapped the curtain around her bed, holding Alma's hand and passing her some tissues. They stayed like that for a while. When the sobbing had stopped, Alma tried pulling herself together. God, what had she done?

Nineteen

···

Laura came to visit later on that day. Alma was sleeping when she arrived, but woke to finding Laura sitting next to the bed.

'Hey sleepy head, how are you?' Laura kissed Alma on the cheek.

'I'm okay.'

'You look flushed, do you want me to get you anything?'

'I need to change this nappy.'

'Okay, let me help you.'

Alma was fine walking, but felt uncomfortable – the nappy she was wearing was not very flattering. Laura got a nurse to assist Alma with the change.

'Will I be leaving tomorrow?' Alma asked the nurse

'The doctor is coming round a bit later, so he will decide this evening.'

Once back in bed Alma felt very drowsy. She spoke a little to Laura, but felt herself drifting in and out of sleep. The next time she woke up, Laura had gone. Her appetite had returned with a vengeance, and she finished everything put in front of her. By eight o'clock Alma was told she would be leaving the following day, much to her relief.

Alma spent the next couple of days at the flat. She had booked the time off work and Mami and David were none the wiser. It had been a relatively straightforward procedure. She had not heard from Luke since that day, either. It was hard to erase him from her mind, he was constantly in her thoughts, no matter how much she tried to shut him out. Feeling sad, she pulled out a big blue and pink box from under her bed, and started looking through the contents. Everything from Ireland was in there, all the letters to which she still hadn't responded. She stared at the letter on the top and instantly recognised William's writing. She wondered what he was doing. She reached out and she smiled as she flicked through the photos, longing to be back there.

***

'Thank you so much for being there for me, I don't know what I would have done without you,' Alma looked up at Laura as she laid dinner out on the table.

'You would have done the same for me right?'

'Of course I would.'

'Well, there you go, don't mention it. That's what friends are for. You gonna be okay going back to work tomorrow?'

'Yep, I need to get back into a routine.'

'Luke came looking for you today.'

'Oh god.'

'Don't worry, I told him to do one.'

'He just won't get the message, will he?'

'He didn't look that hot…I think he's feeling guilty.'

'I don't care, I just want him to go away for god's sake.'

'Do you really?'

'Yes,' Alma took a mouthful of food.

'Here, I brought us a nice bottle of wine, it was on offer.'

'Thanks,' Alma took a glass and put it up to her mouth. She could smell the aroma, it relaxed her. She instantly felt all the turmoil in her stomach disappear, with just a couple of mouthfuls.

'Laura, I have been thinking of going back to Honduras to see my dad, what do you think?'

'Gosh, where did that come from? You sure? You haven't mentioned this before.'

'Well Mami has been going on and on at me for a while. I think it may be a good idea to get away for a bit. I think I'd like to go and meet him, to see what he's like.'

'Well do it, before you change your mind!'

Later that evening, they watched a film, but Alma could barely concentrate. Her mind was on Papi. Would she recognise him? Would he recognise her? She was going to do it, she decided, but first she needed to speak to Mami.

CHAPTER 12
Papi

Alma could feel the heat. She had stayed in a Miami airport hotel the night before, with no air conditioning, but it was nothing on this. When she first stepped off the plane, it was hard to breath, and she had to squint to see where she was going.

After taking the first few steps, she got her bearings. Looking down, she could see some soldiers waiting to one side. In the middle was a slightly smaller, stockier man wearing big sunglasses, in different uniform to the others. Alma stared hard. That was him, wasn't it? He seemed to be staring straight at her.

Alma's hands were clammy, and she almost missed the last step. When she reached the bottom, Papi moved towards her. The other soldiers moved with him. Papi looked at her for a minute or so, holding her by her shoulders, then he grasped her tightly to his chest. A lump rose in her throat. All this time, and now he was there with her, holding her tightly. He spoke to her in Spanish, telling her how beautiful and how proud he was of her. He introduced her to the other soldiers, telling them that this was his daughter from Inglaterra.

Passport control was quick and easy. Papi took her to the front and spoke to the individual behind the glass window. She didn't quite catch what he said, but in no time at all they were through to the baggage collection area. Alma heard Papi chatting to the soldiers. He spoke so quick that she could hardly catch a word he was saying.

'Almita, Almita, dios mio, Almita,' she heard a voice coming from behind her. Looking around, Alma spotted a group of people approaching.

'Hola Alma!'

She recognised Aunty Maria and Uncle Oscar from the photographs that Mami had shown her, but none of the others. They all hugged, and Aunty Maria cried and kissed Alma time and time again on her cheek. She shook hands with Alma's father, exchanging greetings and nodding. There was some discussion that they would all be going back to Aunty Maria's, and that Alma would travel with Papi.

As they exited the airport, two small children approached Alma, hands outstretched. They were wearing old torn clothes and were very dirty. They had bare feet. She instantly reached for her bag, but her father grabbed her arm, pulling her along at full speed, telling her not to give them anything. She turned and looked at the children, feeling sad, their blackened faces staring back at her in despair.

She would never forget her trip back from the airport. They travelled in a huge pick-up truck, with all six soldiers in the back. Everyone beeped their horns for no reason, there didn't seem to be much attention paid to the road, other vehicles had men stood up in the back drinking and waving their beer bottles in the air, cheering for one reason or another. Alma looked on in amusement. Girls were being wolf whistled, it all seemed a bit chaotic. It was a total contrast to England. Papi's driving was erratic, and Alma clung to her seat. He glanced over at her a couple of times, but no words were exchanged. She looked down. Déjà vu, the gun in its holster was prominent. Like Papi, all the soldiers were armed.

They eventually pulled into a small lane and then in through some white gates. *La Rancha*, that was the name of the house. It was beautiful. Her father muttered a few words to himself, and then looked at Alma and smiled.

As they entered, Aunty Maria ran over to Alma, hugging her once more, and then a crowd of people appeared from nowhere. A few of them seemed nervous about the soldiers' presence, but soon, food and drinks were being served and music played loudly. Alma drank beer, but it tasted strange. She was grateful that everyone there understood her Spanish. They spoke so quickly though, especially her father. After a while she relaxed and found herself mingling. Luciana was one of the housekeepers, Alma instantly took a liking to her, she was short, round and very bubbly. Then there was Aunty Martha and Aunty Estella, and so many other relatives that Alma couldn't possibly remember all their names.

Suddenly, Papi was next to her. He put his hand on her shoulder. '¿Vamos a caminar, Alma.' *Let's go for a walk.*

They headed off towards the gardens.

'¿Como esta tu vida en Inglaterra?' *How is your life in England?*

'Bien gracias.' *Good, thank you.*

'Tienes tres hermanos, no pueden esperar para conocerte.' *You have three brothers, they cannot wait to meet you.*

Alma stared at him, were these three brothers from the woman he'd left Mami for?

'Y vas a conocer a tu abuelo.' *And you're going to meet your grandad.*

It sounded like he had a lot of plans for her. As they sat down admiring the view, they could see an elderly man pruning some plants in the distance. He took his sombrero off and gestured to them. Alma waved at him and her father nodded.

'¿Como esta tu mama?' *How is your mother?*

Alma looked up. Papi had removed his sunglasses. His eyes were red…had he been crying?

'Ella esta muy bien gracias.' *She's fine, thank you.*

'Ella me envio muchas fotografias tuyas, estoy muy orgulloso de ti Alma, y la quiero mucho.' *She sent me lots of your photographs, I am very proud of you Alma, and I love you very much.*

Within a few hours everyone started leaving. Papi told Alma that he would pick her up the next day, at ten o'clock. She was so excited that she could hardly contain herself. Hugging him tightly, her heart raced, and as she saw him depart, she was almost counting the hours before she saw him again.

The next morning, when Alma woke, she could hear chattering downstairs. It was strange to hear so much Spanish. Over breakfast Aunty Maria, Martha and Estella recounted the tales of when Alma was little, and how naughty she would be. Then they told the story of how, when Alma lost Dolly, they'd spent all day trying to find her, only to discover that she was tucked up in Alma's bed, underneath one of the pillows.

When Alma asked about Papi, Aunty Maria recounted how upset Mami had been when she found out that he was marrying someone else. They told Alma that they had not been able to forgive her father for the pain and anguish he had caused her mother, but after seeing him yesterday they didn't think it was right for them to carry those feelings any longer, not if it was to jeopardise the relationship between a father and a daughter. They just hoped that he had changed and that he could be sincere.

The day ahead wasn't at all what Alma had expected. First, they travelled to her father's home. She met her three brothers, and Miranda, her father's wife. She looked old and weary, had long grey hair, and her voice was gravelly. Miranda was the woman her father had left her mother for. It was a huge house, with land and horses and chickens, but everything in the house was basic. There was no indoor toilet, and no electrical appliances. Sitting in the kitchen, Alma felt an overwhelming sense of gratitude for what she had back in England.

Later on, they travelled to town, where they looked around the shops and market stalls. Alma found it all fascinating. Miranda told Alma to ensure her handbag was closed, and to make sure she held it tight and close to her, as there were a high number of robberies and murders in Honduras.

From out of nowhere, a young man grabbed onto Alma's arm.

'¿Puedes arreglar mi pasaporte fuera del país? Senorita, por favor, te pagaré.' *Can you arrange my passport out of the country, Miss, please? I'll pay you!'* He started pulling her. Miranda grabbed the man and pushed him off, and Alma's father shouted at him. The man scurried away.

Alma's father explained that they could tell from a mile off that she wasn't a local, just from her skin and her clothes. Alma was amazed. She was Honduran. She had been born there, wasn't it obvious to them?

Alma, Papi and Miranda ate in a small restaurant and drank beer. While Papi was in the toilet, Miranda told Alma about how she'd always been desperate for a daughter, but had only ended up with sons. She seemed like a nice lady, Alma thought. She couldn't feel any malice towards her, as much as she wanted to.

'Almita dile a tu madre que lo siento mucho.' *Tell your mother how sorry I am.*

'Dile a ella que lo se, lo que ella ha experimentado, un Corazón herido, lo siento, lo siento mucho.' *Tell her I know what she's experienced, a broken heart, I'm sorry, I am so sorry.*

Alma looked at her. Miranda's eyes were wet with tears.

That evening, Alma and her father went out to a bar at the army camp, where one of the local bands, Los Gatos Bravos, would be playing. It was an amazing atmosphere. The bar stretched from one side of the room to the other, in a semi-circle, and people were dancing frantically to the sound of the music. Three men approached Alma and Papi, shaking hands with Alma's father, and then leading them to a table.

After a few tequilas, Alma felt completely at home. Tapping her feet to the music, she wanted to dance so badly. One of the men said something to her father, and he nodded in approval.

Turning to Alma, the man beckoned Alma. She didn't hesitate, and followed him straight out onto the floor. Carlitos was a great dancer. He was in the army too, and knew her father very well. He tried speaking to her in broken English a few times, but soon realised it was easier to speak Spanish.

As they returned to the table, Alma saw Papi talking to a woman. Her back was to Alma, so she couldn't see her face, but the woman's figure was amazing. Her dress was tight, hugging at the waist, and her legs finished in high red stiletto heels.

'Almita,' her father beckoned her towards them. 'Meet Sophia.'

The woman turned to look at Alma. Alma guessed she was in her thirties, very heavily made up. Her cleavage was almost popping out of her dress. As she looked at Alma she smiled, and her white teeth gleamed. Her lips were full and bright red. They shook hands, and Papi told Alma that Sophia was a doctor. That was surprising to Alma, but she didn't say anything.

Suddenly, a voice on stage announced that Los Gatos would be appearing shortly. Everyone took their seats, with Sophia on one side of Papi, and Alma on the other.

From that moment, the evening changed. Papi hardly paid Alma any attention. Instead he spent most of the night teasing his fingers up and down Sophia's back, and kissing her neck as she threw her head back several times, laughing at something he'd said. A couple of times she glanced over at Alma, and then muttered things in Papi's ear.

Alma was furious. Where was Miranda? Did she know about this? Alma found out soon enough. In the middle of dancing with Carlitos, Papi pulled her to one side.

'Si Miranda pregunta, estuve contigo toda la noche.' *If Miranda asks, I was with you all night.*

Alma glared at him, disgusted.

'No menciones a Sophia bajo ninguna circunstancia.' *Under no circumstances mention Sophia.*

She felt betrayed. She was being made a scapegoat for her father's pleasure. He had hurt Mami, and quite evidently was going to do the same thing to Miranda. He didn't care about Alma, all he wanted was to show her off. He was arrogant, self-centred, and didn't care about anyone but himself.

Alma came back and sat with Carlitos and the other guys. Over on the dance floor, she could see her father and Sophia wrapped around each other. It made her sick to her stomach.

Papi arranged for a taxi to take Alma home that night. He kissed her on the forehead and slurred that he would ring her the following day, apparently there was a wedding that they were going to in a few days' time. Alma didn't care about going anywhere with him, but nodded politely.

Riding home in the taxi was an experience. The driver was intrigued that Alma was from England. Why was she there? How long was she there for? Would she consider moving back to Honduras? He was nice enough, but Alma wasn't in the mood to make idle chit chat. She felt drunk, but not drunk enough to numb the pain.

As she climbed the steps to the house, Aunty Maria opened the door and hugged Alma, asking her how her night had been.

They both sat, and Alma told her of the evening's events. She could see the pity in Aunty Maria's face. Aunty Maria knew what Papi was like, she must have witnessed it before Mami had decided to leave. Over the next hour, Aunty Maria told Alma about how Papi was a very proud man, who wanted a woman with intellect and from a good background, and that like many men in Honduras, he was not made to be with one woman. For Alma, it was staggering. If you behaved that way in England, you'd be branded a tramp. Yet that was how Luke and Titch had treated her.

Alma sat on the edge of her bed and thought about Luke. Soon, the tears came. It was like being on a rollercoaster. The previous day she was on cloud nine, yet now she felt like shit. Her heart ached, making it hard for her to breath. 'This is senseless,' she whispered. She couldn't make her father love her any more than she could make Luke love her. She heard Aunty Maria moving around downstairs. Alma wondered what Papi had actually felt when they left Honduras. Was he at all bothered? Probably not. How could any human being be so cold and heartless? Did they really mean that little to him? No wonder Miranda was grey and looked the way she did.

A few days later, they attended the wedding ceremony. The bride was one of Miranda's cousins, and looked stunning in an ivory dress and veil. The dress had a sweetheart neckline. Miranda's cousin was getting married in a church, with a large statue of Jesus on the cross. Papi's side of the family were all Catholic. As for Mami's side...she didn't even know. Staring at the statue, Alma's thoughts were suddenly with God. What was it all about?

Despite the church being small, there were an enormous number of people at the ceremony, many of them already there when they arrived. With the exception of Miranda, her father and her brothers, everyone else was a stranger to Alma. Papi led her over to a table, where an old man was sitting.

'Almita este es tu abuelo.' *Almita, this is your grandfather.*

Alma smiled, and took his hand, but he looked at her blankly. Papi interjected, speaking in English. He told Alma that her grandfather was eighty-seven years old now, and didn't really know what was going on around him. He'd lost half of his right leg, due to a diabetic condition. The man sat and gazed at the room. Papi gave him a sympathetic pat on the shoulder, and showed Alma over to another table.

During the rest of the ceremony, Papi spent a lot of time bragging to other people about Alma and her life in England. It made Alma feel embarrassed, and she was even more embarrassed when he started making things up. He told everyone that Alma was a high flyer in the insurance world, and that her salary was probably three times what anyone her age would earn in Honduras. The guests cooed at her father's words, but Alma felt incredibly fake. At one stage Papi asked her to make a little speech in English, and said he would translate it back to the group. She hesitated, but eventually spoke for a couple of minutes thanking everyone for being so accommodating and saying how much she had enjoyed the day and her whole stay so far. Papi translated something completely different. By the end of wedding, Alma needed some space from him.

The reception was being held in a plush hotel in the town. Everyone walked there as a big group. Alma welcomed the chance to get away from Papi. She pushed on ahead. Walking up to the entrance of the hotel, she could see beggars, mainly children, crowded outside. She looked around, checking to see whether anyone was watching, then delved for her purse. She quickly handed some money to the nearest child. Within seconds, there was a swarm of kids around her, crying out and pulling at her bag.

'¡ESTÜPIDA!'

Alma turned to see Papi's furious face. He dragged her away from the scene, and virtually shoved her inside the hotel entrance. Alma could see one of her brothers scowling at her. What had she even done? Surely it wasn't a crime to help starving children?

'No les des nada!' *Don't give them anything.*

Alma looked at him furiously.

'El dinero que les das no es para comida, es para drogas y alcohol.' *The money you give them isn't for food, it's for drugs and alcohol.* Papi took Alma's arm and marched her further into the room. She looked back at the children, feeling guilty. If only she could talk to them.

Over the course of evening, several different men approached Papi, asking for permission to dance with Alma. Watching them, she felt irritated. Why did she need his permission to dance with someone? She was nineteen, for god's sake. Approaching the bar, she ordered a wine, tasted it and then put the glass back down on a table. It tasted awful. Looking around, Papi was nowhere to be seen. She went back to the bar and ordered a tequila, where she got chatting with a group of men. They wanted to learn English, and had her repeat certain phrases, then tried to say them themselves.

Some time later, her father reappeared. He was with a new woman now, who he introduced as Gabriella. Alma was feeling very drunk by that point, and she decided she didn't care about Gabriella. Papi could do whatever he wanted, it was nothing to do with her. She turned back to the men at the bar.

Papi came up close behind Alma.

'Me voy Almita, Louis te llevara a casa.' *I'm leaving, Almita. Louis will take you home.*

Alma watched him leave. His arm was entwined with Gabriella's, and one hand was on her bum. Suddenly, Alma felt angry. How dare he. Who the hell did he think he was? He couldn't just treat her like this, leaving her with strangers.

Downing her tequilla, she asked one of the guys to hold onto her bag, and marched up to Papi. She pushed him hard. He stumbled, and then turned around in a rage, not realising who had done it.

'Hijo de puta!' *Son of a bitch!*

Alma went to slap his face, but he was too quick. He forced both her hands away, and Gabriella shrieked, almost falling over.

'You arsehole! Who do you think you are? You ruined mine and Mum's life and you carry on like nothing's happened!'

'¡Hija por favor, cálmase!' He was telling her to calm down.

Alma sobbed. People were staring at them, but she didn't care. She hated Papi so much, she wanted to hurt him as much as he'd hurt her.

Her father motioned to the chap who was taking her home. The man raced over and led Alma outside, handing her bag and drink to her. She walked to the side of the hotel and sat on the brick wall, taking deep breaths. The man waited patiently. Finally, motioning that she was ready to go, Alma stood up and let him lead her to the car. They didn't say a word on the way back. When they got back to Aunty Maria's house Alma thanked the man and got out of the car. She was tipsy, and stumbling, but somehow she managed to open the front door and let herself in.

Needless to say, Alma and her father did not communicate for a few days. Whenever he rang, Aunty Maria told him that Alma was out, but eventually they couldn't pretend anymore. Alma finally agreed to meet him for lunch. Papi said that there was someone he wanted her to meet. Alma was intrigued. More family members?

He picked her up the same afternoon, and they travelled out of town, arriving at a little restaurant on the side of a busy road. Getting out of the car, Papi turned to Alma and said, 'Are you ready to meet your sister, Almita?'

Alma stared at him in disbelief.

'Well?'

Was he joking? He didn't look like it. In fact, he looked proud. Alma followed him into the restaurant. At the back of the restaurant was a table and at the table a young girl and a woman who looked the same age as Papi were waiting. Her father introduced them as Lola and Valeria. Lola was eight years old. Alma sat down, stunned. It was almost laughable. How many other siblings were there? Lola had a small doll with her, and when Alma asked what the doll's name was, the little girl didn't answer. Instead she clutched onto her mother's arm and hid her face.

After lunch, they took a walk. Lola was hesitant at first, but eventually held Alma's hand. *She's probably as confused as me*, thought Alma. They stopped at a park, where Lola played on the swings, with Papi pushing her. Valeria told Alma that it was lovely to finally meet her. She seemed genuine, but Alma couldn't help but wonder how she felt being just one of Papi's mistresses. Watching Papi lift Lola up off the swings, kissing her several times, Alma felt slightly jealous. Had he been like that with her, before they left? Did he feel any love for her? She turned away and scuffed her foot along the ground, feeling miserable.

As they returned to the car, Papi gave Valeria a kiss on the cheek, and gave Lola one last kiss and a cuddle. Alma hugged them both. Would she ever see them again? She doubted it. Lola was the sister she would never get to know. And how many more of them were there? Feeling sad, she got back inside the car.

The journey back was slow. Eventually, Papi pulled over outside a little seaside bar. They sat on the terrace of the bar and watched the waves crashing against the shore. Salsa music was playing in the background.

Alma couldn't hold it in anymore. She had to ask.

'¿Por qué nos dejaste, Papi?' *Why did you leave us, Papi?*

Papi looked at her, surprised.

'¿Fue porque mami era costurera, no era maestra?' *Was it because Mami was a seamstress, not a teacher?*

Papi was silent. He put his beer bottle to his lips, staring directly ahead of him. After a few moments he said, 'Los quise mucho a los dos.' *I loved you both very much.*

'¿Por que, Papi?'

'Me esforcé tanto para evitar que te fueras.' *I tried so hard to stop you going.*

Papi looked at her. He took her hand. 'No sabes el dolor que senti cuando te fuiste.' *You don't know the pain I felt when you left.*

Alma stared at him. She wanted to believe it. She was desperate to hold onto that little inkling that he felt, perhaps, just a tiny amount of love for her.

Papi caressed Alma's fingers. His cheeks were wet with tears. 'Te quiero mucho, creame.' *I love you very much, believe me.*

Feeling a lump in her stomach, Alma reached up and kissed his forehead. He was her father, he always would be. She needed to know that he hadn't abandoned her, that he hadn't forgotten about her. And in some way, she thought, he needed to hear the same.

***

Eventually, her final day arrived. Two weeks had flown by. Alma was sad to be leaving, but more than ready to go home. She'd only spoken to Mami and Laura a couple of times since she'd arrived, and she missed them terribly.

The goodbyes were not pleasant. She tried hard not to cry, but it was impossible. They were family, regardless of how far apart they lived, or how long it had been. Papi wasn't there, he'd been too busy to come, but Alma forgave him. She understood, finally. As she walked towards the departure lounge, she could see Aunty Maria sobbing, and waving frantically. Then, suddenly, there was a loud voice from across the room.

'¡Espere Almita!' *Almita, wait!*

And then she was running, and Papi held out his arms. He was shaking as he held her close. 'Te quiero hija. Te quiero mucho.'

He didn't need to say anything else. Alma clung to him, crying loudly, not caring who was around. Despite everything he was her father…they had a bond, and she would always love him, no matter what. But finally, it was time to go, and with one final sob Alma untangled herself from his arms. She kissed him on the forehead, gently, and walked towards the departure lounge doors.

As the doors closed, Alma took one last look behind her. Papi's face was streaked with tears, and his hand shook slightly as he waved her goodbye, yet he stood proud and upright in his uniform – the perfect military man.

Alma would remember him that way, always.

CHAPTER 13
Trust Me

Mami laughed so much when Alma told her about Aunty Maria and Oscar's round the clock arguments, but she cried later when Alma showed her the photographs. Aunty Maria had given her a letter for Mami, and Alma could see how much that meant to her.

'I met Miranda too,' Alma said.

Mami looked at her, slightly confused.

Alma told her everything, from the trip to her father's house to the incident in the bar with Gabriella. Mami was sympathetic.

'I feel sorry for her, it must be a very sad life.'

'Yeah well at least you got out of it,' Alma squeezed her mother's arm. 'Oh and I didn't tell you, I also have a little sister – Lola.'

'¿Dios mío, ese hombre, que le pasa?' *My god, that man, what's wrong with him?*

'She's very cute…younger than Yoli, and her mum was lovely too. I just couldn't get my head around it really.'

'¡Nada cambia con tu papa!' *Nothing changes with your father.*

They spent the next couple of hours trawling through the pictures, and were only disturbed by the sound of a key turning in the front door, followed by the clip-clopping of school shoes running through the hall.

'Almaaaaaaaaaa, where are you?' Yoli came through like a flash, jumping on top of Alma.

'Oh my god, you have grown so much in the last fortnight!'

Yoli threw her arms around Alma's neck. Alma pushed her off gently.

'Okay, okay, I'm home!'

'Did you bring me a present?'

'No, why on earth would I do that?'

'Because I'm your little sister and you love me!'

'Is that so?' Alma tickled her sides and Yoli folded up in fits of giggles.

'Come on, I'll show you what I got you...'

'What is it? Is it clothes? Toys? Sweets?'

'You'll have to wait and see,' she led Yoli up to her bedroom, where there were a number of bags on her bed.

Yoli's eyes widened as she opened each present, a t-shirt from Aunty Maria and Oscar, a small leather purse from Martha.

'Who are all these from? Do I know them?'

Alma explained to Yoli that they had family in Honduras. She had already told her this several times, but she seemed oblivious.

'This one is from me,' Alma handed her the bag and waited for Yoli to open it.

'Ahhhh a little doggy, he is so cute,' she pulled the stuffed dog out of his box. He was chocolate and white and had a waggly tail. 'I am gonna call him Sam!'

'Why Sam?'

'Because that's her boyfriend's name,' Mami had entered the room.

'Noooo, he isn't my boyfriend,' Yoli jumped off her bed and ran out of the room, clutching Sam.

Sam was slightly younger and followed Yoli everywhere, they had become inseparable over the last few weeks. This became apparent the following day when Alma dropped Yoli off at school. Sam was waiting by the gates for her. He was tall for his age, skinny, with curly blonde hair and large brown eyes. As Yoli and Sam walked off through the school gates, Alma couldn't help wondering what Yoli would be like when she got older. Would she smoke? Drink? God, it just didn't bear thinking about. She had only been in secondary school for two years, after all. Smiling as she got back into her car, Alma remembered that Laura had arranged for them to go to the cinema that evening. They hadn't really had a chance to catch up yet.

As Alma pulled into her road, she noticed a strange car parked outside their flat. It was a Lexus, navy blue. She parked up, and the driver of the Lexus got out of the car. It was Luke. He was wearing a cream blazer with a light blue and white shirt, with sunglasses over his eyes. He walked over to her.

'Can I get in?' she read his lips through the glass.

She wound down her window. 'Why?'

'Because we need to talk, Alma. You disappeared on me without a word, I had to drag it out of Laura.'

He opened the passenger door and got in next to her. The same aftershave, his good looks…he looked tanned. God, why did he make her feel that way?

'I don't think we have anything to talk about,' she leaned back in her seat, looking defiant.

'I have to talk to you, I just need you to listen, okay? Can you do that at least?' he'd taken his glasses off and looked quite serious. 'I love you, Alma. I can't tell you how much I have needed to see you and tell you this. I haven't felt like this about anyone else, you have to believe me.'

'Less than three months ago you told me you were too old to be with me, or have you conveniently forgotten that?'

'I know, I know. I was scared Alma, I was bloody scared, you sprung the baby word on me and I panicked! I was just being a typical bloke, I made a mistake. These last two weeks I've been miserable. Just ask Ken, I've been a bloody nightmare. I missed you so much.'

'Well there is no more baby, Luke, so that mistake has been taken care of good and proper, and you no longer need to panic. I have to go now, I'm going out shortly,' Alma began to get her bag together. 'Oh and you also said you had things you wanted to do. In other words, you had no time to be tied down, especially to a stupid, young, naïve girl like me.'

'I didn't say that, Alma…I know what I said and what I'm saying now is something different, I still want to do those things but I want us to do them together, if you'll have me that is.' He reached into his pocket and pulled out a small green leather box.

'No, I don't need any more of your expensive gifts! I have a room full of them, you don't get it, do you? You can't buy me, Luke! You can't just keep turning up with jewellery and perfume and expect me to forget everything that's happened. You're probably doing this to so many other girls, do you really think I'm stupid?'

Luke gave her a serious look. He opened the box, 'Will you marry me, Alma?'

Alma stared at the ring. It was a beautiful ring, with a small stone in the centre, shining in the sunlight. Her hands were shaking.

Luke leant over to kiss her. Alma froze. What the hell was going on? She didn't trust him.

'No I won't marry you, Luke. I wouldn't marry you if you were the last bloke on earth, are you seriously kidding me? Is this some kind of fucking joke to you, you can't keep treating people like this,' she went to leave the car, but he reached out, holding onto her arm.

'It's no joke, Alma. I tried so hard to find out which hospital you had gone to, I waited outside your office, I begged Laura to tell me where you were. I was going stir crazy not being able to see you. I want to spend the rest of my life with you and yes I am shit scared hearing those words come out of my mouth, but I bloody well mean them. I've been a complete tosser and I don't want to lose you.'

Alma stared at him.

'I didn't want us to lose our baby,' Luke continued, 'and that's something I will have to live with for the rest of my life because I was such a dick not owning up to my responsibilities, as usual burying my head in the sand. I told Ken everything. He knows how much I love you, he's the only one that knows.'

Alma's eyes were welling up. Oh my god, he wasn't joking. Her heart felt as though it would burst. He did love her, maybe a little, in his own way.

'I need time, Luke. I just can't pretend nothing's happened…I'm not like you. I have feelings you know, I can't just forgive and sweep everything under the carpet. I had our baby growing inside of me. Do you know how much that hurts? Do you?'

Alma burst into tears. He hugged her tightly as she sobbed into his chest.

'I have to go.'

'Can I call you?'

'I don't know…' Alma got out of the car, leaving Luke sitting there. She stumbled towards the front door, without turning around, and inside she grabbed a bottle of wine. When she went to look outside of the living room window, she could see that Luke's car had disappeared. She shrugged, and swigged from the neck of the bottle.

Later that evening, Laura burst through the door, excited.

'Come on girlie, are you ready? We gotta go…Alma, where are you? We need to hurry up.'

She slowly pushed the bedroom door open, Alma looked up.

'Bloody hell, what's going on? How much have you had?' Laura snatched the bottle away from Alma and put it down on the dresser.

'Are you okay? What's happened? Why are you crying?'

'He wants to marry me,' Alma giggled.

'What the hell are you talking about?' Laura looked around. There was an empty bottle of wine at the foot of the bed.

'Laura, Luke wants me to marry me! He showed me the ring, a big sparkkkkly stone! For me, a ring for me!'

'Right, come on, let's get your coat. We'll get a coffee and something to eat at the cinema. You're a right state, Alma.'

The film was boring. Alma slept through most of it, although she occasionally heard Laura laughing away to herself. She sat there staring at the screen, sipping on her coffee. Slowly beginning to sober up, she thought about her wedding. What sort of dress would she have? Who would she invite? Mami and David would flip, she knew it, they didn't really like Luke, not as husband material anyway. He wouldn't have asked her if he didn't mean it, would he? She jerked upright in her seat. What the hell was she thinking? She couldn't marry this guy. He wasn't right for her, not one bit. He was too old, too vain, too self-obsessed...and yet he was also kind, good looking, wealthy, intelligent...caring in his own way. He wanted to spend the rest of his life with her, she couldn't quite believe it. He could have any girl he wanted, but he'd chosen her.

Back home, Alma felt sober enough to tell Laura how she really felt.

'I'm going to say yes, I'm going to marry him.'

'Are you out of your fucking mind? Do you really think he would be faithful? Get a bloody grip, Alma, he isn't the right guy for you. I am telling you as your friend and in case you hadn't realised, I happen to care what happens to you.'

'I think he's changed, you should have seen him. He wasn't like the old Luke, he was quiet and honest for a change. My god, he showed his true feelings, which is saying something. I have been thinking long and hard about it, Laura, I want to marry him. I think we would make a good couple. I need to believe we can make a go of this. If I don't give it a go then I will never bloody know, will I? I'll regret it for the rest of my life.'

'Think about the baby, Alma. He didn't give a shit, he made you have an abortion for god's sake, he is a complete waste of fucking time I'm telling you, but if you wanna carry on being treated like shit then that's up to you.'

'No he didn't, he didn't make me do anything. It was my decision. You sound like you hate him. He hasn't done anything to you, why do you hate him so much?'

Laura stood up and walked into the kitchen, coming back with a small glass of water.

'Listen, I don't hate him, okay? I just don't want to see you get hurt, not again. I've had to see you go through so much since you've been with him and it has just made me angry. You're a big girl, if you wanna marry him that's your decision and yours alone, I will always be there for you, Alma, you know that.' She put her glass of water on the coffee table and gave Alma a hug.

'I love him, Laura. I want to spend the rest of my life with him.'

Laura smiled and held her hand.

'I know you do, you're bloody mad. Listen, I just want you to be happy. Besides, I do love a good wedding.' Laura went into the kitchen and fetched a bottle of champagne. 'I know you've probably had enough booze today but if this is what you want then let's celebrate. Fuck it, let's get wasted!'

Alma woke to the sound of her alarm. She groaned. It couldn't be that time already. Christ, how much had they drank? She couldn't really remember much, but she recalled her conversation with Luke. Jesus, had she agreed to marry him over the phone? What a nutter, he wouldn't have taken her seriously, surely? She tried so hard to piece the conversation and the night together, but nothing came back.

Going back to work was awful, and halfway through the day Alma thought about just going home, but a couple of coffees made her feel better. At six o'clock, as she was leaving, Luke was outside the door. He was holding a bouquet of roses.

'How's your head today?'

Alma glared at him. She wanted to knock that smirk off his face. 'Do you remember what you said to me last night?'

'Oh god, Luke, I'm so sorry. Laura and I had so much to drink.'

'You said you would marry me on one condition…that I had to convince your mum and dad, because they don't like me.'

Alma prayed for the ground to swallow her up. She hadn't said that, had she? Bloody hell, she was so embarrassed.

'They do like you.'

'No, they don't. I've known that all along, Alma. I knew I would have to persuade them anyway, so I've been to see them, and they've both given me their blessing.'

Luke handed her the roses, and then kissed her tenderly on the lips. Her legs felt like jelly. She got into his car, slightly dazed. She tried imagining Mami's face when Luke told her, it must have been quite a picture. Luke took her to a bar in town, where he proposed again, placing the beautiful ring on her finger. It fitted perfectly. 'You have made me the happiest man, do you know that?' He kissed her knuckles, and swept her up into his arms.

The date was set: Saturday 14th August, exactly four months away. It wouldn't be a big affair, with just family and close friends invited, but Alma knew that it would be the biggest day of her life. Alma was organising the wedding herself, with a little assistance from Mami and Laura, and Yoli, of course. Yoli was so excited about being a bridesmaid. Luke had asked Ken to be his best man, and Ben and both of Luke's brothers were to be ushers. One of Luke's brothers was travelling over from Jamaica to attend. Alma was surprised to hear that he was coming, because Luke wasn't particularly close to him.

Mami was making the bridesmaid dresses, they were pink with ivory criss-cross bodice stitching down the front, and full skirt. The shoes were simple, pink silk ballerina style, and they would each wear a headdress of both cream and pink roses. Mami and David had not really spoken about the wedding, only saying that they were happy for the both of them. Mami had once spoken in the kitchen about trust and loyalty, and asked Alma if she was sure about the whole thing, but other than that they had remained quiet about the whole affair.

On the Thursday before the wedding, Alma was greeted by all her colleagues in the office. They had decorated her desk with pink and silver *BRIDE TO BE* banners, and the same colour scheme for the balloons. There were presents on one side of her desk, and her chair had been draped in light pink material, with everyone's good wishes written in silver pen.

'Oh my god! You guys, what have you done?'

'Congratulations, Alma!' they hugged her in turn, and Mr Saddler cleared his throat to make an announcement.

'Alma, before the mayhem of the day starts, we wanted to congratulate you on your forthcoming wedding. We wish you all the happiness in the world and at lunch time we will be closing the office for a couple of hours to go to The George to celebrate with you.' Everyone cheered. Alma felt overwhelmed.

'Thank you so much everyone, I just don't know what to say!'

When they got the pub, Ben made his way to the bar to order a round of drinks for everyone. Alma sat down at the table, and as she did so, a man approached. He looked like Luke, slightly taller, and just as good looking.

'Sorry to interrupt, just wanted to say hi. I'm Michael, Luke's brother.' He leaned in very close and pecked Alma on the cheek.

'Oh hi, lovely to meet you at last. I didn't know you were arriving today, Luke said tomorrow.'

'Yeah, well, he doesn't get many things right in his life, except you, by the looks of it.'

He looked Alma up and down, which made her uneasy. She laughed off his comment and introduced him to her friends. Alma noticed that he was wearing a lot of gold jewellery, and his clothes looked very expensive. Later that evening, when they returned to The George. Luke arrived with his other brother in tow. They spent the whole time playing snooker. Alma guessed that they had a lot to catch up on.

On the morning of the wedding, everyone gathered at Mami's. Alma had stayed there the night before. Nerves were starting to kick in now. She needed a glass of wine, but it was only ten in the morning.

'Hey, Alma! I brought us some champagne!' Laura came into the bedroom overloaded with bags. She was the maid of honour, and her dress was a slightly darker shade of pink than all the others.

'You are an angel, how did you know? I'm dying of nerves.'

'Well we ain't besties for nothing, are we? What do you think of the hair?' she put everything down and did a little twirl.

'Oh it looks gorgeous. Your head dress is next door.'

'Where's your dress?'

'Mami is doing something with it…' and at that moment, Mami walked through the door, holding a massive bundle of material. Alma had chosen a princess style dress, elegant, and not over the top. It was ivory coloured. The moment she saw it, she knew it was perfect.

'God I feel sick.'

'Here, give me that, you girls get ready. I'll ask David to open it,' Mami hung the dress up and took the champagne from Laura.

'Or do you want some water instead?' Laura laughed.

'No I bloody don't!'

The doorbell rang, it was the hair and make-up lady. Mami ushered her through to the bedroom.

Alma had chosen to have her hair up, with curly wispy bits coming down at the sides. She had toyed with the idea of having it down, but made a final decision only the day before. She didn't want to be heavily made-up either. The thought of sweaty foundation and melting eyeshadow was too much.

'Flippin ek! How the hell are you going to breathe in this thing?' Laura yanked tighter on the bodice. It came in, forming a little triangle at the waist. Mami was fussing at the bottom of the skirt, muttering to herself in Spanish.

'There, all done, look,' Laura stood back.

As Alma turned around to face the mirror, she didn't recognise herself. She felt like she was in a movie. The dress was beautiful. For a moment, she felt a bit worried about how much cleavage was on show, but quickly put it to the back of her mind. It was her special day, and she could wear whatever she wanted.

'You look gorgeous,' Laura gave her a kiss on the cheek.

'Bien linda hija,' Mami welled up as all three of them hugged and looked in the mirror.

'He's a very lucky man, he better appreciate you,' Laura smiled.

'The car is here,' David stood in the doorway. Wearing a grey suit and pink tie, his face was a picture of pride.

Mami then asked everyone to leave the room. She closed the door behind her and came over to Alma. *Here we go*, thought Alma, *another lecture*.

216

'I want you to be happy hija, I hope this is what you really want.'

'Yes, Mami, of course it is.'

'Marriage isn't a game, you will both have to work very hard at it, dios mio some days it will be hard, but if you both love each other then it will work out fine.' She kissed Alma on the cheek. 'Now, let's get going. You have a very special day ahead of you!'

Alma took one last look at herself and patted down her dress. Her stomach was aching, and her heart was racing, but it was excitement more than fear this time. It was time to become Mrs Giles.

A LETTER TO HER OLDER SELF

Dear Alma,

You'll probably open this letter in the future and wonder what the hell is going on. I am writing this on the above date. I thought it would be interesting to see where you are in ten years' time.

I am on cloud nine at the moment, married the man I love, just feel like life cannot get any better. I hope this lasts forever. We have talked about children already, so hopefully by the time you open this you will have maybe one or two little tinkers. This will obviously depend on how long it takes. It will be fun trying though, right?

I know whatever happens you will have done your best, I will be proud of you whatever. Did you keep in touch with Papi? I still have his photos in my bedside, although to date I haven't heard back from him after writing. Mami says he will write back soon…

Are you still living near Mami, David and Yoli? David is due to retire from the army in two years, did they move to be back near Nanna and Clive?

Things have felt a bit strange here, moving in with Luke into this big house. I do feel really grateful but it doesn't feel like home yet. Maybe in ten years' time you will have moved somewhere smaller, or maybe not, if you have kids.

Whatever happened to your nutty friend Laura? Did she ever settle down in the end? I know you felt a bit guilty leaving her in the flat, did she manage to get anyone to rent with her?

Healthwise, I remember you said that after getting married you were going to go on a diet, start running again and cut down on the booze, did you stick to that? I think the first two would have been easy but the third may have been a bit of a struggle hahaha! Especially if Laura had anything to do with it.

Writing this at nineteen years of age, it seems strange to think that you will open this letter and read its contents when you're older. I hope that you have achieved what you've wanted in this time, I wish you every happiness and that married life has treated you well.

Upwards and onwards with the next chapter of your life.

Wishing you all the happiness, don't forget who you are and in those hard times remember you are stronger than you think.

Much Love

Alma Giles

xxxxxxx

CHAPTER 14
Luna Ariana

'It's a girl, it's what you wanted.'

She was perfect, five lbs, three ounces, tiny, and so adorable. Luna Arianna Giles. It suited her perfectly. Black hair, chocolatey skin. Big, dark brown eyes, with beautiful wispy eye lashes.

Mami, David and Yoli had moved into the big house with Alma and Luke. There was more than enough room. The annexe at the back was perfect for Mami and David, and Yoli occupied one of the bedrooms on the first floor of the main house. David had retired from the army, and they had contemplated moving back to be nearer Nanna and Clive, but Luke had asked them to join them. He said it would be good for Alma and the baby, especially since he was away on business quite a lot. They were having money problems. In the midst of a recession, Luke had been forced to sell his shop, and none of his properties were making money, meaning he was forced to travel up north, leaving Alma pregnant and alone.

Things got worse once Luna was born. Luke was not a good father. He didn't seem to know how to bond with Luna. He would hold her and change her occasionally, but after a while, he just seemed to give up. He would grunt and go and sit on the lounge sofa, leaving Alma to deal with her.

'Luke, you've got to try harder,' she said.

'I am trying, you're just being paranoid.'

Alma felt like a single parent. This wasn't the way it was supposed to be. Looking down at Luna in her cot, the love she felt was indescribable. The same could not be said for Luke. She loved him, but he'd been distant ever since Luna was born. Yes, their sex life had dwindled since Luna came. Yes, money was tight. But Alma was tired of nagging him, and tired of feeling like she was raising Luna all by herself. It would be okay though, she thought, it was just a phase.

'I am just not gonna be able to make it back in time.'

'Why, Luke? It's her birthday, I've arranged it all now.'

'Listen, I have to get this project finished and it's gonna take working through the weekend to do it. We can do something separately, okay?'

'Okay, maybe we can do a picnic or the beach?'

'Sounds perfect, give baby girl a kiss from me and I will speak to you later.' Alma put the phone down and went back downstairs. Mami was in the lounge.

'Luke isn't gonna make it back.'

'Why not?' Mami sounded angry. 'It's his daughter's birthday, can't work wait?'

'No they're behind, they need to get it finished.'

'He needs to get his priorities right, Alma, he's never here for that child.'

'He hasn't got a choice.'

'Oh don't give me that, of course he does, he could sell this place…get something smaller. Me, David, and Yoli can get our own place…he seems to be making more work for himself.'

'Mami, he's worked hard to get this, the last thing he wants to do is lose it,' Alma said, frustrated. Mami didn't realise how hard Luke worked, just trying to keep everything together.

Luna's birthday was a huge success. They had all the kids out in the swimming pool, and followed that up with party games and food. By six o'clock Luna was a heap on her bed. She managed to say a few words to Luke down the phone, before curling up in Alma's lap and falling asleep.

Mami and David had left after doing most of the clearing up, and Yoli was getting ready to go out with her friends.

'Do you like my shoes?'

'Yeah they are lovely, can you walk in them?'

'Yeah look,' Yoli modelled her outfit for Alma. She looked so grown up, with skin-tight black trousers, a white scoop neck top, gold sandals, and a gold handbag.

'Where you off to?'

'It's Jake's sixteenth, so we gonna go to his and then into town.' She picked up her card and present as the doorbell rang.

'See you later,' Yoli hugged Alma.

'Yeah, be careful, okay? And stick together.' Alma checked herself. God, she sounded like Mami.

Luke returned home the next day. He was back for a week now. They took a trip to the beach, and built sandcastles, with Luna shrieking loudly as the water came in and touched her feet. Luke seemed to be making an extra special effort with Luna, and by the end of the week Alma was wondering whether it was her that was the problem, and not him. Was she pushing him too hard? Perhaps Mami had got into her head.

The following weekend, Laura and Ben persuaded Alma to join them for drinks in town. She didn't want to go, and tried hard to get out of it. No more excuses, Laura told her, just get dolled up and let's get out for some fun.

'You look lovely.'

'Do I?' Alma looked down at her outfit, which she had literally thrown together in ten minutes.

'You haven't been out in yonks, it will do you good. Anyway me and Luna are gonna play and have fun, aren't we?' Yoli cuddled Luna, squeezing her tightly and kissing her neck, making her laugh.

'Don't forget bedtime no later than seven-thirty, come here little girl give mummy a cuddle,' she breathed in the smell of Luna's freshly shampooed hair, and Luna nestled her head into Alma's chest.

The taxi beeped outside, and Alma could see Laura in the back applying her make-up. As they pulled away, Luna waved frantically, as Yoli held her up to the window.

'Where's Ben?'

'He's meeting us down there. Michael is over too, did you know?'

'Yeah, well only cause he's been helping Luke with a bit of work, how long is he back for?'

'Well he's talking about coming over permanently.'

Since the wedding Laura had been seeing Michael on and off. She called it a bit of fun. Alma knew differently. Laura was quite smitten with him, but Michael was selfish, and used Laura. She just couldn't see it, much to Alma's surprise. Laura had spent so long telling her about how bad Luke was, yet here she was with his brother being treated the exact same way.

'Are you still messing about with him?'

'Not messing about, just having a bit of a laugh. He is so funny, you gotta have a laugh sometimes, Alma...I think it's something you could do with to be honest. You're turning into a hermit these days.'

'Yeah well I have Luna to think about, it's not that I can just leave her whenever I fancy going out, you know.'

'Why not? Are you telling me your life ends just because you've got a little one? Come on, live a little. You're twenty-two, not sixty!'

They both laughed. Alma knew that Laura was right. She hadn't even had an alcoholic drink since Luna was born.

When they got there, Ben gave Alma a huge hug, 'Oh my god, hello stranger. I haven't seen you for years!'

'Shut up, you saw me at work last week.' Alma gave him a gentle slap.

'Come on, we're outside.'

The club was extremely busy. Alma could see familiar faces as they approached the table towards the back.

'Here you go,' Michael kissed Alma on the cheek, handing her a large glass of wine.

'Oh, thanks.'

At first, Alma felt a little awkward, but things got a little easier after a few drinks. She started to relax.

'So is Luke still up North?' Ben lit a cigarette.

'Yeh he's back next week.'

'How's it going up there?'

'Slowly I think, but seems to be going okay. We'll survive.'

'And how's little one?'

'She's gorgeous, cheeky as ever, but a good little girl.'

'Who is?' Michael chimed in.

'Luna.'

'Oh my niece.'

'Yes your niece, the one that you've probably seen three or four times in two years.' Alma looked at Michael with a disapproving look on her face.

'Alright, alright, don't forget I've not been coming over that often you know,' he fidgeted uncomfortably, sipping his drink.

The waitress brought more drinks to their table. An announcement was made that the food would shortly be ready.

'What food?' Michael's eyes lit up.

'It's their annual BBQ, remember? I got tickets, so you still owe me actually.' Ben put his hand out and Michael slapped down on it hard.

'Oh yeah sorry, will square up with you, mate, but need cash for drinks tonight.'

They queued up for food. Alma put a few things on her plate, but she wasn't feeling all that hungry.

'Is that all you're having? You need to eat more,' Ben looked at Alma's plate.

Alma looked down as she picked at the burger with disinterest. She placed her fork on the plate and drank more wine. God she'd missed having a drink, she hadn't really thought about it for two years now.

'Oh my god who has ordered this lot?' a tray of shots were brought over to the table.

'Just get 'em down you,' Michael started distributing the small glasses.

Music was thumping in the background. The noise levels seemed to double. Alma looked around her. Everything seemed hazy.

'You okay?'

'Yeah fine, just can't believe how quickly those drinks have gone to my head.'

'Well I'm not surprised if you haven't drank for two years,' Ben smiled at Alma. 'Wanna get another?'

'Yeah let's go.'

They made their way to one of the bars. 'Two double vodka and cokes please.'

Alma giggled. Bloody hell, double vodka. *Might as well*, she thought. After all, she had drank everything else that night. They had a few more rounds, and then Alma decided she wanted to dance. She teased Ben, pulling him to his feet.

'Come on, Ben, just once.' Alma grabbed onto his waist, and he moved his feet slowly, clearly a little embarrassed.

The music got louder. Alma was floating. She was beautiful. Everything was moving slowly. She could see Laura across the other end of the garden, with a group of girls. Where was Michael? Alma looked around, and saw him in the corner, talking to a blonde girl. They were standing very close to each other. She watched Michael lean over and whisper something in the girl's ear.

Rage boiled up inside of her. How dare he? How dare he treat her friend like that. She disengaged from Ben and marched over, grabbing Michael by the arm.

'What the fuck do you think you're playing at?'

'Alma…'

'Don't fucking Alma me, you can't just use Laura and then move on to the next one, she cares about you.'

'Hey, hey, wait a minute, me and Laura are cool. She knows it's a bit of fun. We have a good laugh, so don't worry your pretty little head about it.'

'You're fucking using her, and who are you?' Alma motioned to the blonde, who looked bemused.

'Come on, I think you've had enough.'

'Get your fucking hands off me. You're treating my friend like shit and now you're trying to get into this slag's knickers.'

'I don't know who the fuck you are but you better get outta my face,' the blonde girl snapped.

'Or what, what you gonna fucking do about it?'

There was a scuffle as Alma launched at the girl. Michael managed to separate them.

'Listen, Alma, let's go and talk, okay?' he pulled her away and they both walked inside, leaving the blonde nodding her head and smirking to herself.

Ben was with Laura, they were dancing on the spot and singing loudly.

'Where have you been?' Laura grabbed Alma's hands and made her dance.

'Alma wants a fight,' Michael said.

'What?'

'Yeah she wants a fight. I had to intervene. I wouldn't give her anymore alcohol.'

'Ben, please can I have a drink?'

Ben laughed and shook his head, 'No more for you.'

'I'm so bloody hot,' Alma unbuttoned her lacey top.

'What you doing?' Laura was pushing Alma's hands away.

'I said I'm hot, I need this off.'

'No, Alma, you've only got a bra on underneath.'

'So? I want it off.'

Alma wrestled Laura away and took her top off. She threw it to the floor, and stood there in her bra, much to the amusement of Michael and Ben. A couple of other men stared at her.

'I'm a 36DD, bet you didn't know that, did you?' she was yelling, but she didn't know why. Her hands went to her bra, and started fiddling with the strap.

'No, come on, Alma, let's go,' Ben and Laura tried to pull her hands away.

From above them, loud cheers could be heard. A group of men were watching, and joined in by taking their tops off and swinging them above their heads, before chucking them to the floor.

'Do it! Do it! Off off off!' came the chants.

Laura tried hard to stop her, but Alma wasn't having any of it. She was free, dancing hard to the music. The fresh air felt good against her naked skin. This was utter heaven, nothing mattered except from being here, right now, dancing naked in the club.

'Jesus, what the hell are you doing?' she was brought back to reality with a jolt.

'Come on, Alma, put this back on,' someone was helping her, but she had fallen to the ground, and now her legs didn't work. Arms dragged her up to her feet, and suddenly she was being shoved into the back of a car.

'Christ, Alma, when I said you had to have some fun, I didn't fucking mean like that. You are a bloody fruit loop, I seriously think you shouldn't drink anymore.'

'I luuv you, do yoooou know that Laura? I luuuuuv youuuuu, but where's my drink? I need my drink, Laura.'

'No, we are in a taxi, Alma, we are getting you home.'

'But I don't wanna go home, I wanna go dancing.'

'My brother wouldn't have been impressed with that display,' Michael peeked round from the front seat, smiling.

'Do you know what, Michael? I couldn't give a flying fuck! He's never here, he'd rather be working than spending time with his daughter, he doesn't really love me, but then he has…he has to work for his family, so he must love us, he must love us,' Alma burst into fits of giggles.

'Hey, Mr Taxi Driver, do you luuuvv your wife?'

The taxi driver caught her eye in the mirror and quickly glanced away.

'Well maybe he hasn't been working as hard as you think,' Michael said.

Laura punched the back of the front seat, 'Shut up, Michael.'

Alma looked at him. She tried to focus on Michael's face. 'What do you mean? What are you fucking saying?'

Laura interjected, 'Michael, don't say another fucking word.'

'Shut the fuck up, Laura, why can't he talk?'

They'd arrived. Michael handed the driver some cash.

'What's going on?' Alma said.

'Come on, we'll help you inside.'

Laura and Michael got the keys out of Alma's handbag, and helped her up to the front door. The house was pitch black. Somehow, she climbed the stairs, but then she stumbled, and there was nothing but darkness.

***

'Mummy, mummy.'

Alma felt little hands on her face, and then small lips kissing her cheek. 'Mummy, wake up!'

Alma tasted bile. Something was wrong. It all came rushing back, and she sat up with a jolt. She couldn't remember everything, but she remembered well enough to know that something was very wrong. Michael hadn't been joking.

Getting dressed and then sorting Luna out, Alma got everything into the car. It was nine-thirty, Sunday morning. Laura would still be asleep. It didn't matter, she needed to talk to her.

She knocked gently, but there was no answer. Her knocks became more and more frantic, until she could see a figure behind the frosted glass.

'What time do you call this?' Laura opened the door. She was wearing a silk dressing gown. Luna ran straight into the lounge, where Laura helped her turn on the TV.

'Coffee?'

'God, yes please.'

'I bet you feel rough.'

'Yeah just a bit.'

'What's going on?' Michael stepped out of the bedroom, wearing just his boxer shorts. He saw Alma, then quickly went and got changed, joining them in the kitchen. Alma looked at him.

'What did you mean last night, Michael?'

'Listen, Alma…'

'What did you mean?'

'We'd all had too much to drink, I can't even remember what I said.'

'Is Luke seeing someone else?'

Laura made herself busy washing up a cup in the sink. Alma glared at Michael.

'Is he seeing someone else?'

'Alma, he loves you and Luna, you know that.'

'You're not answering my question.'

Laura came over and put her mug on the table.

Michael sighed, 'Listen, he's been seeing this girl, he's known her a while, but it's nothing serious.'

Alma felt a sharp pain in her chest. It was if she'd been impaled.

'Alma, he loves you and Luna, it would kill him if he lost you.'

'How can he love me?' her tears stung her nose. 'We have a daughter, she's two… just two years old.'

Laura handed Alma a tissue.

'I just had this feeling, he's been distant…well you can say that again, distant up north fucking someone else. How long? How long?'

'You know sometimes with us men, we don't really cope too well with certain things, kids for example and other things.'

'What other things, what like not getting enough sex? Is that what you are trying to say, is it?'

'Listen, I don't wanna get involved in your relationship, what you guys do is your business.'

'Did you know about this?' Alma shot Laura an accusing look. Laura looked down sheepishly.

'How long?' Alma heard her voice tremble.

'What do you mean?'

'How long have you known?'

Laura looked at Michael and then down again at the floor. 'A few weeks.'

'And you didn't think about telling me?'

'How was I supposed to do that? How was I supposed to tell my best friend that her husband was seeing someone else? God, Alma, I wanted to tell you. It's not been easy, you know, I just couldn't do it.'

Michael leaned back in his chair, 'You need to talk to him, Alma. He'd be lost without you and Luna.'

'Don't make me fucking laugh, he doesn't know what it's like to love someone. He's only interested in one thing, just like the rest of you! So what's she like this other girl, have you met her? I bet you have all been out together laughing at me.'

'No, Alma, it's not like that.'

'Laura, I need a glass of wine.'

'I don't think that's a good idea…'

'I don't give a shit what you think, please can you get me a large glass of wine, or I will get it myself.'

'Okay, okay.'

Alma sat at the table and drank. Tears splashed down the rim of the glass. Her marriage was in tatters, her husband didn't love her. How long had it been going on? Probably months, maybe a year, maybe even since Luna had been born. It really didn't matter now. She would sit here and drink herself into oblivion, and it wouldn't make a shred of difference.

Laura drove Alma and Luna back. Alma had consumed the whole bottle of wine, and she was already feeling drunk. It wasn't enough though. She wanted to go out that night. She didn't want to think about anything at all, just drink and music and dancing.

Mami and David agreed to look after Luna. When Alma came down the stairs, Mami looked at her and said, 'That dress is too short, Almita!'

'Oh well, it's a good job I have nice legs then,' Alma smiled as she tried to walk on her high heels. She kissed Luna goodnight and thanked Mami and David for having her.

As soon as they had reached the first pub, Laura fixed Alma's make up. Apparently it was caked on and she looked like a slapper.

'Thanks for coming out with me.'

'You don't need to thank me, Alma, you know I'll always be there for you…please don't drink too much tonight.'

'Don't worry, I'm as hard as nails. I'll sort it, it will be fine, you wait and see. All I wanna do tonight is let my hair down before I speak to Luke. Now, missy, let's get some drinks and hit that dance floor.'

Drink and dance…she certainly did that. It was another disaster. The last thing she remembered was the bouncers carrying her out of the club, with Laura and Ben in tow.

***

'Alma, here, drink this coffee. Come on, sit up.'

Alma opened her eyes briefly and then closed them again. Where was she? What time was it? Where was Luna? She opened her eyes again. God, she had the hangover from hell.

'Are you okay?'

Alma looked up. Ben was staring at her, very concerned. He was shirtless, wearing just jeans, and Alma noticed that he was finely toned. She looked around the room. She was in a strange bed and didn't recognise her surroundings.

'Where am I?'

'You're at my place.'

'Why? What am I doing here?'

'You begged me to bring you back here last night, you said you weren't going home.'

'Oh my god, Luna!'

'It's okay, Alma. Laura has spoken to your mum, she told her you had a bit too much to drink and that you were staying at hers…'

She slowly sat up. 'Ben, did we...?' Alma paused, unable to remember anything. Ben came over and sat on the edge of the bed. He looked worried.

'I feel really shitty about this, Alma. You're a bloody nightmare when you've had a drink, all three of us tried to get you home, but you were adamant you wanted to come home with me.'

She covered her face. What the hell had she done? She couldn't remember any of it.

'I should have got you a taxi home, you were making such a scene, but there was no way your mum and dad could have seen you in that state. You peed in the street, taking off your clothes, chatting up every bloke you could see.'

Oh my god, she couldn't hold back the tears. Sobbing into the bedsheets, Alma's body trembled.

'Come on don't cry, things will be okay. You have Luna and your family and friends around you.'

'Did we sleep together?'

'Yes, if you can call it that, I was very drunk too…so I don't think it was a great performance on my part,' he laughed.

Alma nodded her head slowly. She didn't feel bad, or even guilty for that matter, but she certainly didn't find Ben attractive.

'I'm sorry, Alma, I should have been stronger. You weren't taking no for an answer and I, well, I should have known better.'

'It's not your fault, Ben, don't worry I won't say anything. It's between us.'

'God, Alma, he'd kill me. He's supposed to be my mate but when Michael told me what Luke did I was really angry.'

'He won't find out…anyway our marriage is over, so it doesn't matter, thank you for looking after me.'

'Well that's not what I'd call it, but I am glad you stayed with me and not with anyone else,' he leant over and kissed her on the cheek.

Alma felt uncomfortable. Drinking her coffee, she thought about the conversation she would have with Luke. It would be hard. She didn't want to drop anyone in it.

Michael and Laura were parked around the back of the house when Alma turned up. Mami had been pacing, and Alma had hardly set foot in the door when she was firing questions at her. What the hell was she thinking drinking like that? She was a mother. She had responsibilities. It was unacceptable.

'Where's Luna?'

'She's asleep in her room,' Mami looked frustrated.

Alma walked upstairs. Luna was in a deep sleep. Alma bent down and kissed her, then went into the main bedroom and picked up the phone.

'Luke, can you come home? We need to talk.'

'I'm coming back tomorrow, what's up?'

'Just come home today, Luke, it can't wait.'

The phone line went dead, but it was Alma who hung up. She looked at herself in the mirror. It was time to be strong, for Luna's sake as much as her own.

CHAPTER 15
Hole In The Soul

'I want a divorce.'

'Don't be ridiculous.'

'I'm serious, Luke, I want a divorce.'

'Is this still about Sharon? Because that was over a year ago, Alma.'

'No, this isn't about Sharon. It's about us. It's about the way you neglect your daughter. Our marriage isn't working and you've refused to do marriage guidance counselling, despite me asking you so many times.'

Luke gave her a strange look, 'I think you're becoming paranoid, Alma. It's all in your mind, everyone has their ups and downs in their marriage. Perhaps you should try and cut down on your booze intake…you aren't meant to be drinking with those tablets.'

'I don't think you realise how hard I've tried to save this marriage,' Alma said furiously. 'You've made no effort, only now and then when I make such a fuss about everything, and only for a while after I found out about her.'

'You know about my upbringing, Alma, you know what I went through…it's not my fault if I can't be lovey dovey all the time. And I'm sorry I can't give you sympathy all the time either, it's just not me.'

'Okay, so speak to someone then. They might be able to help.'

He walked away shaking his head. Alma looked at him with disgust. She didn't even want him near her anymore.

Luke poured himself a whiskey. 'I love you, Alma. I love you and Luna more than you will ever know, I don't want to discuss our marriage with a stranger. I don't think you love me anymore though… I can sense it.'

Alma paused. She watched him drink his whiskey.

'I've met someone else.'

'I know.'

'How?' she asked, taken aback. How could he possibly know?

'You haven't been the same since you found out about Sharon, and that's something I don't blame you for…but what you have to ask yourself is why I did it. Have you ever thought about that? I mean really thought about it, properly. You pushed me away, you weren't interested in me. In fact ever since Luna was born it's been all about her.'

'Oh my god, are you fucking kidding me? You're saying you were jealous of our baby and that's why you had to sleep with someone else?'

'No that's not what I am saying. I needed you Alma, the intimacy and love disappeared overnight…you changed.'

Alma thought about it. Had she neglected him? It was true, she hadn't wanted him much since Luna arrived…but he hadn't been interested in the baby. He was a selfish bastard, and that had put her off. It wasn't her fault. She hated him just for making her question it.

'I'm not arguing about this, I don't love you anymore, Luke.' As soon as she said the words she felt a rush of air inside her stomach. It was like a weight had been lifted. Luke winced. He looked more hurt than she'd ever seen him.

Good, she thought, *now he knows how it feels.* Her stomach rolled again, but this time with fear. How on earth was she going to tell him about Ben?

Since that night, things had progressed quickly. One night became two, two became three, and soon they were spending almost all of the time when Luke wasn't home together. She loved him, and it felt right, where it had always felt wrong with Luke. Ben treated her properly. He wanted to tell Luke himself, but Alma had argued that it wasn't a good idea. She remembered Laura's reaction.

'Christ, you are bloody nuts. You're playing with fire. You know nothing about him and he's your husband's mate, you are crazier than I thought!'

Alma rolled her eyes.

'Listen, Alma, I've known Ben for years, and we are good mates, but he's got a bad reputation with previous relationships.'

'He's my best friend, Laura. He's my soul mate, he listens to me and he wants to be with me and Luna, which is more than my husband wants.'

'…So who is he?' Luke's voice snapped her out of her thoughts.

'I don't think it's any of your business.'

'Well I think I've got a right to know. If you're seeing someone else that means he'll be involved with Luna and as I'm her father I need to know she's in safe hands.'

'Oh so now you want to play the doting father figure. It's nothing to do with you, I'll decide if Luna is safe. I've done that since she was born, and you've never given two shits before.'

'You make it sound like I don't care about Luna. I do, she's my only child, and I couldn't bear it if she came to any harm.' He walked towards the window. 'You know, I never envisaged our relationship would end up like this. I thought we would be together forever, surrounded by our children and grandchildren.'

Alma looked at him, she felt nothing.

Luke walked towards her and held her shoulders, he was crying now. 'Please, Alma, I don't want to lose you and Luna. Please, we can work this out, I don't want a divorce.'

'I don't want to be in a loveless marriage. I'm sorry, Luke.'

She brushed his hands off her shoulders and went up the stairs. Walking into the bedroom, she started packing clothes for her and Luna. Mami and David had a two-bedroom house about twenty minutes away. *At least we have somewhere to go*, Alma thought.

'How did you find out about Sharon?' Luke was stood in the spare room doorway.

'What does it matter?'

'Well because as far as I'm aware there were only two people that knew, Ben and Michael.'

Alma thought about it. She didn't have an answer.

'Ben knew from the outset and I guess he told Michael, and then he told Laura,' he was watching her intently.

Alma finished packing and went to walk past Luke, but he stood in her way.

'I don't want Ben anywhere near Luna, do you understand?'

God, he knew. He'd known all this time. But how?

'I mean it, Alma. I've known him since school days, he isn't a very nice person, especially where women are concerned. Just stay away from him, that's the best advice I can give you.'

Alma rolled her eyes. 'Okay, Luke.'

'I mean it…if I ever see him, I will crucify him, I promise you. I don't want to do the wrong thing but my daughter's involved, she doesn't have the choice you have.'

Alma ignored him and went out the door. Walking down the stairs, she could feel his eyes on her the whole way. She didn't turn back.

In the car with Luna, Alma suddenly felt anxious. What had Ben done? Laura had mentioned his previous relationships too, but she hadn't given it any attention. Furious with herself, she banged her hands on the dashboard. It was Luke, again, getting in her head. He was just jealous, like always. She couldn't let him win. Ben was a nice guy, she knew that. She resolved to ask him about it later.

Later that evening, sitting in Ben's lounge, she told him about what Luke had said. He took a swig from his can and paced around the room.

'The lying bastard! How the hell does he know about my relationships, he wasn't there. Christ, he's a jealous wanker. What I wanna know is how he found out it was me you were seeing?'

'I don't know maybe Michael told him…and he also said you're not the person I think you are.'

Ben burst out laughing, 'What the hell has he told you?'

'He doesn't want you near Luna.'

'Ha, well we all know why that is…he doesn't want another man doing something he's been shit at. He's an egotistical bastard.'

'No there was something else, Ben. Him and Laura knew something, they wouldn't say what. Have you been in some sort of trouble?'

Ben looked at her and smiled, he drank the remaining beer and cracked open another can.

'Okay, Alma, I was gonna tell you, but I wanted it to be at the right time…when I was younger I got in with the wrong crowd and got into some trouble,' he sat down next to her and held her hand.

'What? What did you do?' she waited with bated breath.

'I spent some time in prison.'

'Prison?! What the hell for?'

Ben stood up, obviously feeling uncomfortable. 'Armed robbery.'

Alma recoiled in horror. She couldn't believe what she was hearing.

'Oh my god! Armed robbery, are you fucking serious, how? Why? Why would you do something like that?'

'It sounds worse than it was. I got in with the wrong crowd, got talked into doing it and we got caught. I spent three years inside, got out early for good behaviour and haven't been in trouble since, okay?'

'Does Mr Saddler know?'

'No, he'd never have hired me.'

'How long ago?'

'Six years...'

'What were you armed with?'

'Look, it's in the past. I've been to therapy and dealt with some anger issues, I've got back on the straight and narrow, been good with my job and I just wanna get on with my life now, you know?'

Alma was in shock, she needed a glass of wine. It had been the last thing she ever expected to hear come out of Ben's mouth... but somehow, she admired him, in a funny sort of way. It must have taken a lot of courage to talk to a professional about his problems, something that Luke would never do, and he'd turned his life around. He was smart, kind, good at his job and had a lovely place of his own. He was a changed man.

'Does this change your mind about us?' he looked concerned.

'No, I guess I'm just shocked.'

'Well I suppose it's good that you found out now rather than later.'

'You would have told me, right?'

'Of course, I said to you I would have told you,' he stood up, smiling, and walked into the kitchen.

Alma followed him. She pushed her head against his chest and wrapped her arms around his waist. Kissing her head, he tilted her chin up so he could kiss her lips, their tongues explored hungrily. They made love there and then, frantically, passionately. She needed him, and any thoughts of his past soon disappeared.

That weekend, Alma met Ben's mother, Eileen, for the first time. It didn't go like she'd expected. Eileen didn't warm to her, and the feeling was mutual. There were no hugs or kisses, just a very limp handshake greeting. Eileen obviously took care of her appearance. She had a good physique, and long polished fingernails. Her hair was bleach blonde. When they first met, she looked Alma up and down disparagingly.

'No little one then?'

'No, I'll bring her next time.'

She gave Alma a false smile and walked into the kitchen. 'Coffee...or tea?'

'Erm, yes coffee please, white no sugar,' Alma looked around the room. Eileen was obviously very house-proud, and the interior decorating was lovely.

Ben waltzed through the door. He smiled broadly and kissed his mum's cheek, 'Alright, Ma?'

Eileen wiped her cheek, as if he'd contaminated her.

'So have you two been getting to know each other?' Ben smiled.

'Just wondered why the little one wasn't here, that's all.'

'Oh...Luna, well don't worry, Ma, there's plenty of time for you to get to know her. Thought it would be good for you to meet Alma on her own first, so you could have a proper chat.'

The rest of the visit was just as uncomfortable and awkward. When it was time to leave, Alma felt a wave of relief. Sitting in the car on the way home, she said, 'God, Ben, I really don't think your mum likes me.'

'Don't be silly, she's always a bit distant when she first meets someone, she'll be fine when she gets to know you.'

'No, I felt it, she didn't approve.'

'Well it's not her you're in a relationship with...' he held her hand and winked. 'You worry too much. My mum's been through a lot with that arsehole, just glad she's finally decided to tell him where to go.'

Ben's dad was a drug addict. They rarely spoke, and he'd treated Eileen extremely badly. Alma's thoughts turned back to Papi, in Honduras, then to Luke. She felt sad that he would only be a part-time father, but she'd tried her best, and she didn't feel guilty. He deserved everything he got. God, she needed a drink.

'Can we stop off for some wine?' she smiled sweetly at Ben.

'Have you been a good girl?'

She giggled like a school kid, 'The best.'

The man behind the counter in the off-license smiled knowingly at Alma. It was her third visit this week. She felt embarrassed as he handed her over the normal three bottles of wine.

Mami and David had Luna that night. Back at Ben's, Alma cracked open the first bottle. Half an hour later, she moved onto the second.

'You've nearly done a whole bottle, young lady. I think you need to slow down!'

Alma prized the second bottle open and saw Ben shaking his head in amusement. 'You've not touched your food.'

'Nah, I'll have something later' she pushed her plate away and curled up on the sofa. Her head was fuzzy, but she loved the feeling.

'Are you okay?'

'Yep, never been better.'

'You know I'm a really lucky guy.'

'Why?'

'Well I never thought I'd end up with the girl of my dreams and a beautiful step daughter.'

Alma looked at him. His face was glowing with pride.

'Who would have thought we'd end up working and being together? I'll always remember the day you came in for your interview, I knew old Saddler would give you the job.'

'Really, why?'

'Well cause he's a dirty old git, that's why.'

Alma laughed, 'Oi! He's been really good to me and not in the way you're implying.'

Ben shook his head, 'I mean...it wouldn't be the first time.'

'What d'ya mean?'

'Oh well I'm not one to spread rumours but he's definitely had his end away a few times.'

'God shut up, he must be in his sixties.'

'What you saying? That we won't be having sex in our sixties?' he tickled her side, almost making her spill her wine.

'Well I've not really thought that far ahead to be honest,' Alma formed a picture in her mind of her and Ben all wrinkly and him struggling to undress her. She started laughing.

'I've brought you something, wait here,' he went out of the room and came back with a large flat box. 'Here you go, a pressie. Go on, open it.'

Alma looked inside cautiously. Whatever it was, it was covered with red tissue paper. She slowly unwrapped it and then held it up to the light. It was a red and black negligee, and very see through.

'Oh my god, I love it!'

'Go and try it on,' he seemed excited.

It fitted perfectly. Alma stared at herself in the mirror. She gulped her wine down and then started posing and laughing at herself.

'Put some music on!'

'What do you want on?'

'Something I can move to!'

248

Hearing the beat from the other room, she started to move, her hips swaying sexily. Ben came into the room and moved behind her, running his hands up and down her thighs, pulling up the material.

'Good fit,' he bent down and kissed the back of her legs, working his way up, hitching the negligee above her buttocks. Alma took a deep breath, her heart racing with excitement. She wanted him so badly. She felt drunk, happy and so in love. The music sounded distant, but somehow it was getting louder.

'I love you,' he whispered. They both fell forward onto the bed.

An hour later, as Ben lay on his back exhausted, Alma got up and took a shower. Wrapping herself up in his dressing gown, she looked around the bathroom. Ben was OCD, she was sure of it. All his aftershaves were organised by bottle size, down to the tiniest millimetre, and his various lotions and potions were meticulously positioned. Every single towel had been placed in size and colour order, with not a stripe out of line. *Well,* she thought, *at least I won't have to tidy up after him.*

After her shower, she climbed back into bed. Ben leaned over.

'Thank you,' he whispered.

'What for?' she looked at him curiously.

'For being with me.'

'Don't be silly,' she kissed him on the nose. Sitting up, she reached out for the third bottle of wine. Ben put his arm out and took it from her grasp.

'No, I think you've had enough, Alma. You're not opening that.'

'Why not?'

'Because that's bloody ridiculous, you've had enough.'

'I'll decide when I've had enough,' she reached out again and tried to snatch the bottle from Ben.

Ben grabbed hold of her wrist tightly. He looked angry. 'I've said you've had enough. Here, have some water.'

'Fuck the water,' she knocked the glass out of his hand, hearing the glass shatter.

'That was a bloody expensive glass,' he pushed her away and rolled out of bed, searching desperately for something to clear up the mess.

Alma got out of bed too. She pushed past him and went out of the door.

'What are you doing?' he grabbed onto her arm.

'Going,' she said.

'You're not wearing anything on your feet, Alma.'

'So? I am going to get some vodka,' she tried to free herself, but she was so drunk she lost her balance.

'Here,' he handed her a small glass. 'Now go and sit down, Alma.'

'VODKA!' she smiled. 'I love you, Benny!'

She downed the contents and lay back, closing her eyes. In that moment, she felt like she could stay that way forever.

After a while, Alma opened her eyes. Ben was somewhere above her, but she couldn't place him. He was taking her dressing gown off. She tried to yank it back, but he was having none of it. The room spun. Ben's mouth was moving, he was saying something but whatever it was didn't register. Alma was a beautiful butterfly. She was flying high, moving her colourful wings seductively, flapping to the beat of some long-forgotten tune. She was too quick, too clever, but something was on her now, and it was weighing her down, and Ben's hands were heavy on her shoulders. He pulled her hair back, and suddenly it hurt. It all hurt.

'Because you've been a bad girl, you need to be punished,' he clicked the handcuffs into place, dragging her and hooking her up to the bedframe.

'Open your mouth,' he said.

She didn't.

Ben started yelling, 'Open your mouth!'

Alma stared at him. He slapped her face, and again he was shouting something, but now it sounded very far off. His hands were prizing her mouth open and then there was something cold inside. She felt it on her tongue, on her gums, and her legs kicked out. Ben fell back on the bed, with the vibrator in his hand.

'Get away, get it away from me,' Alma gasped.

Ben fell on top of her, kissing her on the mouth. She couldn't breath.

'Get off...get me out of these things. What are you doing?'

Then, suddenly, Ben seemed to disappear. But his voice was close now.

'Here, Alma, here. Have some vodka.'

Handing the glass to her, he undid the cuffs. 'Please don't break this one, okay?'

The following day Alma slept a lot. It was one of the worst hangovers she'd ever had, and she could hardly recall anything from the night before. She ventured outside, only to take Luna to the park, but everything felt foggy. She needed more sleep, or wine. Wine would be better.

Passing by the off license on the way home, Alma tried to resist the urge to go in. It was too much. The shopkeeper smiled at her, in that sympathetic manner. He knew, but of course he was too polite to say anything. On the shelf behind him, Alma could see a rack of miniature bottles. They would fit perfectly in her handbag, and besides, she didn't need a lot, just a little to steady her nerves once in a while. Nobody would ever know. As she handed him the change, she felt a tug on her sleeve. Luna was looking up at her. Alma shoved the bottles into her bag hastily.

Later that night, she hardly recalled putting Luna to bed.

***

'What's with the bruises?' Yoli asked.

They were sitting in Yoli's front room. She'd recently moved in with her boyfriend, just down the road from Mami and David.

Alma looked down at her arm and shrugged, 'Dunno, must have bumped into something.'

'Are you okay?' Yoli looked concerned.

'Of course, why wouldn't I be?'

'Are you and Ben okay?'

'Yes, he's brilliant, never been so happy.'

Yoli looked at her, but Alma couldn't meet her eye. She stood up and shouted for Luna. Luna ran into the room. Alma bent down and gave her a big hug, 'I'll see you Sunday, darling, and I'll give you both a call tomorrow.'

Yoli hugged Alma, 'Are you sure you're okay?'

'Yeh, everything's fine, I promise.'

Getting into her car, she felt guilty. It was hard, lying to Yoli, but the truth would be worse. She just needed to be on her own for a while, just for a couple of hours at least, before she saw Ben again.

Looking around to check the coast was clear, she delved into her handbag. They'd run out of miniature bottles, so she'd brought vodka this time. Luckily, it was just the right size for her bag. Alma swigged from the bottle. There it was, that feeling of instant calmness. It worked every time, like magic. She glugged more of it down. Having almost finished the bottle, she screwed the lid back on and placed it back in her handbag. She'd need it later.

CHAPTER 16
Neat Freak

'What the hell are you wearing?' Ben looked her up and down.

They were going on their first holiday together, to Mexico. The plane was due to leave in two hours' time, but Alma was running late.

'You are useless, do you know that? You can't even dress yourself!' he threw an outfit on the bed and walked over to her. 'Have you had a shower?'

'Yes.'

'When? Last week? God, what's going on with you lately?' He came back holding a towel and pushed it hard into her stomach. 'Just hurry up, please, we're already running late.'

'Where's Luna?'

'Don't fucking worry about her, she's ready, no thanks to you. Hurry up!'

He took one last disgusted look at Alma and ran downstairs. She could hear him talking gently to Luna, reassuring her.

Looking in the mirror, she could see more bruises on her arm. They were yellow and purple now, as ugly as sin, and she was running out of long sleeve tops.

'Now that's better,' Ben came up behind Alma and grabbed her round the waist.

'Here, let me dry it,' he took the hair dryer and got to work on her hair. While he did so, Alma applied her make up. Ben went into the wardrobe and came back with jewellery and a handbag.

'I think your tan open toed sandals will go lovely with that outfit.'

Alma nodded.

'Right, got everything?' Ben smiled sweetly.

'Yes,' she picked up her handbag and started filling it up with various items.

'No, give me those, I'll carry them,' he took the passports and tickets from her.

Alma walked quietly behind him. Luna was at the bottom of the stairs. She was in a floral summer dress and sun hat, clutching her teddy bear. Her little pink case was by the front door. She gave Alma an excited smile

'Mummy, are we going on an aeroplane?'

'Yes, darling, we are.'

'Yay! Teddy is coming,' she showed Alma the teddy.

'Course he is,' Alma smiled back at her, wishing she could act so enthusiastic. All she felt was emptiness.

On the plane, Alma made the excuse that she wanted some sleep, she really didn't want to talk to Ben. As she closed her eyes, she thought about the last couple of years. The divorce had not been pleasant. Luke had eventually agreed a lump sum and monthly maintenance, but not without a fight. Shortly after that, she'd moved in with Ben. In truth, she'd known it was a mistake before she did it, but she didn't want to believe it. It started with small things, like moaning about the washing up, and how dirty Alma made the kitchen. Then it escalated. Luna wouldn't be allowed to take her toys out. Everything had to be put in the right place, exactly back where it was before, and if it wasn't...

Luna had become a nervous child. Alma could sense it. She was four years old now, but she looked more like a little boy. She preferred to play with cars and toy soldiers. Her and Ben would play soldiers most weekends. He brought her toy guns and they would chase each other round the house. Alma loved seeing her happy, and Ben was very good with her, most of the time.

They'd discussed work a few times. At first, Ben had suggested that Alma work less, so she could drop and collect Luna from school. Then he said that the finances wouldn't work out, so her hopes were dashed. He did that a lot, Alma found. He would say one thing, then change this mind, then get cross if she questioned him about it. After some more discussion, Ben had eventually taken over all their finances. He gave Alma an allowance each week. She didn't mind this as much as she'd thought, as she didn't really buy anything except alcohol. She had her own private stash that Ben didn't know about. Everything else was taken care of. Food, clothes, holidays, Ben was in charge of it all. *Just as long as he doesn't find out about the drinking,* Alma thought.

The first day was nice. Ben and Luna played in the pool, while Alma sat on the sun lounger and read a book. They had dinner in a Mexican restaurant. The sun was setting over the sea and faint music was playing somewhere in the background. Luna danced with one of the waiters. Closing her eyes, Alma couldn't remember the last time she'd been so happy.

Things got worse from there. Ben seemed unhappy with almost everything. From the food to the hotel service, he constantly had something to say, and argued with the hotel staff. Alma felt anxious and sick every evening, in case she didn't wear the right thing. She found it much easier to just let Ben dress her. He seemed to take such pride in creating a finished look. Luna was not so easy. She refused to let Ben dress her at first, preferring to wear shorts, t-shirts and trainers, but he soon put a stop to that. It hurt Alma inside, watching him shout at Luna. She just wanted peace, but she didn't have the strength to argue with him.

Sitting on her sun lounger, while Ben and Luna played in the pool, Alma thought back to the time when Luna had accidentally broken his watch. She felt sick just remembering it. She'd spent every penny she had on replacing it, only for him to look at her with disgust when he opened the box.

'You've gotta be kidding me…' he said, 'is this the best you could fucking do?'

Alma stared at him. Luna looked terrified.

'Christ, you are so fucking useless it's unbelievable. Do you honestly think I'd wear this piece of shit?'

He threw the box hard across the room, leaving a dent in the wall. Luna started to cry.

'Just take it back, take it back and get your fucking money back. It's not worth what you've spent, what the fuck were you thinking?'

'I was just...'

'Do you know what, Alma? I thought you had imagination. Do I have to do all your thinking for you? You can't even buy a decent present, you just went and brought the first pile of crap you saw.' He stormed out of the room. That hadn't been the first incident, and it wasn't the last either. She could tell Luna was scared of Ben. His moods were impossible to predict.

'Excuse me, is this bed taken?'

Alma looked up from her book. The man standing over her was handsome, dark skinned, with a kind smile.

'No, no, help yourself,' she said, surprised.

The man smiled at her and placed his towel and bag on the sun lounger next to her.

Alma looked back at her book. She could sense the man watching her.

'Don't tell me you're on your own?' he said, glancing at the two beds beside her, complete with teddy and towels.

'No, they're in the pool, I'd rather be in the sun,' she laughed nervously.

'Thought as much,' he looked towards the pool and rolled his eyes, took off his shoes and settled down on the lounger to read his paper.

Alma quickly forgot about the incident, until dinner that was. They had put Luna to bed early, and gone to eat in one of the hotel restaurants. Ben hadn't said much since they got back to the room. He'd been drinking, too.

'So…' he said, looking up from his menu, 'do you fancy him?'

Alma looked confused, 'Who?'

Ben pointed his fork behind Alma. She turned to see a group of men sat at a table across the room. The man from the sun lounger was with them.

'I don't get it?'

'Well you seem to like that type.'

'What are you on about?'

'Come on, Alma. You've got a mix-raced kid, so you must be well into them.'

Alma flinched. 'Just stop it, okay?'

'What? It's not like I'm wrong is it? I bet you even shagged Michael.'

Alma scraped her chair back and stood up.

'Sit the fuck down.'

Alma hesitated.

'Don't make a fucking scene, Alma, I'm warning you.'

Alma sat back down and poured herself a glass of wine. Her face felt flushed, she didn't know what she felt most, fear or anger. They sat in silence for a while, until Ben decided it was time to leave. As they got up, he held onto her arm. Alma froze.

'Look, I'm sorry, okay? I was out of order…it just got me, the way you were flirting with him by the pool.'

'I wasn't flirting, Ben. He asked me if the sunbed was free and I said yes, that was it.'

'Well it looked like flirting to me.'

Alma didn't argue. She was tired and just wanted to go back to the room and get some sleep. Ben had other ideas.

'Hey, come here,' he put his hand on her bum and prized her over to him, kissing her neck. 'Let's go,' he whispered.

Staggering back to the room, they found Luna fast asleep. The babysitter was watching TV. Ben paid her, and Alma went to the bathroom. By the time she came back, Ben was laid on the bed, out cold.

Alma poured herself a drink. She closed her eyes. And then, suddenly, Luna was next to her. Teddy was clutched in her arms.

'Mummy, I'm scared.' Alma could hear her little heart beating fast. 'Please can I sleep with you tonight?'

'Yes of course my darling, let's get some blankets, okay?'

Alma laid on the bed, with Luna's head in her lap. Ben snored loudly. They needed him. Luna needed a father figure, and even with all his faults Ben was still better than Luke. She was determined to make this work.

As if by magic, the remainder of the holiday wasn't so bad. Ben seemed a bit more laid back, and towards the end of the break they had become intimate again. Alma almost felt guilty about questioning him.

The weekend they got back, Luke was supposed to have Luna.

'I've said I'm sorry, Alma, I just can't let these people down. They need to move in as soon as possible.'

'But it's okay to let your daughter down?'

'Don't be like that, you know it's not like that.'

'She's been so excited about seeing you and I have to tell her you're not coming for her…again!'

'Let me speak to her, okay? I'll explain, I'll spend all next weekend with her, I will come and get her early.'

Alma felt that same old disappointed feeling in the depth of her stomach. She sighed deeply and called Luna down from her room. It was painful for Alma to listen to Luna speaking with Luke, and then hearing her ask why so many times. She couldn't stand it, and went out in the garden. After a while, Luna came out too.

'He's not coming, Mummy, he's working.'

'Well in that case what do you say about us going to the park and getting an ice-cream?'

'Yay!!!!!! Yes pleaaaaassseeee!'

...

'So what's his fucking excuse this time then? Christ, I swear he does this on purpose, he does it so we can't have any time together!' Ben growled.

'No, Ben, he doesn't. He's working.'

'Working? Working? That guy doesn't need to fucking work, that's what he wants you to think, just like the measly amount he pays you for child maintenance. He's got money stashed away just doesn't want you to know about it.'

'That's ridiculous, he nearly lost his house for god's sake.'

'You know what? After your ex-husband, your daughter, your mum, dad and sister, I may just fit in somewhere in your life. I know something though, I am nowhere near the top of your list, I am way way fucking down there. Stop making fucking excuses for his arse, he's taking you for a fucking ride and I'm not gonna sit back and let it keep happening.'

With that, Ben grabbed his car keys. He stomped out of the house, slamming the front door behind him.

Alma sat down. She held her hands together to stop them from shaking. Luna came running down the stairs.

'Mummy, why was Ben shouting again?'

'Oh darling, he was just a bit cross, but not with you or me, okay? He's just popped out for a while, come on let's get to the park.'

The park was busy. Luna knew two of the children playing there, and Alma and one of the mums watched them from the park bench. Alma lost all track of time, and it wasn't until the other mum told Alma that it was gone six that she realised they'd been out for over two hours.

As they reached the bottom of the drive, the front door opened. Ben was in the doorway, his face a picture of rage.

'Where the hell have you been? I've been worried sick.'

'We've been to the park.'

'Why didn't you leave me a note?'

'Sorry, I didn't think.'

'No you didn't think, that's your fucking problem you never think...only when it comes to yourself.'

Alma and Luna made their way inside. Luna bent her head forward and went to go up to her room.

'Oh and you need to tidy that room, it's like a pigsty,' Ben shouted at Luna's back.

Alma walked into the kitchen. She felt like she was suffocating. She poured a glass of wine and leaned against the kitchen counter.

'Oh yeah here you go, reach out for the bottle, that's your fucking answer to everything.'

Alma walked past him and went into the garden. Ben followed.

'Do you even love me?'

'Yes.'

'You've got a funny way of showing it, my mum doesn't even know what I'm doing with you.'

'Please, Ben.'

'Please Ben what? I'm sick of the way I'm always at the bottom of your shit heap, things are gonna fucking change around here.' Ben walked inside. She heard him open a can of beer.

Alma sat down on the garden bench. She watched the birds playing on the wooden table, pecking cautiously at the bird feeder. Across the road, a car screeched. Her glass was empty. Walking back into the kitchen, she saw Ben lying on the sofa. There was a black box on the floor beside him, and in his hand was a gun.

'What the hell's going on?'

'What does it look like?'

She stared, 'Where did you get that from?'

'Relax it doesn't work, it's been deactivated. I've got a few, they're my collection.'

Alma walked up and stood in front of him. 'Have you lost your fucking mind?'

Ben glared. 'I told you that it's deactivated, okay? Just relax… do you deliberately mean to wind me up, cause you're getting on my fucking tits. Just go and get drunk, that's all you're good at these days.'

Alma poured another glass of wine. She took it upstairs. Her legs felt like jelly. A gun. It didn't make any sense. She was living with someone she didn't even know. From Luna's bedroom, Alma heard the sound of tiny wheels whizzing across the carpet.

'Mummy, do you wanna play cars with me?' she turned to face Alma, her face full of hope. Tonight her hair was particularly frizzy, but Alma thought it looked beautiful. She couldn't get the image of Ben out of her head. A gun. A gun. Why did he even need to have it? And why was he collecting them?

Alma and Luna played for ages, until they heard Ben coming up the stairs. Immediately, Alma's heart started racing. Her mouth felt dry. Was he coming to finish them off?

Ben poked his head around the door. 'So, what would my beautiful girls like to eat tonight then? Do you fancy going out to eat?'

'Yeahhh, out to eat, out to eat!' Luna shouted excitedly.

'Okay, we'll go out, but first…'

'Yes I know, tidy my cars away.'

Ben stood at the entrance to Luna's bedroom, hands outstretched. He swooped her off the ground and tickled her, making her giggle.

'And make sure you put a pretty little dress on, okay?'

'Oooohhh, can't I wear jeans and my new plimsoles?'

'Okay but a pretty little top to go with them, deal?' he put her on the ground and they high fived each other, both shouting *'deal'* at the same time.

'Perhaps Mummy can make a bit of an effort too,' he winked at Alma. Alma glared. She despised him. She had to leave, with Luna. But how?

The next day was Tuesday. Ben was in London at a big client meeting all day, and Alma was back in the office. The phone hadn't stopped ringing, and Mr Saddler seemed stressed. They could hear him speaking, in a raised voice, to someone through his office door.

'Hello, can I help?' Alma cleared some space on her desk to serve the guy hovering in front of her desk. She'd seen him before, somewhere, but she couldn't work out where.

He hesitated, seeming slightly nervous.

'Please, take a seat.' Alma pointed at the chair in front of her, and the man slowly sank into it. He took a piece of paper from his pocket and slid it across the desk to Alma.

Alma looked at him, 'What's this?'

The man didn't answer. Instead, he got up and walked out of the door.

Alma stared, confused. She opened up the sheet of paper.

1pm Bluebird windows today!

Now she knew where she'd seen him before. Bluebird Windows was a car showroom, two doors down from them. But still, it didn't make any sense. She looked at her watch. The time was twelve thirty-seven.

'Laura, do you have a minute?'

The two girls made their way to the kitchen out the back. Alma told Laura about the note.

'I'll come with you if you want.'

'No I'll go, just wanted to let you know.'

'You know that Ben deals with their account?'

'What? I didn't even realise they were a client!'

'Oh yeah, have been for years, but Ben always goes down to see them…'

At twelve fifty-nine, Alma walked into the showroom. The man who'd come to the office was standing in the corner, watching the door. She walked over to him.

'Wait here a minute, Shak's on the phone.'

Alma looked around. Various men were mulling around the showroom. Suddenly, she felt extremely uncomfortable. This was ridiculous. What did they want with her anyway?

'CJ!' the man shouted something, and then disappeared into one of the back rooms. He came out again shortly, ushering Alma in.

The room had a large steel desk, and through the window she could see a number of brand new vehicles, not yet released to the showroom. Sitting at the desk was a man in a dark suit. He was an enormous man, with huge arms and a shiny bald head.

'Hi. Alma, right? I'm Shak.'

The man stretched out a huge hand. Alma shook it. Shak's hands were covered in tattoos. On his wrist he wore a thick, gold watch.

'Tea, coffee, something stronger?'

'Er coffee, white no sugar please.'

'Thanks for coming over,' he sat in front of her, picking up a pen and flicking it from one hand to another. 'I need the usual, but I need it like yesterday.'

'I'm sorry, what?'

Shak leaned back in his chair, tapping the pen on the desk.

'You're Bennie's chick, aren't you?'

The tea girl brought in their drinks. She smiled at Alma, who thanked her.

'Yes, that's right, what exactly do you want?' Alma sat upright, she could hear her voice tremble slightly.

'I need a back dated cover note for one of our drivers last night. He was involved in an accident and cops need the paperwork.'

Alma stared at him.

'You're joking, right?'

'Do I look like I'm joking?'

'No, but...I don't understand...'

Shak put his hands on the table. He laid his palms flat and scratched his wrist. 'You work at the insurance company though.'

'Yeh, I do.'

'So, in your job you know if someone's got no insurance and they're involved in an accident, that's a problem, right?'

'Yes, I am well aware of that.'

'Well, in this accident, there's been a fatality, so my man needs a quick fix as normal and pretty sharpish.'

'What do you mean like normal?'

Shak seemed surprised, 'Jesus, you don't even know, do you?'

'Know what?!'

'God, he's good. I thought you were both in it together…do you know when he's back?'

'Not until at least this evening.'

'Well I'm gonna need something before then, my man needs to display papers by three o'clock.'

Alma struggled to speak. She could hardly believe what she was hearing. 'How long has this been going on?' she blurted out.

'Listen, I ain't saying shit… I just need this sorted. We've got a deal and we pay handsomely for it. You'll need to try and get hold of him otherwise things could get messy, he ain't let us down yet.'

Alma excused herself, the colour had drained from her face. Driving home, her mind raced. How could he do this? What the hell was he thinking?

She grabbed the telephone as soon as she got indoors. 'Hi, it's Alma from Saddlers & Co. I believe you have Ben Gardener visiting Mr Eccles today. Please could I just leave a message for him to ring Alma at home as soon as possible? It's urgent.'

She opened the fridge and without hesitation took out the bottle of wine. The tears came slowly at first, but the more she thought about the situation, the more they flowed. What a selfish bastard, how long had he been doing this? His job, their home? He'd never get away with it. And why? He didn't even need to. Alma kicked off her shoes. She closed her eyes and then opened them. The gun!

Quickly running up the stairs, trying not to spill her wine, she reached their bedroom and headed straight to his wardrobe. There were boxes and boxes of shoes, trainers, some Alma had never seen Ben wear. Behind a neatly piled stack of t-shirts, she reached out and her hands found a metal box. She dragged it out of the wardrobe. The box was locked. Rummaging around some more, she found a tiny key at the bottom of a drawer. The key turned in the lock, and the lock opened. Alma stared at the contents.

There were three guns in the box, and a large drawstring bag. The bag was filled with money. Thousands of pounds worth of notes were bundled together neatly with black tape. There were letters too, but she couldn't see any stamp on the envelopes. Pulling out one of the letters, she held it up to the light. None of the writing made sense, it was all in code, but there was one name at the bottom that she recognised – *Michael.*

Alma went back into the box. Below the letters were photographs. Girls naked in different poses, a couple of pictures of Ben and Michael from when they were younger. Most of the photos were taken on a beach. There was one picture of Ben and a girl in a tiny, pink flowery bikini. Alma turned the photo over and read the back: *Benny and me – Jamaica 1981 – love you babe x*

Alma put the photograph back in the box. She was just about to look through the rest, when the phone rang. The sound cut through the silent house like a knife through butter.

'Hi, babe, what's up? You okay? Why have you gone home?'

She held the receiver, not quite knowing what to say.

'I just didn't feel too good...and also I had a message from Bluebird Windows, they've been trying to get hold of you. They said it's urgent.'

There was a moment of silence.

'Okay, no worries I'll speak to Shak...just as long as you're alright. Is Luna there?'

'No she's with Mami, she's gonna stay there tonight. What time will you be home?'

'Probably just after seven. Listen, get some sleep, okay? I'll bring something for dinner.'

'Okay.'

'Love you.'

The receiver clicked. Alma took a deep breath. She couldn't believe how cool he had been. She didn't even know the person she was living with.

After putting everything back the way she'd found it, Alma felt exhausted. It was only twenty to three, but she needed to lie down. What was she even going to say to him? He would be absolutely furious. The knot in her stomach became more painful, but a glass of wine helped. Suddenly, she had an overwhelming urge to speak to Luke. *He's not who you think he is.* Did he know what Ben was doing?

Alma poured another glass. There was no way out of this now. She'd have to confront him, there really wasn't any other choice. What Ben was doing was illegal, and he was using the company name to do it. She thought about Mr Saddler, and felt a pang of guilt. The company would suffer. Poor, dear Mr Saddler would suffer. It wasn't right. The clock ticked slowly. In three hours' time, Ben would be home. Alma braced herself.

By the time he pulled up in the drive, it was dark outside. Alma had changed into her pyjamas. She lay on the sofa, huddled under a blanket. She heard the car engine, then the key turning in the lock of the front door. Ben put a takeaway box down on the dining table and smiled broadly at Alma.

'There she is. Come here and give me a hug.'

Alma smelt the stale cigarette smoke on his clothes as he bent down to kiss her.

'How you feeling?'

'Bit better,' Alma said, trying to make herself sound as sickly as possible.

'I got us a Chinese for dinner, just gonna get outta these clothes and I'll sort it.'

Alma swallowed hard. She could hardly breath.

'You wanna glass of wine, babe?'

'Yes please.'

'Ahhh you can't be that bad then,' Ben laughed. He went out to the kitchen and unboxed the takeaway, piling it onto two plates, and also opened a bottle of wine.

'So how was your meeting?'

'Yeah all renewed, that's a good £4500 commission. Eccles was really pleased with our service, he's a cantankerous old bastard though, made me work for it.' Ben stabbed at the chicken piece on his plate and rammed a prawn cracker in his mouth.

Alma took a deep breath. 'Did you speak to Bluebird?'

Ben looked up at her. Their eyes met, for a brief second. He nodded, and took another mouthful of food.

'What did they want?'

'Oh just a cover note, got a new motor needed to get the tax,' Ben opened his can of beer.

'I could have sorted that out for them when they came in,' she watched his face intently.

'They came in?'

'Yeah, CJ…I think that's his name, came in and asked me to go down there, as it was urgent.'

Ben put his fork down. 'And did you go?'

'Yes, I spoke to Shak.'

There was a terrible silence. Panic rose in Alma's chest. Ben was staring hard at the opposite wall.

'Why didn't you tell me, Ben?'

He looked at her. His face was expressionless. 'Tell you what?'

'That you were back dating cover notes for them.'

In an instant, Ben's face changed. His eyes were cold and furious.

'Fucking hell. Fuck, he told you that?'

'He thought I knew, Ben! He thought we were doing this together. What the hell are you doing? How could you do that?'

Ben stood up. He started pacing the room.

'You can't say a fucking word about this to anyone, do you understand?'

'It's illegal! You'll get us both fired. How could you be so stupid?'

'Shut up, for fucks sake. Shut up. Our jobs are fine. I've been doing this long enough, and I'm not fucking stupid, okay?'

'Maybe you're not stupid but sooner or later you'll get caught. And I'm not losing my job because of you.'

Ben marched over to her, putting his hand around her neck. Alma batted him away, but he was too strong.

'Not if you keep your fucking mouth shut.'

Pinned against the back of the sofa, Alma gasped. 'Let go of me.'

Ben gave Alma a disgusted look and threw her back down against the leather.

'How much money do you make out of it? Is it really worth that risk?'

He didn't answer that.

'We could lose our home too, Ben. Have you even thought about that?'

'Listen, I've been doing this for years, okay? I know what I'm doing.'

'Why though? For the money? We've got enough money, I don't understand.'

'No, Alma, we don't. I have debts to clear, okay? I need this money.'

She stared at him, 'What the hell are you talking about? What debts? Has this got anything to do with those guns, cause if it has I want out!'

Ben grabbed her again. He virtually picked her up by the pyjama top and pushed her against the wall.

'You stupid bitch,' he snarled, 'you want out, do you? Well that's not gonna happen. What you think you can just walk out after everything I do for you and that kid? You've been living off my money too, what do you think is gonna happen if you grass me up? I'm all you've got, Alma.'

'That's not true....' Alma wheezed. 'Please, Ben, you're hurting me.'

Ben dropped her on the sofa. 'You better start acting like you're my partner, and not my enemy. Like I told you before, things are gonna change round here...you don't want to know what I'm fucking capable of, Alma.'

She glared up at him. His eyes were full of hate.

'I don't want to hurt you or Luna, but you're not leaving, so get that stupid idea out of your head. And if I go down, then you better know that I'm taking you with me.'

'What?'

Ben bent down close to her face. 'That's right, I'll tell everyone that you knew. You were in on it too, Alma. We did it together.'

He pulled himself back up to his feet, and gave her an ugly look. Then he smiled.

'Now, let's eat! I don't want you worrying about Shak and his boys, I've sorted out what they needed.'

Ben picked up his plate of food. He sat down on the chair opposite, and turned on the TV. Alma stared at him.

'Come on, girl, eat!' he pointed at her food.

Alma picked up her fork. She felt numb. Slowly, she held the fork up to her mouth, but as soon as she did so she knew that she was going to be sick. She heaved, and rushed to the bathroom.

'Oh god,' Ben said. 'I think you better get to bed. I'll fetch a hot water bottle, go on you, get upstairs.'

Alma meekly obeyed. Her head was pounding. She went up the stairs and climbed under the covers in the bedroom. Ben followed.

'Here you go,' he said, and shoved the hot water bottle under her legs. He plumped up the pillows behind her head.

'Listen, Alma, I don't want you to worry about anything, okay? I know what I'm doing, these people need me more that I need them. I just want you, Luna and me to be okay…I'm working towards something big for us, I just have a couple of more payments on this debt and then the money after that is ours. We'll have a bigger house, Luna can go to private school, and you can give up work. You'd like that, wouldn't you?' He looked down at her, lovingly stroking her hand.

'Yes,' she nodded.

'Okay, just let me do what I do and we'll have a good future, I promise.' He bent down and kissed her lips tenderly.

'I love you, Alma. I would never let anything happen to you and my baby girl, do you understand? I don't know what I would do without you.' He planted a kiss on her forehead and turned out her bedside lamp, leaving the room and closing the door behind him.

Alma waited until she was sure that he'd gone downstairs. She sat up, trying to steady her breathing, but it was so difficult. She needed to leave. But how? Ben wouldn't let her out of his sight. Turning on the lamp, she picked up the phone.

'Hello?

'Luke, is that you?'

'Yes, who's this?'

'It's Alma, I need your help.'

CHAPTER 17
On the Run

Two weeks later, it was Ben's birthday. Alma and Luna had given him his present first thing in the morning – a designer shirt and cufflinks. Ben was delighted, much to their relief. Luna had made him a card herself. It was bright red, with a drawing of a big car, and the three of them sitting inside of it. Ben got almost teary reading it.

'Wow, princess. Thank you so much, you did this all by yourself?'

'Yep, Mummy didn't have to help me, did you?' Luna looked up at Alma, who shook her head.

'No, you're a big girl now, you chose all the colours and everything,' Alma smiled at Luna, who looked extremely proud of herself.

Alma went downstairs to make tea. Ever since that night, she hadn't been able to relax. She couldn't stand to be in the same room as Ben. Luke was none the wiser. She'd tried to tell him, but it didn't come out right, and in the end she just stammered about needing more help with Luna.

As was customary, Mr Saddler let them go out to the pub for lunch. Ben was allowed to stay out longer, since it was his birthday. Meanwhile, Alma and Laura headed back to the office.

'Have you got ten minutes after work? I need to run something past you.'

'Course. Are you okay?'

'Yeh, I just need to talk to you about something,' Laura walked back to her desk.

Alma stared at her screen. Was it something to do with Michael?

At the end of the day, Laura and Alma left together.

'Where we going?'

'The George…let's walk fast.'

They got there in record time. Laura ordered two white wines, and they took a table right at the back of the pub.

'God, Alma, I've been wanting to tell you this all bloody day.'

'What's going on?'

'It's about the company.'

'What company?'

'Saddlers and Co.'

'Why, what's happening with it?'

'It's going up for sale.'

Alma looked confused, 'How would you know that?'

'I heard Janet telling Barbara in the kitchen. I was doing my filing and overheard their conversation.'

'So is it because Mr Saddler's retiring, do you think?'

'No, I think something's going on.'

'Like what?'

'I heard Janet say something about us being under investigation.'

Alma gulped her wine.

'I think we're in some sort of trouble, Alma.'

'I'm gonna get us another drink,' Alma stood up quickly and made her way to the bar. God, it was Ben. They must have found out, somehow. He was going to bring down the whole company. She leaned against a barstool, and took deep breaths. Was this really happening? There was no way around it now, she had to tell Laura. She couldn't let this continue.

Alma slowly walked back to her seat. Laura gave her a strange look.

'What's wrong?'

'I have to tell you something, but please don't freak out, okay?'

'Alma…'

'Promise?'

'Okay, fine.'

Alma looked at her, 'I think I know what the investigation is about.' She leaned back in her seat, took a deep breath…and then let it all out. From the cover notes to the guns, Ben's OCD behaviour to his near-throttling her, she didn't spare a single detail. When she was done, she waited for Laura's reaction. Laura looked stunned.

'Please tell me you're fucking kidding me.'

'No, why would I joke about something like that?'

'Seriously, Alma, are you having me on?'

'No! I promise you, on Luna's life, everything I said is true. Did you know he has an armed robbery conviction?'

'A what?'

'Yeh, from when he was younger. He went to prison. And Luke tried to warn me…but I didn't listen. And he even admitted it to my face, Laura, and I still stayed. What the fuck is wrong with me?'

'I can't get my head round this. You have Luna…that little girl, have you not thought about what this is all doing to her? He's got guns, Alma. Christ, are you mad? You need to leave, we need to tell the police.'

She stood up, frantically.

'Laura, please, please sit down.'

'You need to get out of there, Alma. How the hell are you sleeping at night?'

Alma looked at her, 'I think the alcohol helps.'

Laura sat back down. 'Alma…'

'I'm playing the dumb girlfriend. I've been trying to work out an exit, but I'm so scared, Laura. I think he'd kill me if I tried to leave.'

Laura stared at the table, dumbfounded. 'I just knew he wasn't all there…'

'What do you mean?'

'I've known him for a while, Alma, and just some things he said in the past…I guess I just ignored them. I knew he had a temper. Looking back now I should have done something, his ex ended up in hospital a few times with unexplained injuries, think he said something about her having too much to drink and falling…it just all makes sense now.'

Alma's hands were shaking. She felt sick to her stomach.

'You can't go back there, Alma. I won't let you.'

'Listen, you can't act any differently. Ben isn't stupid, he'll sense something's up at work…please let me just do it my way, okay? I know what I'm doing.'

They walked back to the car in silence.

'I'm gonna worry myself sick about you and Luna.'

'We'll be okay, I promise. And not a word to Michael, okay?'

***

Ben was waiting when she got home.

'Where have you been?'

'Sorry, the traffic was bad on the way back from picking up Luna.'

'What, it's taken you nearly two hours?'

'Yes,' she tried not to sound flustered. She was itching for a glass of wine.

The phone rang, and Ben went to answer it. Alma was glad for the distraction.

'Hi, mate. Yeh, no problems…see you in ten mins.'

Placing the receiver down, Ben looked at Alma. 'I'm popping out with Michael, should be back in a couple of hours.' He grabbed his coat, keys and wallet, and then bent down and kissed Luna on the head.

'Will you be back to read me a bedtime story?'

'Wouldn't miss it for the world, princess.'

Alma waited until his car had pulled out of the drive, and then reached for her keys.

'Come on, Luna, let's go and see Nanny and Grandad.'

They drove at least three to four car lengths behind. Ben wouldn't know it was her. Where the hell was he going, anyway? The route he was taking wasn't familiar. Steadying her breathing, Alma loosened her grip on the steering wheel. Eventually, he pulled up outside a block of flats and went in. A quarter of an hour later, he came out, with Michael in tow.

Luna was getting impatient, 'Mummy, what are we waiting for? I thought we were going to Nanny and Grandad's.'

'Just a few more minutes, darling.'

She watched Ben and Michael get into a car. They sped off. Alma followed, staying well behind. What the hell were they up to? Then, all of a sudden, the car stopped. Michael got out of the passenger side and jogged over to a house across the road. He was carrying a rucksack.

Alma had seen enough. She didn't know for sure what was going on, but it was getting late. She drove home.

'But what about Nanny and Grandad?' Luna asked, as they parked up.

'We'll see them tomorrow, I promise.'

When they got home, Luna ran straight up to her bedroom. Alma sat down at the table. She poured a glass of wine, and then another. Halfway through the third glass, she felt a tug on her sleeve. Luna was staring up at her.

'Mummy, why are you always drinking wine?'

Alma put the glass down on the table.

'Well…I guess I just like it, that's all.'

'What, like me and Teddy?'

'Yes, I suppose so,' Alma laughed.

'Ben says you drink too much.'

Alma looked up, startled.

'Oh really and when did he say that?'

'He says it all the time and he says you get silly when you drink too much,' she giggled.

'And what else does he say?'

'Just that it's better to leave you alone when you're drinking. He said I don't have to drink when I'm older and that it's best not to anyway, as it isn't very good for you.'

Alma was fuming. She took a deep breath, trying to calm herself.

'Well, I agree, Mummy isn't going to be drinking soon, she's gonna stop and there is no way that you will have to leave me alone, okay?'

Luna smiled. Alma lifted her up, cuddling her tightly.

'Now, let's have some dinner.'

Later that night, as Alma lay in bed, she heard a car pull up on the driveway. The lock in the front door turned, and then Ben came up the stairs. He opened the bedroom door and closed it quietly behind him. Then she could hear him rummaging around, before turning on the shower. Quickly scrambling out of bed, Alma turned on the bedside lamp. Ben's rucksack was on the floor. She unzipped it. Inside there were small bags of tablets, and then a big brown envelope filled with cash. Right at the bottom of the bag, wrapped in cloth, was the silver gun.

Alma stuffed everything back into the bag. She pulled a jumper out of the wardrobe, scraped her hair back into a ponytail and rushed into Luna's room. Luna stirred.

'Mummy?'

'Shhhh…' Alma silenced her, pulling her out of bed and forcing her into a dressing gown. She listened. The shower had stopped.

Signalling to Luna to be quiet, they both slowly made their way down the stairs. Alma walked on tiptoes. Then, suddenly, there was a soft bump behind them. Luna turned around.

'Teddy! Mummy, Teddy!'

Alma panicked. She grabbed Luna, and the bear, and pulled them down the stairs. Behind them, she heard the bathroom door open.

'Run Luna!' she yelled. They dashed down the drive and into the car. Behind them, she could see Ben standing in the open doorway of the house. Her hands shook as she tried to put the key in the ignition. And then he was at the car door, wearing just his underwear, pulling desperately at the handle.

'Alma, what the fuck? Alma!'

'Fuck!' she screamed. Luna cried out loudly as Ben opened the driver's side door. Reacting quickly, Alma pulled the door back, and reversed at the same time. Ben fell back against the pavement, stunned. Luna was crying, holding Teddy to her face. Alma reversed. She couldn't see anything behind her, but she heard the bump as the car collided with next door's fence. Ben was on his feet again, and he was banging on the side of the car.

'Alma, get out of the fucking car, we can sort this!'

They spun out of the drive. In the rear view mirror Alma could see him standing on the pavement, a look of cold fury on his face.

And then they were gone.

'Hello you've dialled 999. Which emergency service do you require?'

'Police...police please.'

Mami was sitting with Luna upstairs. Alma was in the lounge. She sobbed down the phone as she told the operator about Ben.

'Okay, Alma, listen to me, you need to take a deep breath. We are going to get someone over to you as soon as we can, but you need to give us his location, okay?'

Alma felt a hand on her shoulder. She looked up and saw David, which only brought more tears. He rubbed her arm sympathetically, and gestured for her to pass him the phone.

When he'd finished, David went into the kitchen and made a cup of coffee. He handed it to Alma. 'I don't know how much you've had to drink, and I don't want to even think about you driving with Luna in the car, but you better sober up before the police arrive.'

After drinking the coffee, Alma washed her face. She felt a bit better. But the thought of facing the police was terrifying. What was she even going to say?

When they arrived, the police questioned her for forty-five minutes. Did she have any idea where Ben was? When did she first see the guns? Did she know where Michael was? What had she found in the rucksack? Finally, they said they'd be in touch. Alma felt lightheaded. Was that really it? Just some questions? No arrests, no further information. Her thoughts turned to the next day. There was no way her or Luna would be leaving the house, not until they caught Ben. It wasn't safe with that lunatic out there.

The next morning, Mami woke her up with a cup of tea.

'You need to ring work, and the school too.'

Alma rubbed her eyes.

'How long have you been living like this, Alma?'

'I'm sorry I didn't tell you before, I stupidly thought he would change. He was so good with Luna…and that's all I wanted, you know, after Luke.'

Mami looked at her. Alma couldn't tell whether she was disappointed or exasperated. 'You'll need to get on to a solicitor about the house or you could lose everything.' She got up and walked out of the room.

The first person she called was Mr Saddler.

'Hi, Mr Saddler, it's Alma. '

'Hi, Alma, are you okay?'

'No, not really. I need to talk to you in private and I don't think over the phone is the best way…if I give you my parents' address can you come over?'

Mr Saddler seemed surprised, but nevertheless he was there within half an hour.

'Ben hasn't come in today either,' he said, sitting down at the table.

'Mr Saddler…'

He looked at her questioningly.

'I don't know how to say this, but me and Ben…we're over. Me and Luna have left him.'

'I'm sorry. What happened?'

'Well…it's a long story, but basically Ben isn't who he seems. He's not a nice guy, at all actually. He's in a lot of trouble.'

'Sorry, Alma, I'm not really with you. What's he done?'

She took a deep breath. 'He's back dating cover notes, and using your company to do it. He's also into other things, which I can't really talk about…but I wanted to let you know, Mr Saddler.

I really appreciate everything you've done for me, but the police will probably be coming to see you to talk about Ben.'

Mr Saddler leaned back in his chair. He wetted his lips with his tongue.

'I see,' he said.

Alma looked at him. She hadn't expected that reaction. Then, suddenly, Mr Saddler stood up. He stared at her.

'Well, thank you for telling me, Alma.'

'Mr Saddler…is there anything I can do?'

'No…no. That's quite alright.' He moved towards the door, opened it, and walked out onto the drive. Alma ran after him, but he was already halfway down the path.

'I won't be coming back, Mr Saddler. I'm sorry!' she shouted after him.

Mr Saddler ignored her. He just carried on walking, without a word.

Alma sat down on the sofa. It didn't make sense. She'd expected anger, or some kind of blame, but instead he'd been as calm as anything. Maybe it was the shock? Or maybe she was just being paranoid. Mr Saddler had never lost his temper with her, that was just the type of person he was, calm and collected.

The police were back round that afternoon. Ben was on the run. They mentioned finding evidence at the house, and a lot more besides, but couldn't discuss what they'd found.

'What the hell!? You know we're not leaving here until you find him, right?'

'We'll find him, Alma, don't worry.'

'You do know he's been in trouble before, don't you?'

The two officers looked at each other, and then back at Alma.

'Alma, did Ben ever hurt you?' said the older officer.

Alma looked around the room. She could see Mami and David waiting for her response.

'Sorry, let me put it in clearer terms…did he ever physically hurt you, raise a hand… you know, that sort of thing?'

Alma looked down at the floor, 'Yes.'

Mami turned away.

'And Luna?'

'No.'

'What about verbally?'

'Yes,' she almost whispered it.

'How long had he behaved like this?'

'I dunno...within six months of moving into our house.'

'Why didn't you report his behaviour?'

Alma walked over to the sofa and sat down, clutching her hands together. 'I was too scared.' She felt ashamed. She'd put Luna in harm's way, and all because she was too stupid to listen to Luke, of all people. He'd warned her. Even Luke had better judgement than she did. God, she needed a drink.

Two days later, the news came. Ben had been arrested, and so had Michael. They'd been pulled over for speeding, and when the police checked the registration it was a match. While Alma was relieved, it wasn't all good news. Mr Saddler had been arrested too. Laura called, and told Alma that he'd been frog marched out of the office, and that the whole street was blocked off with police cars. It all seemed so unbelievable. How could Mr Saddler possibly have been involved? In any case, Saddlers and Co was done. The doors were closed, and their contracts were out. She'd have to find a new job, and quickly.

Later that evening, she sat down with Yoli.

'Are you okay?' Yoli looked sympathetic.

'Yeah I'll be fine, I'm just worried about Luna.'

'I can't believe what's happened. Why didn't you tell us?'

Alma looked away, feeling ashamed, 'I was scared, I didn't know what to do or think…I just lost confidence in myself, you know, not being able to make my own decisions. I guess I just resigned myself to letting him take control. It was easier. God, I haven't even got my own bank account anymore.'

Yoli looked aghast.

'It's my own fault, I didn't say a word to anyone, maybe I just hoped it would get better.'

'Why don't you and Luna come and stay with me? I have the sofa bed too…only until your house is sold,' Yoli held Alma's hand and smiled.

Alma nodded. 'Thanks, think I'll take you up on that!'

While Yoli put on a film, Alma leaned back against the sofa. Ben had brought so much sadness into their lives, it was true, but she needed to get a grip. She understood that now. They would come back from this, they had to. Luna was the most important thing in the world, and she would do whatever she needed to protect her from men like Ben. She owed it to her.

CHAPTER 18
The Madness
(five years later)

The two directors of Ballard Jones Retail looked through the annual report once more. Alma felt that familiar anxious feeling in the pit of her stomach.

'Well I think we are happy to go ahead, Alma. Would you agree, Morris?'

Mr Ballard cleared his throat, before turning to the premium page. *Please god, let them renew.* This was the biggest case Alma had ever had. She'd been working on it for months. Yes, their price had increased this year, but Alma had explained that away. All it needed now was a signature.

'The service you've provided over the last twenty-four months has been exceptional, Alma. However, please bear in mind that we do have an insurance budget, and the invite you've put forward is rather more than what we'd hoped for...'

Mr Ballard closed the report. He put it back on his desk.

'We'll renew this year, but I hope next year we can look to trim costs.'

They all stood up and shook hands.

'Mr Ballard, Mr Jones, thank you so much. I'll do my very best with premiums at your next renewal.'

Sitting in her car afterwards, Alma pumped her fist. All the hard work had finally paid off. And she was sitting in the reward. The Mazda was practically gleaming. It purred as she put her foot down on the pedal. It had been a risky buy, she knew, but Mr Ballard and Mr Jones had negated that. It wasn't just the Mazda either. Her credit card balance was through the roof. Now she could pay it all off. With the trial over, she could finally move forward. No more nightmares about Ben, no more hearing his voice behind every corner. They could move forward, just her and Luna.

***

The clock beside Alma's bed said that it was twenty past three. She crept downstairs. It was Saturday morning, and Luna had a full weekend of football ahead. Alma opened the fridge. There was no wine. In the cupboard beside the fridge were two bottles of gin and a quarter bottle of vodka. Football was in six hours. It would be a mistake, surely…

A few hours later, Luna was shaking her.

'Mum, wake up! Wake up! You didn't wake me, we're not gonna make it!'

Alma opened her eyes. She was on the sofa, wrapped in a blanket. She tried to focus on Luna's face.

'Okay, honey, we can still make it, I just need to get dressed… go upstairs and get your kit on.'

Luna ran upstairs, leaving Alma to struggle off the sofa. She discarded the empty gin bottle, and moments later was dry heaving in the bathroom. Later, at training, she made her excuses and sat in the car. As she closed her eyes, trying desperately to sober up, there was a frantic tapping on the window. Alma opened her eyes. A man was staring through the glass, looking concerned.

'I'm sorry, I just wanted to make sure you were okay,' he said, as Alma wound down the window. She recognised him – his daughter was on the same team as Luna.

'Yeah I'm fine, just feel a bit crap this morning, bit of a late night that's all,' she couldn't look at him.

'Oh as long as you're okay, just used to seeing you cheering on the touchline.'

Alma cringed. How embarrassing. Luna had told her off for getting carried away before, and so had the coach.

'Oh god, sorry, I don't even know I'm doing it,' she felt awkward.

'No it's good to get excited, there's been some good games recently…' he looked round and watched the girls running up and down the pitch, 'your Luna is a good little player.'

'Thanks, she lives and breathes football.'

'Ahh a bit like my Sarah, she's exactly the same. Sorry, I'm Lee, by the way.'

'Alma.'

'I'll leave you alone, Alma. Hope the hangover's not too bad!' he laughed loudly.

Alma closed the window and put her head back. It was all she could do not to vomit.

Exactly two weeks later, Lee asked Alma out for a drink. She said no. He seemed like a lovely guy, but he wasn't her type. And besides, she didn't know anything about him.

'Thank you, but maybe some other time.'

'Okay, well perhaps you let me know? No strings, just a drink, okay?'

Alma looked at him. She didn't even know what he did for a living. For all she knew, he still had a wife.

'Well I'm free next Friday.' The words tumbled out of her mouth before she could stop them.

Lee looked delighted. 'You're on. I'll pick you up at seven-thirty, how about the Tavern in Bounty Road?'

'Fine.' Alma scrabbled around for a piece of paper and pen from her car. She jotted down her details.

'Here's my card,' he handed her his business card. *Triumph Couriers, Lee Murray, Proprietor.* 'Don't worry I'll ring you beforehand, just in case you've changed your mind.' He smiled, and walked off.

Behind Alma, the back door of the car opened. Luna got in, looking at Alma suspiciously.

'What were you and Sarah's dad talking about?'

'Oh, we were just talking about you girls and how much you love football.' Alma looked in her rear view mirror. Luna was stuffing herself with crisps.

'Sarah's got older brothers,' she mumbled, through a mouthful, 'they used to play football too.'

Alma thought about Lee and his three children. God, that must be hard work. It put a definite end to any possible relationship. There was no way she wanted or needed that sort of baggage. Alma decided that she'd make her excuses when he rang.

There was a message on the answer phone when they got home.

'Hi Alma, it's David…give us a call when you're home from training.'

There was something off about David's voice. He sounded strained. Alma called back immediately.

'Hi, you okay?'

'I wasn't very good in the night, just wanted to know if you could possibly pick up a few things… sorry to ask but I've tried Yoli and can't get hold of her.'

'Sure, what's wrong?'

'Had chest pains…I think it's a bad indigestion. I just don't really feel like driving if I'm honest and I don't want your mum to have to get a bus.'

'Do you want me to the call the doctor?'

'Oh, no, no…I'll be okay.'

When Alma delivered the items, Mami was fussing over David. He was sat in his armchair, with a blanket round his knees, nursing a mug of soup. Luna gave both Mami and David a hug.

'Are you okay, Grandad?'

'Feel a lot better now, sweetheart.'

Mami and Alma left both of them talking about football and went into the kitchen.

'I'm worried about him, Alma. His appetite is next to none and he hasn't been sleeping, I am sure he's worse than what he's making out.' Mami washed her hands and wiped them on her apron.

'Okay,' Alma said. 'Well let's see how he is. If he hasn't improved in a couple of days I'll call the doctor.'

Mami looked at her, 'Did you know Yoli's met a new chap?'

'What? No I didn't.'

'Yes he was round last night. His name's Neil…he's such a nice guy, which is more than can be said for the last one that left her in all that debt. God knows how long it's going to take her to pay that off.'

'I'll give her a ring.'

'She hasn't rung us back, David tried getting hold of her earlier.'

'Mami, she's probably glad of a lie in. She's been working really hard.'

'I know, Almita. Okay, well just let me know if you hear from her, please.'

'I will, I promise. I'll ring tomorrow to make sure David is okay too.'

···

'Melanie's mum is dropping me off after the party.'

'Oh okay, I thought it was a sleepover.'

'Yeah some are staying but I want to come home.'

Alma helped Luna wrap her present, and then dropped her off at her friend's house. In truth, she was relishing the idea of having time to herself. It was hard, having to get up in the night and drink. At least if Luna was away she wouldn't have to hide it.

By six-thirty she'd finished two bottles of wine. It wasn't enough. She needed vodka. There was always that same craving for more, that feeling of being unfinished, incomplete. She went to the cupboard, and started pouring a glass, but just then the phone rang.

'Hello?'

'Hi, it's Yoli.'

'Are you alright? Mami told me about Neil.'

'I was gonna tell you, just didn't seem like the right time the other night, I'll pop over if you're in later.'

'Yeah, yeah, I'm here. Luna's at a party, and she won't be back till about nineish.'

Later that evening, Alma rooted around under the bed and pulled out some photo albums. Already drunk, she flicked through the pages, gazing over pictures of the old crowd from Ireland. They'd never kept in touch. There were photos of Luke and Ben, and Luna as a baby. It was all too much. She started to well up.

Within half an hour, she was walking to the off license. Tears streaked her face. Behind her, a car horn sounded.

'Watch where you're fucking going, you stupid cow!'

Alma stuck two fingers up at the man. She stumbled into the off license, where the man behind the till looked at her, alarmed.

'Two bottles of vodka, please,' she slurred.

The man shook his head. 'Nah, I'm not serving you love.'

'Two bottles!'

'Nope, I'm sorry.'

Alma giggled, 'Two bottles of vodka!'

The man gave her a disgusted look. Alma started dancing. There was faint music playing somewhere in the back of the shop. She felt so free, moving around the aisles, dodging between the crisps and sweets and magazines, flowing in time to the beat. Everybody in the shop was watching her, wishing they could dance like her, entranced by the hypnotic rhythm of the beat…

Alma woke to heavy pounding on the door.

'Alma! Alma!! Open up!'

She dragged herself up off the sofa. It was still dark outside. She stumbled over to the door and pulled it open. Luna was stood there with Yoli, who had a look of thunder on her face.

'I've been banging on the door for ages.'

Luna ran past and scurried to her bedroom, without a word.

'Are you drunk?' Yoli pushed past Alma and into the kitchen. She looked around at the empty bottles.

'What's going on?'

'What you on about?'

'You've been drinking, Luna tried to get hold of you for a lift home from the party but you were too out of it to talk down the phone…' she walked towards Alma with a disappointed look on her face. 'What's happening to you? Look at you, why do you get like this?'

'I had a few drinks, Luna said she was getting a lift home.'

'A few drinks! You call this lot a few drinks,' Yoli started picking up the empty bottles and discarding them into the bin. 'I don't understand it, Alma. You have everything. You've got a beautiful daughter who loves you so much. Why, Alma? I don't get it.'

Steadying herself against the kitchen worktop, Alma felt anger bubbling up inside of her. How dare she. How dare she lecture her.

Who the hell did she think she was, coming into her house and reading her the riot act. What the fuck did she know?

Yoli continued, 'Do you want to lose everything you've worked for? Mami and David have been worried about your drinking for ages, and to be honest until now I didn't realise how bad it was. Maybe you should get some help, Alma.'

Alma snapped. She launched herself at Yoli, catching her by surprise. Grabbing Yoli's hair, Alma let out a terrible scream, pushing her sister back against the kitchen table. They tumbled to the ground, with Yoli desperately trying to fight back, but Alma was too strong. She pinned Yoli to the floor.

'Who the fuck do you think you are? What do you know about my life? Don't you fucking lecture me about things you know nothing about, do you hear?'

'Get off me, get the fuck off me!' Yoli struggled to break free.

'You're nothing but a spoilt selfish bitch who only thinks about herself. The most difficult thing you have to deal with is what to make yourself for dinner. You don't know what it's like to have a father walk out of your life, your father loves you! He loves you! You've had a fucking walk in the park when it comes to having a normal life and don't you ever, ever tell me how to bring up my daughter!'

Alma climbed off Yoli and leaned against the table. Yoli got up immediately, and pushed her finger towards Alma.

'Yeh well at least I'm not a fucking drunk. You're a disgrace, Alma, even Luna can see that. And for your information, you do have a dad who loves you, you just can't fucking see it.'

There was a shrill cry from behind them. Luna burst into the room, wailing hysterically.

'Stop it! Just stop arguing, please!'

Yoli walked towards Luna, 'It's okay, baby, it's okay.' She gave Luna a hug and a kiss on the forehead, and with a glare towards Alma, walked out the door.

Alma watched Yoli leave. What the fuck had she done? What the fuck was she doing? It was all too much. She collapsed to the floor, sobbing into her hands. Luna came over and gave her a gentle hug.

'It's okay, Mummy, it's okay.'

Yoli told Mami and David about their fight. Mami was disappointed with Alma, and David gave her a stark warning – she needed to curb the drinking. Alma vowed that she was off the stuff for good now, but even she knew it was an empty promise. She'd tried ringing Yoli to apologise, but it was no good, and Yoli never returned her calls. Alma laid on the sofa for most of the next day, wallowing. She could barely believe what she'd done. She'd attacked her own sister. And for what? It seemed like an out of body experience. Even Luna seemed to be avoiding her. She'd gone out to a friend's house again, this time for a sleepover. They'd barely spoken since the previous night, and Alma was too embarrassed to bring it up. She sat on the sofa and sipped her water, barely paying attention to the film on the TV.

At six o'clock, the phone rang.

'Hi, Alma, it's Lee.'

'Hi.'

'Just wanted to check, are we still on for tonight?'

Alma hesitated.

'It's just as friends, like I said.'

'I'm sorry, Lee, I don't feel like it today.'

He sounded disappointed, 'Okay, well if you change your mind then just call me.'

Alma hung up. She went over to the cupboard, opened it, and then closed it again. Even the thought of vodka made her sick. Switching off the TV, she pulled a blanket over herself. If she couldn't drink, then at least she could sleep. Anything to stop the emptiness.

The next day was Saturday. Luna had football training first thing in the morning, and Alma was up and ready for it. She picked up Luna from her friend's house, and smiled as Luna got into the backseat.

'How was your night?'

Luna looked at her, 'Good thanks.'

'Great. Are you excited for training today?'

'Yes, Mum.'

They drove in silence for the rest of the way. When they got to training, Luna bounced out of the car and ran out to greet the rest of the team. Alma sat, watching her. After a while, she got out of the car, and made her way to the sideline. Across the pitch, parents were chatting with each other. Alma stood alone, in her coat, shivering.

'Hey, Alma!'

She turned to see Lee. He was with another mum, whom Alma had seen before.

'How's it going?'

'Fine thanks…listen, I'm sorry about yesterday.'

Lee smiled, 'Don't worry about it. Are you feeling better?'

'A bit. I didn't mean to ruin your plans or anything.'

'It's fine,' Lee smiled at the woman next to him. 'You missed a good night though.'

'Oh, I see.'

'Sorry, where are my manners? Have you met Louise? She's Jennifer's mum.'

The other woman gave Alma a brief smile. Alma forced a smile back.

'Maybe next time you can come with us?' Lee said.

'Yeh, okay.'

'Is everything alright, Alma? I mean I know you said you were feeling better…'

'It's fine,' Alma said. She turned around, without another word, and went back to the car. Her insides felt like they were melting. *Have you met Louise?* Louise was tall, blonde, pretty. She didn't stink of booze. She got up in the mornings and did her hair and put her makeup on and had men like Lee eating out the palm of her hand. Of course there was another woman. *There's always another woman.* Alma backed out of the car park. She put her foot down on the accelerator and made it home in record time.

The fridge beckoned. She practically threw it open. Nestled in the bottom drawer were two beautiful bottles of wine. It was all she could do not to scream. Was she sick? Perhaps. Either that or she was crazy. Glug, glug, glug. She loved that sound. It filled her with calmness. It made everything better. More glugging. More wine. She needed more wine. She emptied the cupboards from top to bottom. In the bottom drawer of the cupboard she found a small bottle of vodka. It would do, but it didn't last long. The calmness disintegrated. Suddenly, Alma was on her hands and knees. There was a pool of something, and she was lying in it. It didn't smell like blood, but it didn't smell like vomit either. Her trousers were wet. Rolling onto her side, Alma shook violently. Her heart was beating as fast she had ever felt it beat. This was madness. The madness to end all madness. Just one more drop, just to calm it all down. She reached up and pulled a bottle of wine from the counter. It was empty. There was nothing left. Nothing at all.

The blackness was total.

***

Alma knew she was in hospital before she opened her eyes. She recognised the smell, the sounds, the muttering voices in the background.

'Mum!' Luna gasped.

Alma gave her a weak smile, 'Hello darling.'

Luna frowned and touched Alma's arm, 'They put this horrible thing on you.'

David stepped forward. Mami was sitting on a chair next to him. 'That's so your mum gets water and vitamins inside her,' he said.

At that moment, a nurse came into the room. She asked if Luna, Mami and David could move to the waiting room, as the doctor wanted to do his rounds.

Doctor Potts wasn't smiling. He made Alma feel like a naughty schoolchild.

'Are you still taking your anti-depressants?'

'No.'

'Why not?'

'Well because I've been on them for years and years and I thought it would be a good time to come off them.'

'You thought it would be a good idea?'

'Yes.'

'Did you consult your doctor before doing so?'

'No.' Alma could feel herself losing her patience with him. She wasn't a bloody child.

'Well, we've carried out some tests and you have a small amount of damage to your liver.'

'What do you mean?'

Dr Potts gave her a serious look, 'It's been caused by alcohol abuse.'

Alma stared at him.

'You must have made some mistake, I don't even drink that much.'

'It's not serious at this stage, Alma, but I must warn you if you keep abusing your body the way you have been, the consequences could be catastrophic. Cirrhosis of the liver is not a laughing matter.'

'But…'

Dr Potts interrupted her. 'Do you think you have a drink problem?'

'I don't know,' she said quietly.

'I'll leave you this information to read, it may just put things into perspective,' he handed her a leaflet. 'We'll be discharging you tomorrow and I will be writing to your general practitioner. It may be worth you making an appointment, as I think you should discuss your medication, okay?'

'Okay.'

Dr Potts wrote some notes on his clipboard, and placed it back on the end of the bed. He nodded, and then moved on to the next patient.

Alma stared at the leaflet. Alcoholics Anonymous. Alcoholic? She wasn't an alcoholic. She worked for god's sake, and earnt good money. She had her own house and a car. Alcoholics sat on benches and drank day and night. They were dirty, scrawny, mostly old, men. They sat in town…she'd seen them! She wasn't anything like that, and even the thought made her livid. She shoved the leaflet under a magazine on the bedside cabinet. They'd made a mistake, she was sure of it.

That evening, lying in the hospital bed, Alma fished out the leaflet. Curiosity had gotten the better of her.

Have you lost control of your drinking?

Have you tried stopping but been unable to?

Alma stared at the leaflet. She hadn't lost control, had she? But yes, she had been unable to stop. And it was true, one drink never seemed to be enough. In fact she always carried on until she was too drunk to continue.

Alcoholism is a disease. It can happen to anyone.

At the bottom of the leaflet there was a list of AA meeting locations. To her surprise, they seemed to be everywhere. In fact there was one just down the road. She couldn't go there, though. What if somebody recognised her? Alma came to her senses. This was ridiculous. She wasn't an alcoholic. Why was she even thinking about it? She had Luna to take care of, a perfectly good job…maybe even a date with Lee, if Louise hadn't got there first. She'd made a mistake, but it would be the last one.

The doctors discharged Alma the following morning. Mami and David dropped her and Luna off home. Alma had been hoping that Yoli would come to the hospital, but she hadn't showed.

There was a pile of mail under the letterbox. Alma flicked through it. Bills, bills, insurance…and then an official, formal looking letter. She sat down at the table and read through the contents.

Dear Mrs Giles

I am formally writing to advise you that Luna has been caught selling confectionery to the other students. She has also been wearing boys' school uniform. Both of which are not acceptable.

Please can I ask you to contact the school to make a mutually convenient appointment where both matters can be discussed.

We look forward to hearing from you

Yours Sincerely,

Mr D. L King

Deputy Headmaster

Alma put the letter down on the table. She could hear Luna upstairs, playing in her bedroom. Luna's schoolbag was in the corner. Alma picked it up and opened the contents out on the table. Trousers and a shirt, neatly folded. A school tie in a plastic bag, and a stretchy vest top. Cigarettes and a lighter.

Alma stared, taking it all in. She struggled to control her breathing. The clothes she could deal with, but cigarettes? It didn't make sense. And yet, in some way, it did. Luna had been distant with her lately. They'd barely spoken the last two days, and Alma had just left her at training. She felt a pang of guilt. Was she a bad mother? Was it her fault?

She looked at the letter again. There was no two ways about it, she'd have to attend the meeting. But what would she even say? How could she tell them the truth?

CHAPTER 19
An Opportunity

'I don't understand, why would you even choose to wear boys' clothes? You were asking to get into trouble.'

Luna undid her seatbelt as they pulled into the school car park.

'I just find them more comfortable. I don't like dresses or skirts, you know that.'

'Yes I'm aware of that, Luna, but at home and when you're playing football you can wear what you want. You know at school you have to wear school uniform, and as for the sweet selling… that isn't right either, is it? You're taking children's lunch money, what are you doing with the money apart from buying cigarettes?'

Alma turned around and looked at Luna. She had a stroppy look on her face.

'So you've been going through my stuff?'

'When did you start smoking?'

'Ages ago.'

'Oh really and don't you think that's going to affect your fitness?'

'Everyone does it,' Luna shrugged. 'I bet you were smoking at my age, anyway.'

'I did smoke, but not that young, and besides you've told me you wanna be a personal trainer. This isn't gonna help, is it? Your future customers won't be impressed if you have a cigarette hanging out of your mouth, that's not going to set a good example. You do realise if you get caught with those cigarettes you'll be expelled?'

Luna stayed silent.

'Come on, we better get in there.'

They were both told to wait outside Mr King's office. Alma had taken the morning off work, but it was early, and none of the other children were even in school yet. She needed a coffee.

'Mrs Giles, Luna, please come in.' Mr King was tall. He wore thick rimmed glasses and walked with a limp. He shook Alma's hand. Mrs Fox was already seated. She gave them a friendly smile.

'Can I get you both a drink?'

'Oh, I'd love a coffee please, milk and no sugar.'

'Luna, how about you?'

'I'm fine thanks.'

Mr King went out to the staff kitchen and came back with a tray of drinks. He set them down on the table.

'Right, shall we begin?'

Luna was playing with a loose thread on her trousers. She didn't seem particularly interested.

'Mrs Giles, just confirming you've read the contents of our letter and that you know why we've asked to see you both.'

'Yes I understand.' Alma smiled nervously, clasping her hands in her lap and trying to catch Luna's eye.

'Firstly, can we talk about the sweet selling? As you're aware Luna was caught selling sweets in the playground. She told us she was doing this on behalf of a friend, but we now know this wasn't the case. Luna, can you please explain to us why you were doing this?'

'Well because everyone was moaning there wasn't much choice at the tuck shop, so I saw it as an opportunity. I had some pocket money and went to the shop on the corner of our road, they always have sweets and bits in the sale baskets.' Luna looked straight at Mr King not showing any sign of remorse. 'I didn't think there was anything wrong with it, I was gonna start selling drinks and other stuff too.'

'Luna, can I ask why you thought there was nothing wrong with what you were doing?'

'Cause the kids were asking me to get the stuff, I think they should have a choice on what they spend their money on, not everyone wants a sandwich and an apple for their lunch, Sir.'

'So were you making a profit?'

'Yes of course, there was no point in me doing it otherwise. That's why I took the time to go and get the stock.'

Alma stared at Luna, shocked. Mrs Fox opened the file on her lap.

'We've had several complaints from parents, Luna, and this has to stop. Children need to spend their money on lunch not sweets. You'll receive detention for three days after school next week, and you'll write a letter of apology which I can pass on to those parents, is this understood?'

'Yes, Mrs Fox,' Luna looked down at the floor.

'Now turning to the matter of your school uniform…' Mr King said, '…why have you been wearing the boys' school uniform, Luna?'

'Because I prefer it, I don't like dresses or skirts.'

'I'm sorry, Mr King, but Luna doesn't possess a skirt or a dress at home, she lives in tracksuits and jeans.'

'Yes well that may be the case at home, Mrs Giles, but Luna isn't at home here. The school has a strict policy on school uniform. We can't have Luna wearing boys' uniform just because it's more comfortable or because she prefers it.'

Luna looked angry.

'Luna, do you understand?'

Luna nodded. Her bottom lip wobbled.

Mrs Fox put the folder on the desk. 'Luna, is there anything else that is bothering you that perhaps you want to discuss?'

Luna looked at her. She wiped her eyes, 'No.'

Mr King stood up and tucked his shirt into his trousers.

'Right, well if that's all, then please excuse me – I have a meeting to attend. Luna, I believe your first lesson starts in fifteen minutes.'

As Alma drove back to work, she mulled over the conversation. Christ, a profit? Luna sounded like she was on her way to starting her own business. Alma smiled, recalling Mr King's horrified expression. It wasn't funny, but at least Luna had been honest and that was all she could have asked for.

Later that afternoon the school rang Alma. They asked her to pick Luna up. She'd burst into tears mid-lesson, and nobody had been able to calm her down. The school thought it would be better if she went home. Feeling guilty, Alma explained the situation to her boss. She wasn't impressed, but grudgingly allowed her to leave.

The drive home from school was silent. Alma had tried to talk to Luna, but she wouldn't speak, and as soon as they got home she disappeared into her room. It was two o'clock, and too early for a glass of wine, but Alma needed it. She sat on the sofa, and within half an hour the bottle was almost gone. Then there were footsteps behind her.

'Luna! Are you okay?'

'Mum, I think there's something wrong with me!' Luna slumped on the sofa.

'No, what do you mean? There's nothing wrong with you.'

'Yes there is, I hate myself.'

'Oh darling, please don't say that. You're beautiful, you're intelligent…you have so much going for you.'

'I don't want to be a girl. I have my period and I feel dirty, I hate my boobs, I should have been a boy.' Luna looked at Alma, her eyes full of tears. 'Look, I wear this because I hate them so much,' she lifted her football top up and Alma saw the same vest that had been in her gym bag.

'This squashes them down so you don't notice them, I just feel happier with it on,' she looked down. 'I don't know why I feel like this, but I do. I'm so unhappy with my body, I hate the way I look.'

Alma took a gulp of wine. 'Luna, darling, listen…sometimes we hate our looks and bodies. As you get older you'll come to appreciate what you have, and you'll end up accepting who you are.'

Alma reached out to hold Luna's hand, but Luna pulled away. She looked hurt and angry.

'No, no, you don't understand, you're not interested, you're not even listening to me.' Luna stood up, raising her voice, 'All you're interested in is that!' She pointed at the wine bottle.

'Luna…'

'That's all you've ever been interested in, even when Ben tried helping you, you pushed him away. I miss him so much, and it's all your fault.'

'No, Luna. Ben wasn't a good person, but he was good at pretending. He didn't love us, he lied to us.'

'No you're the liar, you only think about yourself. He loved me, he told me he did. He told me he loved you but you couldn't love him back, he said it wasn't your fault you drank. I think Ben understood me more than anyone else in the world.'

'Luna, please, he had us fooled…both of us. I'll try cutting down on my drinking, I promise.'

'You've been saying that for years! You don't love me, you only love the bottle. You're a liar and I hate you!'

Luna ran upstairs, slamming the bedroom door behind her. Alma sat on the sofa, stunned. It had been five years since she left Ben. How on earth was Luna still thinking about him? Alma rooted in the drawer next to the telephone, and then picked up the receiver.

Twenty minutes later, the doorbell rang.

Lee beamed at her, 'Hello!'

'Hi. Thanks for coming.'

'Are you okay?'

'No, not really,' she let him in, grabbing her purse off the table. She handed him a twenty pound note. 'Please could you go out and grab me another bottle of wine?'

Lee gave her a funny look. He put the money on the table.

'What's happened?'

'My daughter hates my guts.'

He sat down on the chair opposite, 'That's not true.'

'Yes she does. She wants me dead.'

'They're at that age, Alma. Hormones all over the place, she doesn't mean it.'

'I'm a fucking shit mother. I love her so much, why can't I sort my life out? She says she hates herself, my baby. Why would she say that?'

Lee stared at her, dumbfounded.

'I'm an alcoholic, Lee.'

'Alma, don't be silly.'

'I mean it. The other day…when I left training, I came home and drank two bottles of wine. They had to take me to hospital.'

'Why?'

'They said my liver is damaged.'

'No, I mean why did you do that?'

'I got upset, seeing you with that woman.'

'Who? Louise?'

Alma tried to get up from the sofa, but her legs didn't work. She flopped back down again. Tears were streaking her face.

'Alma, come on.' Lee helped her get to her feet. He gave her a hug. Alma pushed him away.

'No, no, I know why you're here. You're all the same.'

'Who?'

'Men! I thought you were different but you're all the fucking same. You only came because you thought you were getting some.'

Lee gave her a serious look, 'Look, Alma, I barely know you. I like you, but I didn't come around here for that…you called me, remember?'

Alma sat down on the sofa again. She put her head in her hands.

'I'm an alcoholic, Lee. I'm a fucking alcoholic.'

Lee sat next to Alma. He put his arm around her.

'Listen, Alma, I don't know how much you drink or why you feel you need to drink to excess, but maybe you should go to a meeting. That's a start, isn't it?'

'And if not?'

'Well we can talk about it further, but please don't feel like you're alone in this, okay? I'm here if you need me.'

Alma hugged him tightly.

'You should go and speak to Luna, she needs you.'

'She doesn't need me, not really.'

'Of course she does, you're her mum, Alma.'

Alma looked miserable, 'I'm doing a shit job of it.'

Lee stood up. He put out his hands and pulled her up.

'That's not true,' he said. He looked Alma straight in the eyes, 'Now, you're going to go up there and speak to her, like an adult, and make sure she knows her mum is there for her.'

She nodded.

'Okay? Good.'

'Thanks, Lee, genuinely.'

He gave her a hug, 'It will be fine, Alma, I promise.'

Alma watched him walk down the driveway, then made her way upstairs. She knocked on Luna's door. No response. She knocked again. Still, no response. Gently, Alma pushed it open.

Luna was lying on her side, with her chest rising and falling slowly under the bedcovers. Alma could smell cigarettes. As she crossed the room, her foot banged into something, and she nearly tripped. Bending down in the dark, her hands closed around something hard and smooth. She held it up close to her face. It was a diary, with one of the pages folded over at the corner.

Alma held the diary up to her face. The light from the landing illuminated the page.

No-one understands how I feel not even my own mum, why can't she understand? It's so difficult to talk to her, I hate her for what she did to Ben. I want to have the operation, I am going to speak to the doctor about how I feel and then there's Melanie, she is so beautiful how can I tell her how I feel about her? One day when I'm a boy when I have short hair and wear smart suits the world will know me for who I should really be, maybe mum will see me too, if she stops drinking. It says in that AA stuff she's got that she could die if she doesn't stop, why can't she see what she's doing. If she loved me she would do something wouldn't she? That's how I know she doesn't love me.

Alma couldn't breathe. She stifled a sob and placed the diary carefully back in place. Her daughter thought she was an alcoholic. God, this couldn't continue. Closing the door behind her, Alma grabbed her keys. It was time to sort this out.

***

The church carpark was busy, and there were various people milling around, greeting each other. *Surely they're not all alcoholics?* Alma thought. She got out of the car and walked up the pathway towards the church, keeping her head down.

'Hi, are you looking for the AA meeting?' the girl seemed very friendly and was quickly joined by a smart young man in a suit.

'Errr yes, it's my first time.'

'Welcome, I'm Trisha and this is Baz,' they hugged Alma in turn, which was most unexpected.

'I'm Alma, sorry I don't really know what to do, I feel a bit nervous.'

'Oh, don't worry, come on I'll take you in.' Trisha led Alma into a large hall, where there were chairs laid out, with some people already sat down. A table at the front was piled with books, and had various slogans and scrolls hanging off it. 'Alma, this is Judy and Karl. They'll get you a drink, and then I'll introduce you to a few others.'

Within a quarter of an hour, Alma had met so many different people. They all seemed happy, joking and laughing. But where were the real drunks? She looked around the room, all the seats were now taken. Then a bell rang, and a man stepped forward at the front of the room.

'If you think you have a drink problem, you are in the right place.'

There was a woman next to the man. He introduced her, and informed the group that she would be sharing her experience, strength and hope with them.

Alma sipped on her coffee, trying to stop her hands shaking. The woman at the front was a mum – a career woman – and she was also an alcoholic. She had been unable to stop drinking, and it was only when she became desperate, and hurt enough people in her life, that she decided to come to AA. Alma could hardly believe it. This woman had money, a beautiful home, a husband who loved her, but none of it had been enough to stop the drinking. The woman spoke about a 'higher power', and claimed that this was what had persuaded her to come to AA meetings, and break a twenty-year habit.

Once the woman had finished speaking, the man stepped forward again. It was time for sharing, he said. This was a newcomers' meeting. This was their chance to open up. They went around the room, with people giving their stories. Alma cried while listening, some of the stories were much worse than hers. Finally, though, it was her turn.

'Hi, I'm Alma. I'm…I'm not sure if I'm an alcoholic.'

'Hi, Alma,' the whole hall replied.

'I don't really know what to say, but I am just desperate to get some help…' Alma trailed off, trying hard not to cry. 'I drank last night. I drink every night and it's not pretty. It's causing me problems with my daughter, my sister… my whole family really. I know it's going to start affecting my job sooner or later, I've tried so hard to stop, but I just can't seem to do it. It's taken every ounce of willpower for me to come tonight, instead of staying at home and getting drunk…' Alma couldn't continue. She burst into tears.

'Thank you, Alma,' the group replied.

The meeting lasted an hour. By the end of it, Alma felt utterly drained. She bought some books from the table, and was also given a list of telephone numbers. As they told her, if she needed a drink, all she had to do was call someone on the list. Soon, she would have a sponsor, but for now she just needed to attend as many meetings as possible.

When she got home, Alma flopped down on the sofa. For the first time in a long time, she didn't want a drink. It was bizarre. She felt a sense of something in her stomach, not quite calm, but something close to it. Somehow, a weight had been lifted.

***

Doctor Ellis leaned back in his chair, waiting for Luna to speak.

'It's okay, take your time, there's no rush.'

Luna shuffled her feet. She looked uncomfortable. 'It's so hard, I find it hard to talk about.'

'What is it that you find hard to talk about, Luna? Is it the whole thing or is it one particular thing?'

'I've been feeling sort of weird…I don't want to be a girl.'

'Okay, is that something you have felt for a little while?'

'I don't know, I just don't like myself as who I am?'

'Do you prefer doing boy things?'

'Yes.'

'And do you prefer boys' clothes?'

'Yes.'

'Did you play with boys' toys when you were younger?'

Luna looked across at Alma, as if looking for reassurance.

'Yes, Doctor Ellis, Luna has always played with boys' toys since she was very young, and dressed like a boy from whenever she could dress herself.'

Doctor Ellis looked at his computer and started typing something.

'Okay, Luna, I am going to suggest you see a counsellor… someone who specialises in gender dysphoria.'

'Gender what?' Luna looked scared.

'From what you are describing to me, it sounds like you may be questioning your gender identity, and it would be good if you could talk to someone who is an expert in this field.'

'Is there something wrong with me?' Luna sounded desperate.

'No not at all. Luna, don't worry, you are not the first person on earth to feel like you do, it's becoming more and more common these days. I am confident you'll get the help you need. The most important thing is not to worry, okay?' he wrote some notes down and handed a piece of paper to Luna.

'I've written down some details that may help you in the meantime, whilst you await your appointment. Alma, I think it's a good idea if you go to the first few sessions, Luna is going to need a lot of support.'

Alma wrote to Mr King, advising him that Luna would be seeking outside counselling, and explaining why. She asked if it was possible for Luna to wear grey, stretch smart trousers – not boys' trousers but slightly different from the normal girl uniform, and the school polo shirt with a blazer. To her relief, Mr King replied the next day, informing her that this would be acceptable.

'Oh, Mum, wow I can't believe they've agreed to it,' Luna read the letter and smiled. 'Can we go get them, I mean today, as you're off work?'

'Okay, let's go now then, I've got a meeting later.' She grabbed her keys and headed for the door. Luna didn't follow.

'What's wrong?'

'I just want to say thank you, Mum. I know how hard this must be for you, I don't want to be a burden…I'm sorry if I have been,' Luna began to well up.

'Hey, come here,' Alma hugged her, 'you are never a burden, okay? If anything I'm the burden. I'm so proud of you, you just remember that.'

She looked Luna in the eye, 'You have to be strong, Luna. There are people out there who won't understand, some of them will be ignorant, and I certainly don't want you to keep anything to yourself. God knows we don't even understand what is going on ourselves, but I just need you to be strong. We'll only tell everyone else once you're ready.'

At that evening's AA meeting, Alma felt like a different person. It had been four sessions in total now, and every single one was better than the last. Her sponsor was named Gaynor. Gaynor was an older woman, who had been recommended to Alma by some other people in the group. They met once a month, to check on Alma's progress. Since the first time she attended, Alma hadn't had a drop of alcohol.

Walking home from the meeting, she started to notice things that she hadn't before. The greenery of the trees, the way the air felt on her skin. She felt alive. Under her breath, she muttered the serenity prayer:

'God grant me the serenity to accept the things I cannot change, the courage to change the things I can and the wisdom to know the difference, amen.'

CHAPTER 20
The Unexpected

It was a Wednesday evening. Alma and Luna had just got back from their second appointment with the psychiatric specialist. It had gone well, Alma thought, but Luna didn't seem so sure.

As they walked through the door, the phone rang.

'Hello, is that Alma Giles?'

'Yes.'

'Hi, Alma, it's Sister Bewley from Trings hospital. We have your dad with us…he was brought in by ambulance about half an hour ago. Your mum is here with him.'

'Oh my god, is he okay? What's happened?'

'He's suffered a heart attack…if you could make your way over as soon as you can.'

'Okay, I'm on my way.'

The journey to the hospital was a blur. When they got there, the receptionist smiled politely at Alma and Luna.

'Hi, my dad was brought in earlier this morning…David, David Jennings.'

The receptionist looked at her computer.

'Oh yes, he's in ward four. Go down the corridor, take the lift, it's on the second floor.'

David was in the cardiac unit. Mami was in the hallway, with her hands to her face. When they got there, David was being wheeled out of the room on a hospital bed.

'Alma, gracias a dios,' Mami was beside herself. Yoli was there too, comforting her.

Alma could see David wasn't conscious, 'Where are you taking him?'

'We're getting him into a side ward, if you can stay here and we'll call you through in a moment.'

Mami sobbed loudly. 'He wasn't good in the night…he said he had chest pains and couldn't breathe. Then he turned as white as anything.'

'Okay, Mami, don't worry, just calm down.'

Moments later, two more doctors rushed into the side ward. There were several people in the room with David now, what the hell was going on? A nurse came out of the room and ran down the corridor, shouting something at one of the other nurses. Alma stared through the glass. She could see David being hooked up to machines, surrounded by hospital staff.

One of the nurses came out of the room. Yoli grabbed her arm.

'Excuse me, is my dad okay?'

'I will get the doctor out to you shortly, we are doing all we can.'

Mami broke down in tears, distraught. Yoli, Alma, and Luna cuddled her. They all collapsed against the wall. Alma closed her eyes and started to pray. *Please let him be okay. Not today, God, not today.*

David died at five fifty-four in the morning. He was sixty-one years old.

They were allowed to go into the room, to say a final goodbye. Mami and Yoli went in first, together. Through the glass, Alma could hear Mami's wailing, and the painful sound of her crying David's name over and over again. Luna went in next, and finally it was Alma's turn.

David was laid on his back against the white sheets. He looked peaceful, and when Alma held his hand, it was still warm.

'We all love you, David. Don't worry about Mami, we'll take care of her.'

She bent down and kissed his forehead.

'I'm sorry I wasn't a better daughter for you…' and then the tears came, and she couldn't stop them. Alma closed her eyes

321

and beat her hands against the bedsheet. It wasn't fair. Why now? How could this happen?

Mami, Luna and Yoli were waiting for her outside the room.

'Yoli, why don't you take Mami and Luna home? I can stay and sort out everything here,' Alma hugged Mami.

'I don't want to leave him,' Mami sobbed. She walked back into the room and kissed David on his head, crying loudly.

'Come on, let them have some more time,' Yoli pulled Alma and Luna away. Alma followed, in a daze. It all felt so surreal. David was gone, just like that. She would never see him again.

***

'Hi, I'm Alma. I'm an alcoholic.'

'Hi, Alma.'

'I am so relieved to be in this meeting tonight. I need to share this…I'm in so much pain. I guess I'm also angry, angry with God. I'm struggling, if I'm honest, I just feel so let down, it's like nothing will ever take this pain away. My dad has left us and my daughter is suffering with her problems. I need to be strong to be there for her and for the rest of my family…but I'm so scared I won't get through this…' Alma struggled, but continued. 'I guess I'm having to deal with real feelings now I'm sober. I feel real pain, you know? Something I just used to be able to numb before…' People around the room were nodding appreciatively.

'Anyway, thank you to everyone here, and to my sponsor…I don't have anywhere else to go to talk about all this, so I'm really grateful. Thank you so much for listening.'

Following the meeting, Alma was overwhelmed by the number of people who came up and reassured her that she'd done the right thing. In many ways, they were the same as her. They were all trying to live their lives sober, one day at a time. But Alma was determined not to fold. The moment they got home from the hospital, she'd promised herself that she wouldn't let this push her off the rails. She had to be strong. It was what David would have wanted.

Yoli and Alma prepared all the funeral arrangements. David's death had brought them closer together again. That, and a sincere apology from Alma. Looking back, she could barely recognise who she'd been that night. It had only been a few weeks, but it seemed like years. The turnout for the funeral was wonderful, and the procession itself couldn't have gone better. Luna had made a speech about her grandad, and how inspirational he was. Watching her at the front of the church, Alma swelled with pride. Luna had been so brave, helping Alma to plan the funeral. Lee had also helped, to her surprise. He was spending more and more time at their house, these days, and Alma had to say that she didn't mind it at all.

When they returned home from the funeral, Luna crashed out on her bed immediately. Alma called her sponsor.

'Hi, Alma, thanks for calling me. How did it go today?'

'I just feel exhausted, to be honest.'

'I know, it must have been a very long day. Listen, we'll talk tomorrow, okay? You get some rest, just as long as you're okay and remember I am always here for you.'

Alma cried that evening. She cried for hours, even when Lee came round to see how the funeral went, she couldn't stop. It hurt so much. She hated God. How could he do this?

The next day, Luna and Alma had their third session with the psychiatrist. Luna came down the stairs wearing dark denim jeans, with a red t-shirt.

'Do I look okay in this?' she asked.

'You look fine, darling.'

'Will you come in with me again?'

'Of course I will.'

The session didn't go well. The psychiatrist asked a lot of questions, but Luna seemed reluctant to open up. As they came to a close, he said, 'Luna, can I ask one final question for today's session?'

Luna nodded, 'Yes.'

'Can I ask you what your biggest fear or worry is about transitioning from female to male? Have you ever had a chance to think about what that might be?'

Luna stayed silent for a few seconds, before looking over at Alma.

'I worry for my mum.'

Alma felt a lump in her throat.

'Why?'

Luna's eyes filled with tears.

'Because all she ever wanted was a girl and I don't want to hurt her.'

'Mrs Giles, can I ask you to respond to that? If you want to, that is.'

Alma swallowed hard. She looked at Luna. She hadn't really thought about her own feelings, she just wanted Luna to be happy. Would she miss her, as a boy? Would she like the person she became? She would have a son. Alma didn't know anything about boys. It didn't matter though, and she knew that. Whatever her gender, Luna was her child.

'Luna, I want to tell you that I will love you whatever happens. I guess I'm very fortunate that I will have experienced having both of you in my life.' Alma tried not to cry, and blinked several times.

'You are both going to experience feelings you've never had before,' the psychiatrist said. 'I can't deny that some days are going to be harder than others. Luna, for you it's important to open up and be as honest as possible, do you understand? It will help you so much more if you can express exactly what you are feeling no matter how trivial or embarrassing you think it is, okay?'

Luna nodded, Alma could see how hard this was for her. But inwardly she was glowing with pride. They would get through it, together.

A LETTER TO MY YOUNGER SELF

Dear Alma,

To say it's been a rollercoaster ride is an understatement.

I've experienced so much in my life, and I am still learning things every day. Thinking back to when I was growing up, and how little about life I knew, there was always that eagerness to be part of the crowd and to seek attention. If only I knew back then what I know now…the problems I would encounter, the emptiness and loneliness that went far deeper than I ever could have imagined.

You see, Alma, I didn't know there was something wrong with me. I knew I felt different, but I could never work out why I didn't feel included, why I felt so lost and fearful all the time. I know now that I suffered with deep rooted mental health issues from a very young age. No-one can say for sure whether it was because Papi left, or whether coming to England was the start of it, but I knew something wasn't right.

I've had to experience some very painful situations. I used to think I was a bad person for some of the things I'd done in my life, but these days I have learnt to forgive myself. We are all different. We all come from different backgrounds and all follow our own paths, I just chose a really difficult one. Because I couldn't cope with the guilt and anguish, I dealt with the pain the only way I could – drink was my saviour, or so I thought. It became my best friend, and I couldn't be without it. I drank for so long that I had forgotten what real life was about. I was a slave to the bottle, and got to the point where I couldn't live with or without it.

Today I am free and sober. I have never felt better, but sobriety has been hard. Some days I really struggle, and the depression comes at me like a bolt of lightning, without any warning. But now I have the tools to deal with this. You see, my alcoholism was a mere symptom of my real illness. Without Alcoholics Anonymous, I don't think I would be here today, at least not mentally anyway. I can never have another alcoholic drink for the rest of my life, but that's okay. If you'd said all of this to me just a few years ago then I would have laughed at you, as there was no way I was giving up the drink, not for anyone. With the help of AA, and outside counselling, I am free. Free from the buried emotions which caused so much pain in my life.

In the past, I craved the good life. I wanted someone to love me, but I now know that I was looking for something that didn't exist. There is no such thing as a perfect life, or a perfect relationship. Today, I have found someone very special to me. He is loyal, courageous, and loves me without trying to control me. He understands that I need to go to my meetings every week, and his support for me is never ending. Losing David was one of the hardest things I've ever had to go through, but I have to be there for Mami, Yoli and Luna. They need me, just as much as I need them.

It's amazing how a life can turn around. The key, I have discovered, is 'live and let live.' Stay out of drama. If I let my spiritual health improve, then it will. If I am ever struggling, then it's because I am still hanging onto my old ideas.

Yours truly,

Alma

CHAPTER 21
No Escape

Alma yawned and climbed out of bed. She put her hands to her stomach. It was six months and four days to the morning that she'd taken the test, and the baby was starting to kick. Lee groaned in the bed beside her. He opened his eyes.

'What time is it?'

Alma smiled and kissed him on the top of the head. 'Seven o'clock.'

He rolled over and shut his eyes again. Alma quietly closed the door behind her. After getting herself ready, she walked down the drive. She thought about Lee's reaction. Initially she'd worried about what he would say, they hadn't even moved in together when it happened, but to her relief he was over the moon. Luna was delighted to have a sibling on the way, and Lee was now an essential part of the family. She put her hands on her stomach again and felt a warmth spreading down to her toes. It was almost too good to be true.

An hour later, she was sitting opposite Gaynor at a local café. They ordered two orange juices.

'You know, Gaynor, I don't know how I would have got through all of this without you. I still have to pinch myself to believe I haven't touched a drop of alcohol all this time.'

'I'm only doing what you'll be doing in the future, when you are someone's sponsor,' Gaynor smiled sweetly, sipping her orange juice. 'Alcoholism is a disease, just remember that. I learnt the hard way. After four years, yes four whole years, I had this insane thought that I could drink like normal people. After six months I was at Haywood Mental Institution after two suicide attempts. I couldn't live with or without alcohol at that stage. Alma, please don't ever kid yourself that you can drink normally, that is something that no alcoholic can do.'

Alma shivered at the thought.

'You see, Alma, it doesn't matter whether you are a day sober or twenty years sober, you are only one drink away from that downward spiral. It never leaves you…your illness is always there, waiting. It's a progressive illness, so there is no win-win situation here.'

Alma checked her watch, it was almost eight-thirty, and she was due in at nine. Gaynor stood up to hug her goodbye.

'How are you feeling about today? It's an important meeting, isn't it?'

'Just a client meeting, but then our new boss is coming into the office.'

'Okay, well let me know how it goes, please.'

'I will. And thank you, Gaynor.'

By the time Alma got to work, it was nearly nine. Laura looked up from her computer.

'Jeez, cutting it fine!'

Alma scowled, 'I'm here, aren't I? When's the new boss coming in?'

'Not till four o'clock, but the inbox is packed. And Sarah is already waiting for you!'

Alma made herself a coffee, took off her suit jacket and then knocked on the door of the office across the way. Sarah was on the telephone. She beckoned Alma in.

'Okay, thank you. Yes, I know that. Thanks again.'

Sarah hung up, looking frustrated.

'Right, sorry about that Alma.'

'It's okay.'

'So anyway, I've got exactly three months left here, god knows how I'm gonna manage to handover in that time…I need your help. Please can I give you a few things so as to free some of my time?'

'Of course!'

Sarah started going through various things on her computer. Alma pulled her chair closer, and scribbled furiously in her notepad. By the time they'd finished, it had gone lunchtime. The client meeting was at two o'clock. Laura had gone out, but she'd left a cup of coffee and a penguin chocolate biscuit, with a picture of a love heart, on Alma's desk.

As Alma drove to the meeting, her thoughts turned to Mr Saddler. She was lucky, in many ways, that she'd managed to get a job working with Laura. Laura had been there for a while before Alma joined, so she'd shown her the ropes. *And in many ways,* Alma thought cheekily, *she's lucky to be working with me!* Since Michael had been arrested, there had been a few men in Laura's life, but none of them were keepers. She came round for dinner at least twice a week, and Luna often referred to her as 'the big sister I never had.'

The client meeting was difficult, but she'd expected that. They'd chosen a small pub for lunch, not too far from the client's premises. Alma thought that by paying for lunch he might soften his view on insurance as a whole, but at the end of the meal he turned to her and said, 'I appreciate the offer, Alma, but I need to let you know that I have spoken to a couple of other insurance companies for quotes. So I won't get back to you until I've heard from all of them.'

Alma nodded, feeling annoyed.

'At the end of the day, as I'm sure you'll agree…money is the bottom line. If you want to retain us as a customer then we need to make sure the premiums are as low as possible.'

'Thanks, Mr Edwards. I look forward to hearing from you.'

Driving back to the office, Alma was distracted. *The cheek of him,* she thought. He hadn't even said thank you for lunch. It wasn't just a matter of courtesy, the least he could do was consider her offer and treat her with a bit more respect…

The vehicle came out of nowhere. Alma's head flew towards the dashboard, and immediately the airbag inflated. The car collided hard with the rear of the vehicle in front, and span out wildly across the pavement. There was a furious beeping behind her.

Alma disengaged from the airbag. What the hell had happened? She put her hand to her head…there was no blood. Suddenly, there was a tapping on the window. Alma wrenched open the door.

'I'm sorry! Are you okay? Oh my god you're pregnant, what have I done?' the woman was shaking, and tears were rolling down her face.

'Don't worry, I'm okay,' Alma got out. 'I wanna make sure the people in front are alright.'

Ahead of them, an elderly couple were stepping out of their vehicle. They looked shaken, but not injured.

'I just don't know what happened. I thought I'd braked…but then it's like the car didn't stop.'

Alma shook her head sympathetically, 'It's fine, honestly.'

The woman looked confused, 'I was expecting a mouthful.'

'Don't be silly, these things can't be helped. No one was hurt, that's the main thing.'

She took down the woman's insurance details. There was a big dent in the back of the car, but Alma felt relieved as she drove away. It was a near miss, but she'd escaped in one piece.

When she arrived back at the office, Alma went straight to the bathroom and fixed her hair and makeup. It was almost time to meet her new boss.

'Well, how did it go with the lovely Mr Edwards?' Laura grinned.

'Oh he was his normal charming self…'

'Are you okay? You look a bit pale.'

'Yeh…I just had an accident on the way back. Some lady drove straight into me, bless her, then I hit an elderly couple in front.'

'What the fuck!'

'It's fine, nobody was hurt.'

'That's terrible. I'll make you a cuppa. Stay here.' Laura scooted off into the kitchen. While she was there, Sarah came out of her office.

'He's here, Alma. Are you all set? We'll be having the meeting in the boardroom downstairs.'

Alma nodded. She reached into her drawer and took a couple of pain killers. She took a deep breath, and then followed Sarah down the stairs.

As they reached the boardroom, Sarah stopped. Her phone was vibrating in her pocket.

'Ugh, sorry Alma, I really have to take this. I should only be two minutes. Would you be okay to go in and introduce yourself?'

'Sure, no problem.'

Alma knocked gently, and stepped into the boardroom.

The boardroom consisted of a round wooden table, with red cushioned chairs spread in a neat circle across the room. There was a projector above the table and a mounted wall screen, rolled down to the carpet. A man was sitting at the table, with his back to Alma. His hair was slicked across the top of his crown, and he was wearing a crisp, navy blue suit. On the wall behind him was an oil painting of boats and a pier, with a fisherman throwing rope out over the sea. The light from the projector screen cast an eerie glow across the table.

Alma coughed. The man turned around. He grinned.

'What the fuck?'

'Hello, Alma.'

Alma stared at him. Her legs wobbled. It couldn't be him, surely.

'Have I surprised you?' Ben said. He smiled again, a familiar look, his eyes dark and venomous.

'What the fuck are you doing here, Ben?'

Ben tapped the table with his pen. 'Now, that's no way to talk to your new boss, is it?'

Alma felt sick. She slumped back against the wall.

'No need to be so upset, Alma. This is going to be super interesting, don't you think?'

Sarah came back into the room. She looked at Alma, concerned.

'Alma, Laura just told me that you've been in a car accident. Are you okay?'

Alma could barely speak. She muttered something incomprehensible. Her breath came in short shallow gasps.

'Alma...here, sit down, I'll get you some water. Give me a minute.'

Sarah dashed out of the room. Ben smirked.

'Did you honestly think you wouldn't see me again?' he said.

'I don't know...'

'I've been out for a year now, did nobody tell you that? A whole year. I had no money, my mum passed away...I've had to start from scratch, but I've done it. And here we are.'

Alma stared at him. He was relishing every moment of it.

'There's no way I'm working with you.'

'I loved you, Alma. I loved Luna too…but you took that away from me. You destroyed me. And now, you are gonna know what it feels like to be on the end of that.'

'I'll quit, I don't have to work for you.'

'And you think that will be the end of it? I don't care about whether you work here or not. And besides…' he glanced at her stomach, 'looks like you can't afford to lose your job.'

Alma's head was spinning. She felt bile in her throat.

'I'm gonna make you pay, Alma. I'm going to show you what it feels like to lose everything. Did you think I was just gonna let this go? I've done my homework. Maybe later on I'll pay a trip to Sunhill Secondary, I know Luna will be pleased to see me.'

Sarah came back into the room. She smiled warmly and put a cup of water down in front of Alma.

'There, drink that, you'll feel better. I take it you two have got acquainted?'

Alma's hand was shaking. She sipped the water, but she couldn't swallow.

Ben smiled. 'Yes, it's nice to meet you, Alma. We were just about to start discussing Alma's contract, actually. I have some changes I want to implement…'

Alma closed her eyes. This couldn't be happening. And yet, it was. And through the darkness, Ben's voice became louder and louder, until she couldn't shut him out any longer.

There was no escape.

Printed in Great Britain
by Amazon